A

CANDLELIGHT REGENCY SPECIAL

CANDLELIGHT REGENCIES

THE
BELLE OF BATH

Dorothy Mack

A CANDLELIGHT REGENCY SPECIAL

Published by
Dell Publishing Co., Inc.
1 Dag Hammarskjold Plaza
New York, New York 10017

Dell ® TM 681510, Dell Publishing Co., Inc.

ISBN: 0–440–10617–6

Printed in the United States of America
First printing—July 1981

CHAPTER ONE

All but one of the several occupants of the large family parlor were engaged in a lively and occasionally contentious game of speculation. They were seated at a circular table situated in a corner near the long window doors that opened onto a stone-paved terrace. The single exception was a female seated in a capacious wing chair drawn close to the fireplace to enable her to derive maximum benefit from the cheerful blaze that was still necessary in the evenings, though June was already far advanced. She had been plying her needle assiduously for some time, but was not so absorbed in her task as to be prevented from directing an occasional quiet-voiced reminder to one or another of the players when a shifting of the fortunes of the game gave rise to an access of passion that momentarily overcame good manners.

In the dying light of day and the dancing light of the fire it could be seen that she was a woman past her first youth certainly, but not yet of an age to be the parent of even the youngest of the group of noisy young persons stationed around the table. The word that would rise unbidden to the top of a person's mind on first viewing Miss Agnes Greyson was *drab*. Her eyes were hidden behind thick spectacles that she habitually pushed more securely up onto the bridge of her undistinguished nose with the middle finger of her left hand, and her hair, pulled tautly back from a high forehead, was almost entirely concealed by an unbecoming muslin cap. What little could be seen appeared to be a dull color, neither brown nor gray, and her skin, though finely grained and unmarred by the least suspicion of a wrinkle, also seemed to have a grayish tinge, which would invariably give cause for speculation concerning her health had not Miss Greyson's erect bearing and firm step immediately given the lie to this line of thought. Her hands, busy with her needlework, were her best feature—graceful, long-fingered, with smooth white skin and tapering nails. They paused now over her work as a minor altercation at the card table threatened to escalate in intensity.

"Livvy, you little fiend!" wailed a charming voice edged with a tinge of exasperation. "That's the third time you've turned up the ace of trumps as dealer. I declare, you must have made a pact with the devil to be so lucky!"

"Hah!" exclaimed an extremely young man with bright red hair. "She's made a pact with the devil all right, Juliet, but luck had nothing to do with it; she's cheating! I saw you pull that ace from the bottom, Livvy. Do not bother to deny it, and take your hands off that pool! The deal passes to Mellie."

"It does not! I did not cheat, Bertram, I didn't!" came the passionate rejoinder from the alleged miscreant, a schoolgirl of some fourteen or so summers whose healthy good looks were dimmed at the moment by a hectic flush suffusing her cheeks and a ferocious scowl creasing her forehead as she glared at her brother. Her darting fingers closed tightly over the bowl in the center of the table, and she dragged it toward her while continuing to protest her innocence with vigor. "The pool is mine! Mellie knows I didn't cheat, don't you, Mellie? Tell Bertram!"

Thus, directly appealed to, the fourth player at the table, who had been staring appalled from brother to sister as the argument raged, swallowed with difficulty and ventured with timid earnestness, "I don't believe Livvy would cheat, Bertram."

This offering was brushed aside brusquely, though not unkindly, by the accuser, who remained unmoved in his determination to avenge the misdeed.

"You don't believe anyone would cheat, Mellie. Well, all I can say is you do not know Livvy as well as you think if you haven't learned after ten years of associating with her that she'll cheat at every opportunity if she thinks she can get away with it. Drop that pool, Livvy, or you'll be sorry!"

His twice-maligned sister stigmatized him as the greatest beast in nature and tightened her grip upon the bowl containing the counters, whereupon he leaned across the table and grasped her wrist between strong fingers.

"Drop it!"

"Bertram, take care you do not hurt your sister."

This quiet remonstrance came from the fifth participant in the game, breaking the silence he had maintained throughout the squabble. The speaker was a young man in his early twenties, a quiet-faced man possessing regular features who stared at the world from intelligent hazel eyes. His serious gaze met and held the boy's irate one until the latter finally wavered.

"Dash it all, Chris, she can't be allowed to get away with cheating at her age. Mark my words, one of these days she's going to disgrace the family in public." Bertram's fingers reluctantly loosened their grasp, but his glance challenged his tutor's, and the latter hesitated for a second.

The lady near the fire came unexpectedly to his rescue.

"A true gentleman, Bertram, restrains his passions even under extreme provocation," she proclaimed coolly. "If Olivia did indeed cheat, then you may be sure her conscience will punish her, but now, since no one else observed a misplay,' I believe you will have to let it pass . . . *this* time," she ended with some severity as Olivia speedily gathered in her winnings with a sound suspiciously akin to a crow of triumph.

At a look from his tutor the youth muttered, "Oh, very well, I beg pardon, ma'am," but spoiled the effect of this apology by issuing his sister a dark warning in the next breath. "I shall be watching you like a hawk from now on—we all shall—so do not crow too quickly, Livvy!"

Her immediate goal having been accomplished, Olivia subsided with a wholly spurious meekness that deceived no one. Ceremoniously she presented the cards to Amelia on her left, and the game resumed. After a moment Miss Greyson took up her sewing again, but her thoughtful gaze continued to dwell on one or another of the players from time to time as her meandering mental processes kept pace with her needle.

A pair of smiling gray eyes beneath an unruly cap of red hair met hers briefly, and her own eyes warmed and her pale lips curved slightly in response. The crisis past, Bertram's normally good-humored disposition reasserted itself almost immediately. He was not one to cherish a grudge, and no one, allowed Miss Greyson with a somewhat rueful glance at Olivia's untroubled countenance as she blithely played a card, was more aware of this characteristic than his younger sister, who took frequent and shameless advantage of what she considered to be a weakness in his armor.

Bertram was a nice lad, a trifle impetuous perhaps and not always above being irked by the disadvantages of possessing two volatile sisters, but he was sound to the core and would no doubt moderate his behavior, if not his strictly held ideals, as he attained maturity. Sixteen was a difficult age—he was neither boy nor man at present—and sometimes his boyish enthusiasms and strict judgments clashed head-on with an emerging sense of a man's responsibilities. It was unfortunate that an infectious complaint contracted last winter had left his strength too debilitated to enable him to return to Eton for the spring term, but his new tutor, Mr. Christopher Ryding, was providing his young charge with an excellent model to emulate. Recently down from Oxford himself, he possessed all the attributes of intelligence, athletic ability, and worldly experience to dazzle the eyes of a boy approaching manhood, and the character to use his superiority solely for Bertram's good. The two had hit it off from the start and got on amazingly well together. Despite the difference in their ages and conditions, a very real friendship had grown up between pupil and teacher that might even survive Bertram's eventual departure for Oxford. This event, however, was problematical at the moment, for not all his respect and admiration for Mr. Ryding could keep Bertram's nose in his books for sufficiently extended periods to guarantee steady progress in his studies. To Miss Greyson's mind he appeared to possess the requisite native intelligence to succeed at university, but at present the greater portion of his enthusiasm and interest was divided among various sporting proclivities, to the detriment of his studies. Nor was he by nature nearly so serious minded as his tutor.

A few months observation had revealed that Christopher Ryding combined a scholarly bent with an overriding interest in social problems. Had his background been more affluent, he would most likely have gravitated toward a career in government in the course of time. Unhappily, though his birth was gentle, the senior Ryding was merely an impecunious clergyman whose slender resources were not augmented by the good will of someone powerful enough or well-connected enough to establish his youngest son's feet firmly on the first rung of the ladder leading toward prominence in public life. As matters stood, Miss Greyson could not but wonder what the future might hold for such a promising but sponsorless young man when his association with the Brewster family came to its inevitable end. Her forehead assumed a faint vertical line as she stared fixedly at the work in her hands and then slowly pushed her needle into the fabric once again.

A few moments later a silvery laugh drew the older woman's eyes back to the group gathered about the table, more specifically to the laughing face of her primary responsibility, Miss Juliet Brewster. The first sight of Miss Brewster's enchantingly pretty countenance had on occasion drawn forth gasps of astonished appreciation from unprepared and susceptible young men, and generally evoked a considering, narrow-eyed interest or open admiration from members of her own sex, according to the various temperaments of the onlookers. Not even the most determined fault finder (exclusively female) could detect the least flaw in Miss Brewster's person upon closer scrutiny, however.

She was, conceded her duenna in a fair-minded spirit, quite simply the most beautiful girl she had ever beheld. In a society where divine fairness had long been established as the epitome of feminine perfection, Juliet's dark vivaciousness caught the eye instantly. Yet hers was not the exotic olive-skinned appeal found in women of Mediterranean ancestry. Although her dusky curls were nearly blue-black, the face they framed so charmingly was of a dazzlingly white-skinned perfection whose appeal undoubtedly owed something to this contrast in coloring. It also owed much to a pair of enormous black-fringed eyes of a deep sapphire blue, set under beautifully arched black brows. Her nose and rosy mouth could have been modeled by the foremost sculptor of the day engaged in creating the ideal female, but her high cheekbones and delicately pointed chin gave the heart-shaped face a distinct individual charm.

Nor was there the least fault to be found with Miss Brewster's figure. She was neither too tall nor too short, and her youthful slimness in no way implied an immaturity of form. Some quite satisfactory feminine curves above and below her narrow waist were emphasized by this feature, as her delicate wrist defined the well-rounded arm above it. Her small hands and feet were in keeping with the overall perfection, and her movements held all the inherent grace unconsciously expected from such an exquisite creature.

She was an engaging girl, too, with no more than a minimal share of those less appealing characteristics that, perhaps inevitably, accompany unusual beauty and are generally traceable as much to the effects of others' treatment as to inborn character defects. Deprived of a mother's care and good sense since shortly after the birth of her young sister, she had been cosseted and doted upon by her adoring father until it was scarcely surprising that she was a trifle spoiled and inclined to be demanding at times.

Even so, there was an underlying sweetness of character that made her genuinely appreciative of others' efforts on her behalf and helped to nullify her occasional spells of pouting when matters did not fall out quite as expected. Her beauty having been remarked on continually almost from birth, it was not to be imagined that she could have

11

escaped some degree of vanity and excessive concern for her appearance, but Miss Greyson had been relieved to find her gregarious charge quite willing to accord other, less favored females their share of attention and admiration. In fact, Juliet was a warm-hearted girl with a fierce loyalty toward those she loved.

Miss Greyson's own arrival at Fairhill less than six months ago as a newly hired companion-chaperon had been met with a polite but cautious reception from the young girl that had soon warmed to an unforced cordiality, much to the older woman's relief. If there was no real affection in their association as yet, at least there was, on the youngster's part, a mild pleasure in her mentor's company and a good-natured acceptance of the former's superior knowledge of the behavior expected of a young lady on the threshold of her entrance into society. So far Juliet had proved amenable to suggestion, but as Miss Greyson's assessing eyes switched from the girl's face, alive with mischievous delight, to the slight discomfiture apparent in the expression of Mr. Ryding, she knew a small anticipatory qualm.

It was gradually becoming apparent that the lovely Miss Brewster was possessed of a strong coquettish instinct. It was not to be wondered at that the flattering attention she received from gentlemen of almost any age should have turned the head of such a young girl, but at this point in time she hadn't acquired the experience to deal with the attentions such flirtatious tactics invited. At present her acquaintance was strictly limited to young men she had known for years, with the occasional addition of a visitor in the neighborhood, but all too soon her horizons would be greatly expanded, and then the job of chaperoning one who was destined to become an overnight sensation would cease to be the sinecure it was while the family resided quietly in Essex.

Miss Greyson noted with approval that Mr. Ryding had succeeded in diverting Juliet's attention from himself. He was always to be depended upon to help keep any situation firmly within the bounds of propriety. His demeanor toward the sisters of his pupil was a model of punctilious civility; always conscious of his position in the household, he never allowed himself the luxury of sinking into an informality of manner that might encourage Juliet to form an unwise attachment to one who was, after all, totally ineligible.

As firmly as Miss Greyson, was he convinced that Sir Reginald cherished the highest ambitions with respect to his lovely daughter's future. That Juliet shared these ambitions was attested to by her frequent airy references to all the unknown titled gentlemen who would soon swim within her orbit when she made her appearance at Almack's next season, but this treat was in the future. At the moment there was an exceedingly personable young man, who had the advantage of accessibility, on whom to practice her wiles. It was evident to Miss Greyson that Mr. Ryding's seeming immunity to the charms of her protegée represented a constant challenge to the youthful Circe, but she saw no immediate solution to the implicit problem. Unless some new interest captured Juliet's fancy, she would continue her so far unavailing assault on this intriguingly impregnable fortress.

A sudden soft squeal of delight brought Miss Greyson's attention to the youngest member of the card party. Little Amelia Wrenthorpe, having won all three tricks, was eagerly adding the entire contents of the double pool to her depleted stack of counters. The woman smiled in sympathy with the child's pleasure and noted with satisfaction that the two oldest Brewsters at least were regarding their guest's unusual vivacity with tolerant affection. Even Olivia, whose precarious sportsmanship was being strongly tested, was merely heard to comment mildly on the rarity of being dealt the ace, king, and queen of trumps, and to urge her brother not to be so slow with his dealing. The game went on as before. Miss Greyson observed with passing regret how quickly the glow of triumph receded, leaving Mellie once again the little mouselike creature whose plainness was rendered even more obvious by contrast with the vivid Brewster girls. She would never be a beauty, but there was a sweetness of disposition that was reflected in her soft brown eyes and the gentle regularity of her features. One felt that Amelia would develop into a charming woman whose looks would improve tenfold if she were loved by the right sort of man.

She was a year younger than Olivia and cherished an almost worshipful regard for the spirited girl with a character so strikingly opposed to her own gentle nature. That this mismatched friendship had existed for so many years was a tribute to Mellie's meek tolerance of Olivia's bossiness and her resilience and forgiving nature in the face of the occasional snubs and general callousness on the part of her friend. Miss Greyson's lips tightened as Olivia administered another such rebuke for a mistaken play on Amelia's part that caused the timid girl to color up to her eyes with abject embarrassment.

It was an exercise in futility to wish that just once Amelia might take a stand against the strong-minded Olivia. It simply was not in her nature to pit her own desires against a stronger character, and there was no denying that Olivia's was a very determined personality. Perhaps growing up motherless as the youngest of three children, with the additional handicap of being cast into the shade by her sister's extraordinary beauty, had inevitably formed her character along such decided lines, if she was to be noticed at all.

Though not possessed of Juliet's ethereal beauty, the younger girl bid fair to become a heartbreaker in her own right. She shared the same blue-black hair and white skin as her sister, but her eyes were a cool gray and her features were somewhat less delicately chiseled. The two girls were of a height, but Olivia's frame was sturdier. Though none of the Brewster offspring were inclined to be bookish, the youngest was possessed of a shrewd intelligence and a mind that worked quickly, especially when it was a question of her own advantage. Part of Miss Greyson's responsibility was to act as governess to Olivia whenever her duties with regard to Juliet permitted the expenditure of her time in this manner. She had found her young charge to be a quick and generally willing pupil as long as her teacher did not demand concentrated study for long periods of time. She demonstrated a real aptitude for the pianoforte and harp, though she had to be coaxed to practice, but neither coaxing nor coercion succeeded in imparting any degree of skill with a needle. Olivia resisted all such efforts to turn her into a competent needlewoman with apparently endless subterfuges and stratagems. Neither did occasional sulky compliance lead to any improvement in her stitching skills. She was forever losing her thimble, pricking her fingers, or knotting her thread until Miss Greyson was more than willing to allow her to escape to some other activity while she proceeded to remove the badly set stitches and smooth out the work in preparation for the next session.

Olivia was dealing the cards and chattering brightly to Mellie. Her governess saw her hands pause briefly as she looked around the circle for a reaction to her remark before resuming the deal. *Oh, that wretched girl!* Miss Greyson held her breath, hoping for the sake of peace that her pupil's last action had escaped the eagle eye of her brother, but such good fortune was not to be.

"Livvy, that card belongs to Mellie, not you!" Bertram said sharply. "It's a misdeal." He started gathering in the other hands as he spoke.

Olivia protested at the top of her lungs and put a protective arm in front of her cards and Mellie's to prevent Bertram from sweeping them up, but he darted a hand in over this makeshift shield and triumphantly turned over an ace from amongst his sister's cards.

"I told you I'd be watching you, my girl," he remarked with offensive smugness, displaying the ace of hearts for all to see.

"That wasn't even the last card!" came the shrill protest. "It was the first card dealt, Bertram, you horrid sneak." Olivia was taking in a breath of air before continuing her attack when a welcome diversion was created by the entrance of Penniestone, the butler, announcing the arrival of Sir Malcolm Wrenthorpe, come to carry his young sister back home.

Sir Malcolm's appearance was greeted with relief by all present, with the possible exception of Bertram, who had been about to see his vigilance repaid.

At Penniestone's first words Miss Greyson had directed a warning look at the young combatants. Now she was slow to perceive the presence of a second gentleman approaching her chair. She greeted Sir Malcolm with a smile, then turned a politely inquiring glance in the stranger's direction. The hand she had extended to Sir Malcolm paused in midair, and she dragged her eyes away from the newcomer's face to fix an unfocused stare in the vicinity

16

of the fingers that Sir Malcolm was saluting with formal politeness.

"Good evening, ma'am. I trust I find you well and beg you will excuse the informality of bringing a stranger in amongst you unannounced." At her faint nod he continued: "May I present my good friend, Mr. Simon Kirkland, who has just arrived to spend some time with us at the Manor. Simon, this is Miss Greyson, who is Miss Brewster's companion and Miss Olivia Brewster's governess."

Miss Greyson directed a brief, impersonal glance at the newcomer. "How do you do, Mr. Kirkland," she said with unsmiling civility, unresponsive alike to the penetrating stare the dark-eyed man bent on her and his polite murmur acknowledging the introduction before she made him known to the others in the room with a practiced ease of manner.

For his part Mr. Kirkland more than matched Miss Greyson's social ease, responding with a cool charm that nicely blended propriety and pleasure at being presented to a half dozen persons, none of whom could be likely to arouse any lasting interest in him. The youngsters had deserted the card table en masse to acknowledge the introduction with varying degrees of eagerness but uniform civility, thank heavens. The two youngest girls curtsied demurely, but only Olivia's reply was audible, since Amelia was too shy to attempt a coherent remark under the circumstances. Bertram, eying the impressive width of the stranger's shoulders beneath a perfectly tailored coat of blue superfine, gazed at him in some respect and executed a stiff bow. Mr. Ryding's bow was a more graceful effort, and he shook hands politely. If he had any opinions of Mr. Kirkland, they were well concealed behind a faultless manner.

17

Not so Juliet's reaction, however. Miss Greyson noted with a trace of unease the instant brightening of that young lady's eyes and the radiance of the smile she bestowed on Mr. Kirkland along with her hand. This feeling deepened to dismay at Mr. Kirkland's response to Juliet. His eyes had widened slightly at first sight of the lovely young girl, and though his greeting did not go beyond the accepted social formula, the expression in his eyes went far beyond mere civility, and he released her hand with a reluctance that was obvious, at least to the governess. The only thing that saved him from looking like a mooncalf, thought Miss Greyson disgustedly, was his age. He appeared to be some few years older than Sir Malcolm, who was six and twenty, and he had the assured mien of a man of the world. It was in his bearing and the ease with which he maneuvered himself into the chair next to Juliet as the party regrouped. The younger girls wandered over to the game table to put away the cards and counters.

"I fear our arrival has spoiled your game," Mr. Kirkland murmured apologetically.

The remark was general, but there was no doubt that the words were addressed to Juliet, who responded gaily: "You and Sir Malcolm arrived in the nick of time. Bertram and Olivia were about to come to blows over a misdeal, and for my part I am excessively thankful to be done with it since I played only to oblige the children." She smiled blindingly at Mr. Kirkland, ignoring her brother's glowering look at being thus relegated to childhood by one who was generally ready for any game or lark in the offing. He opened his lips to let her know in no uncertain terms that her airs and graces cut no ice with him, then subsided at a warning look from Mr. Ryding and contented himself with a mild reminder to the effect that Juliet wasn't dragooned into the game.

18

Miss Greyson moved smoothly into the breech before Juliet's pitying smile, directed at her brother, further aroused his ire.

"The game had gone on quite long enough in any case. I have frequently observed that social activities and games have a self-limiting span beyond which they tend to become a trial to be borne."

"Very true, ma'am," replied Sir Malcolm with the air of one making a discovery.

"The trick is to recognize that point before reaching it," contributed Mr. Kirkland with a smile that displayed strong white teeth.

Juliet trilled a laugh. "Well, your timing was excellent tonight, sir. You will surely stay and take tea with us? We cannot let you drive back to the Manor without some sustenance, can we, Aggie?"

Miss Greyson agreed that the demands of hospitality forbade sending guests out into the night unfed and rang for tea.

Conversation became general over the tea tray. If Juliet gave Mr. Kirkland every opportunity to monopolize her attention, his manners were too polished to avail himself of the invitation, though he managed to convey his admiration for her plainly enough to have her in a glow of pleasure by the time the small party embarked on the short drive to the Manor, having first made plans to meet the following day to show Mr. Kirkland the sights of the locality on horseback.

Miss Greyson had performed her role perfectly, remaining discreetly apart from the young people's talk unless some quiet diplomacy was required, but the interlude had seemed to drag on endlessly. Even the departure of their guests and the dispersal of the family members to their various bedchambers did not signal the end of what had become an exceedingly long day, since an excited Juliet showed every inclination to prolong the evening by a cozy visit in her companion's room.

Miss Greyson, seated on a cane-backed chair, kept a faint smile pinned to her face and listened patiently to a bubbling category, of Mr. Kirkland's obvious and imagined virtues. She concurred pleasantly that he was indeed more handsome than any of the gentlemen residing in the immediate locale, adding as a rider that this depended, of course, on whether one cared for that bold, brash type. When this remark met with disapprobation on the part of Miss Brewster, she apologized easily, adding with a placating smile that it was a fortunate circumstance, surely, that not all females preferred precisely the same type of man, or clothing for that matter, for that would insure excessive competition for a dwindling supply. Juliet flounced indignantly on her companion's bed, but she managed to utter a polite, "Just so, ma'am," in a wooden little voice.

Her sense of humor partly restored by the young girl's successful effort to keep to herself her thoughts on her companion's probable taste in men or clothing, Miss Greyson smiled kindly at her charge and agreed that Mr. Kirkland's presence in the neighborhood should certainly prove amusing. It would also very likely give rise to some seasonal festivities as the local hostesses sought to entertain him. This prediction gave Juliet an additional morsel to dream over, and she was finally persuaded to get some rest so as to be in her best looks for the ride arranged for the next morning.

"I beg your pardon for keeping you up so late talking, Aggie," she said contritely from the doorway. "You look terribly tired. Does your head ache? Shall I ask Mrs. Murchison to prepare a tisane for you?"

Miss Greyson quickly lowered the fingers that had been kneeding her temples and smiled warmly at Juliet.

"No, thank you, my dear. I am a little tired perhaps, but a good night's sleep is all I need to set me to rights again. I'll see you in the morning."

CHAPTER TWO

As the door finally closed behind Juliet, Miss Greyson acknowledged wearily that a good rest was the last thing she was likely to achieve tonight. Her fingers started kneeding her forehead again, then as they came into accidental contact with the spectacles, curled around them suddenly and dragged them from her face. She flung the spectacles to the bed with a violent gesture and moved jerkily over to the door, where she turned the key in the lock before dashing the back of her hand across wet eyelashes. She lumbered over to the same chair she had occupied a moment before, her heavy movements in striking contrast to the light-footed grace that was habitual. As she sank onto the rigid chair, the panic that she had suppressed for the last two hours rose in a tide and overwhelmed her physically. Her hands were actually trembling, and her throat felt horribly dry. The small cake she had forced down with her tea after Olivia had reminded her they were her favorites was now lodged in the pit of her stomach as though made of lead. If that were not enough to ruin her sleep, the headache she had denied was causing her temples to throb like a striking clock.

She wrung her hands together in her lap, dry eyed now, her mind churning with fears and doubts. What malignant twist of fate had brought that dreadful man to this particular spot? Suppose he recognized her, suppose he exposed the lie she was living, what would become of her? Her shaking hands crept up to cover her face, feeling momentarily cool on her hot cheeks. She had tried so hard to fit in, had submerged her personality, her own desires, to fullfil to the best of her ability the position she had obtained by deception.

Deception! Such an ugly word, but the correct word for what she had done. At the time, six months ago, she had been so desperate that this position with the Brewster family had seemed like a lifeline, and she had seized it, using the only means possible. At first she had been in a state of constant apprehension lest the deception be discovered, but as the months passed without incident, she had settled comfortably into the role she had assumed and had long since ceased to freeze inside each time a door opened. She had been completely unprepared tonight when a man who could ruin her had walked casually through the doorway and into their lives.

"Of course he did not recognize me!" she told herself in a fierce whisper. Determinedly she struggled against her cowardly fears, and forced herself to breathe slowly and deeply as she tried to recall everything that had occurred in the parlor during Mr. Kirkland's visit. She was almost positive that he had not recognized her, although there was no denying that he had studied her intently when they had been introduced. Possibly her face had betrayed some of the shock that had coursed through her body at the instant of recognition. Her recovery had been swift; surely she had given him no additional reason not to accept her at face value, and besides, he had been too absorbed with Juliet's charms to notice a plain governess well past the age to interest a man of his type.

Even as she comforted herself with this rationalization,

24

honesty forced her to recall that more than once during the conversational interval she had discovered his eyes fixed on her face in a look that could not be dismissed as casual. He was curious of course; that was not to be wondered at after her startled reaction to the sight of him. It was just a momentary curiosity that she would take care not to arouse again. Why should he recognize her when they had only met once, and briefly on that occasion? Why was she sitting here worrying that he might pierce her disguise when in all likelihood he would not have remembered her even had she looked exactly as she had seven months ago at their initial meeting. Neither had found favor in the other's eyes on that occasion.

"But you remembered him," a little voice reminded her relentlessly.

Abruptly she got up from the chair and walked over to a mirror above the chest of drawers, after detouring by the bed to pick up the discarded spectacles. She settled them on her nose, tucked a strand of hair beneath the cap, and studied her reflection in detail before removing them again along with the cap that covered her hair. She turned her back on her reflection and went to wash her face with the warm water in the pitcher on the mahogany stand. After patting her skin dry, she set about removing the hairpins and deliberately unplaited her hair. Still with those same deliberate movements, she took a brush from the top drawer of a small dressing table and began to brush the gray powder from her hair. Not until the long, thick tresses began to shine once more did she return to the mirror for a second look.

Gone was the drab spinster governess on the wrong side of thirty. In her place stood a young woman of no more than twenty or twenty-one years with gleaming chestnut-colored hair in striking contrast to white skin of an alabas-

25

ter smoothness and black-lashed green eyes that slanted intriguingly. The transformation was spectacular enough to bring reassurance that no one would be able to make any connections between the lively and popular Miss Virginia Spicer, formerly of Bath society, and the dull companion-governess to an unknown Essex family. It was a faint comfort to know that the unhappiness and anxiety of the past six months had not actually robbed her of her youth, but her eyes were sober, and she pressed her lips firmly together to discourage a tendency to tremble as she removed the unfashionable dark brown gown that was just enough too large to disguise her elegant figure and prepared for bed. For the moment the crisis was past, she trusted, but she could only look forward with apprehension to a closer association with Mr. Simon Kirkland.

She had been relatively successful of late in living from day to day and keeping memories of the past at bay, but the unexpected appearance of someone from her former life brought the memories rushing back to torment her. Lying in bed with wide-open eyes staring at the gathered silk lining of the canopy, she was recalling the circumstances of her first meeting with Simon Kirkland. The encounter had been quite brief, and she might well have forgotten him by now had not a subsequent incident infused the episode with equal parts of amusement and annoyance.

It was at a ball in the Lower Rooms at Bath that someone had presented Mr. Kirkland to her. She had taken one long look at his smiling face and promptly decided she did not care for too-handsome men who radiated self-assurance to an offensive degree. Consequently it was something of a pleasure to deny him the dance he politely requested. It was perfectly true that her card was full, but perhaps she had permitted something of her satisfaction in refusing him to manifest itself in voice or expression. She hurried over this unpalatable aspect of her own behavior, knowing her manners had been at fault, and passed on to the scene she had inadvertently overheard an hour or so later. She had been about to reenter the ballroom after a trip to the ladies' retiring room, where a maid had helped her to pin a torn petticoat, when the sound of her own name coming from the other side of the wall caused her to pause before going through the entrance arch.

"What, leaving already, Kirkland, without securing a dance with Miss Spicer?" a jovial masculine voice had asked. "What's happened to that vaunted London address of yours?"

"Ahhh, Miss Ginger Spice! Is she the local belle?" The mocking tones were unfamiliar, but Virginia had caught the name, and a picture of a self-assured stranger floated in front of her eyes as the voice continued, "I am totally cast down, gentlemen, to be compelled to admit that the fair damsel did not take to me. She refused to make room for me on her programme."

"I sh-shouldn't wonder at it if y-you c-called her Gi-Ginger!" The speaker's slight stammer identified him to the listening girl, who grinned at the horror he expressed at such a faux pax. Ned never had possessed a sense of humor.

"Indeed not." This was the first voice again. "Some select few people, such as your humble servant, are permitted to address Miss Spicer as *Ginny.*" The exaggerated condescension changed to a note of laughter as he added, "But even I, who claim the privilege of a childhood friendship, have not dared to call her Ginger since she was eight years old. I still have the scar where she kicked me on that occasion—about three inches below my right knee," he

27

appended with a nostalgic sigh that elicited a chuckle from Mr. Kirkland.

"A temper to match the red in her hair, eh? I guessed as much. But I wish you will tell me, either of you, what there is about Miss Spicer to warrant such popularity. There are two or three girls here tonight who eclipse her *au fait de beauté*. The coloring, I grant you, is glorious, with that lovely white skin and chestnut hair, and I'll even concede that her eyes are magnificent if one is partial to green, which I confess I am not—too much like a cat's for my taste; but what else does she have to raise her above the ordinary?"

"Ordinary . . . M-Miss Spicer?" Ned had echoed, scandalized. "Why, th-that is the l-last word that c-can be applied to her. Sh-she is unlike any other g-girl in the world. Who else is so b-blazingly alive? Who else p-possesses s-such sparkling wit, such gr-grace on the d-dance floor, such . . . such . . ."

"Such a superb figure," put in the original speaker laconically when Ned's evidently rapturous thoughts refused to be articulated further. "And such a superb seat on a horse."

"Enough, gentlemen, enough!" Mr. Kirkland had protested laughingly. "You have convinced me that Miss Spicer must indeed be something quite out of the common run of young ladies. It is unfortunate that I shall not have the opportunity to improve my acquaintance with her since I am leaving Bath on the morrow, but perhaps that is just as well, after all, since spoiled darlings are not quite to my liking. I infinitely prefer to concentrate my efforts on improving my acquaintance with heiresses."

Turning restlessly on her bed, Virginia had no trouble in recalling the challenging words verbatim. At the time she had been torn between amusement and the irritation most any female would experience on discovering that a gentleman is unimpressed with her charms, which irritation bears no relation whatsoever to the degree of liking the girl has for the man in question. While listening absently to Ned's vehement defense and her old friend Randall's less impassioned description of her as "sound to the core," she had toyed with the idea of disconcerting the offensive Mr. Kirkland by strolling around the corner and stopping to speak to the trio. She would have enjoyed watching their faces as they tried to guess just how much she might have overheard. However, a twinge of conscience about her earlier rudeness to the stranger, plus a shrewd notion that Ned and Randall would be the only persons embarrassed by such a gesture, had caused her to stifle the impulse, and she had altered her course to avoid the men. She had not seen Mr. Kirkland again, and although it rankled for a bit, the trivial incident was soon forgotten.

She had overheard that conversation seven months ago in Bath when she had been a carefree and popular young woman, the adored daughter of a local landowner. The ball had taken place in November. Before the Christmas season had arrived, her father was dead by his own hand, and Virginia's carefree youth was over.

She had started life as the eagerly awaited child of the only remaining son of a prominent Somerset family. The loss of his young wife when their only child was barely out of leading strings had proved a devastating blow to Mr. George Spicer. He had never remarried, but after an extended period of wandering about the Continent and the Far East, he had finally returned to England when Virginia was twelve. Over the outspoken protests of his elder sister, he had removed the daughter he barely knew from her care and reopened his house just outside Bath, where he had installed the young girl with no other woman to lend her countenance than a timid middle-aged governess. In time father and daughter had grown very close.

It was an unconventional upbringing for a young lady and one that drew forth much criticism from his female relatives, finally resulting in complete estrangement from his only sister. Virginia, who had never felt her aunt regarded her care as anything other than a duty to be performed, remained undisturbed by the controversy, quite content to be her father's companion. She had emerged from the schoolroom at sixteen and had functioned as her father's hostess thereafter, taking no notice of the censorious whispers of local matrons.

The Spicers were an old, respected family in the area, but the last of the line was living in reduced circumstances, due in great part to his proclivity for all forms of gambling and a marked lack of success in any that stretched back over a number of years. When it was high tide with Mr. Spicer, he denied his daughter nothing. She was mounted on the best horseflesh, drove her own phaeton and pair, and was indulged with a dress allowance fit for a duchess. It was several years before the inexperienced girl came to have a more realistic picture of the family finances. Then she cheerfully retrenched, giving up her phaeton and hunters and retaining only her favorite hack, despite her father's protests that they would come about soon. It cost her only a slight pang to refuse the promise of a London season as an extravagance they could ill afford. She had sufficient opportunities for social contacts with other young people right in Bath, thanks to the good offices of two of her mother's old friends, and by the time she was nineteen had refused several suitors, despite her lack of dowry.

Mr. Spicer, on the other hand, was desolated to think

he could not provide for his daughter on the same scale as his father had done for his sister. He became a trifle secretive and would disappear for days at a time without explanation. Virginia worried about him at these times but was powerless to help him. She tried to convince him that she was happy with the life she led, and certainly there were periods of renewed optimism when Mr. Spicer was persuaded his luck would change. At these times he would become again the wonderful companion his daughter missed. It was during one of these halcyon periods that Virginia had met Mr. Kirkland.

The shock of her father's death, and particularly the manner of it, had nearly prostrated the girl. Even now, seven months later, she could not readily recall the period directly afterward. For the first time she deliberately attempted to bring those two weeks before her mind's eye for review, but with limited success. Her aunt had arrived to take charge, and the grief-stricken girl had done as she was told, following orders with the mindless compliance of an automaton. She accepted her aunt's dictates regarding funeral arrangements and household management without protest, and at first barely comprehended her own situation as the true extent of her father's financial obligations gradually became apparent. Eventually it was abundantly clear that her father's credit had been so overextended that everything he owned would have to be sold to meet his debts.

Two factors occurring almost simultaneously were responsible for bringing Virginia out of the trough of numb despair into which she had been plunged at his death. One was the knowledge that she no longer possessed anything of value—even her mother's jewelry had been sold—and the second, and even more alarming fact, was the dawning realization that she was expected to take up residence in her aunt's household once more, but under very different circumstances this time. No longer would there be a steady financial contribution toward her keep; now she would in truth be an object of grudging charity. This would be the least of it, however. If Aunt Henrietta planned to avail herself of every opening to level accusations against her dead brother's character, as she was doing at present, an enforced sojourn in her house would be tantamount to a term in purgatory, but more hopeless, since purgatory was considered to be a temporary stage, while a dowerless female must be considered to be a permanent liability. Virginia found the prospect perfectly insupportable and began to cast around in her mind for some alternative.

Lying sleepless in the comfortable bed in the charming room that had been allotted her at Fairhill, she experienced anew the devitalizing sense of futility that was the lot of a penniless female trying to make her way unaided in the world. Because the prospects were frankly nonexistent. The only possible occupation for a woman of gentle birth was teaching, either in a girl's seminary or in a private home, and to secure such a position, assuming one had the required accomplishments, one needed a personal recommendation from someone known to the prospective employer. This was equally true of the allied position of hired companion, which demanded less in the way of academic achievement, but was less appealing because all too frequently it was difficult to distinguish between a companion and a personal slave.

Virginia knew herself to be no more than moderately well educated, despite the best efforts of the meek Miss Eddleston, whose reign over the schoolroom had been so abruptly terminated when her pupil was barely sixteen. Her musical training was extensive, and she believed herself equal to the task of imparting her knowledge to others, but she was the first to admit to severe deficiencies in the realm of artistic attainments expected of well-bred young ladies. No one had ever been able to discern the slightest merit in her childhood sketches, and her few attempts at watercolor painting had left Miss Eddleston thoroughly depressed. Like most women of her class, she could sew and embroider beautifully, but only where the creative aspect had been taken care of by other, more talented hands. She could not design clothes or draft patterns and was a total loss at trimming hats. She spoke French prettily enough, but her command of the Italian tongue was limited to those phrases necessary to the pursuit of musical studies. Her Latin background was meager, to say the least, and she had no Greek; nor would she wish to compare the scope of her reading with that of a top-notch governess.

A basically serene and optimistic nature did nothing for Virginia at this point in her life. She was tortured with vague regrets and feelings of guilt that she had not known how to comfort her father or guessed the depths of his despair so that she might have prevented his tragedy. In the course of her considerations as to how she might become self-supporting, the conclusions she reached with regard to her qualifications left her overwhelmed by the extent of her own inadequacies. The combination rendered her unable to take the smallest of decisions without agonizing over it.

She revealed as much to her good friend, Miss Agnes Greyson, when she came to condole with Virginia the week following Mr. Spicer's interment. Miss Greyson, who was shortly to leave her position as governess for a local family in order to be married, rounded on the apathetic girl and took her strongly to task for her defeatist

33

attitude. Once she accepted that Virginia was serious in seeking employment, she proceeded to make a list of her qualifications in a businesslike fashion, concluding that though the young woman might not suit the most exacting employer, that did not necessarily mean there were *no* situations where her combination of talents would be welcome.

"Then you believe I shall be able to secure employment with a family or in a seminary?" Virginia asked hopefully.

"Not an established seminary, I fear," replied Miss Greyson decidedly. "I should not think you are well enough trained in any subject except music to satisfy their requirements. No, it must be a family, and the right sort of family, too." There was a silence while Virginia waited expectantly. Miss Greyson appeared sunk in thought and at last resumed almost reluctantly. "The position I had accepted before Mr. Dobson made me an offer would be perfect for you except for one factor, and I fear that presents an almost insuperable obstacle."

"What factor could be so important?" asked Virginia, her eyes clouded with anxiety.

"Your extreme youth, my dear girl."

At this the dear girl's face fell ludicrously. "But I am of age, Aggie." She swallowed with difficulty and went on in dulled tones, "My father was buried on my birthday."

Miss Greyson patted her hand in wordless sympathy, but after a moment returned to her original line of thought, drawing each word out slowly.

"Prospective employers have a decided prejudice against very young or very pretty governesses and, forgive me, my dear, but you share both these handicaps."

The pale-featured girl smiled somewhat bitterly at her friend. "Young and pretty? I feel as plain as a pikestaff and easily double my age. It's an effort just to get out of bed in the morning."

"That feeling will pass, believe me, my dear, a lot sooner than you will attain sufficient years to make an employer willing to take a chance on you as a member of his household, especially if there are young men in the family."

"Perhaps my age will not be a consideration in a family with quite young children?" suggested Virginia.

"Perhaps," agreed Miss Greyson but with no conviction in her usually decided voice. "Is there someone who could help you to secure a post, someone who would be willing to give you a character?"

"There are one or two of Mama's friends who might be helpful, but I feel sure they will try to persuade me to take up residence in my aunt's household."

"And would you not be better advised to do just that? After all, she is all the family you have left. It need not be a permanent arrangement if you find, when your first grief is somewhat eased, that you cannot deal together."

"Aggie, I could not. We cannot be in the same room together for above five minutes before she begins criticizing Father. We should be at dagger drawing before a sennight had passed, but I would be trapped there forever without any funds."

"She won't live forever," stated the practical governess dryly. "As her only living relative, you are bound to inherit something."

"Taking into account the clash of our personalities, she will be much more apt to cut me out of her will entirely unless I can relinquish every bit of my independence and submit to her every whim. Surely I would find employment in a congenial family more to my taste, as well as being more rewarding financially." Virginia became aware that her friend had grown increasingly pensive during this earnest speech. "Have you thought of something, Aggie?"

"Ye . . . ess, perhaps, but it would never work, and the danger of discovery would be too great." The older woman shook her head as if to dismiss the aberrant idea, but she continued to examine the girl's face with peculiar intensity until the latter laughed with real amusement.

"Having gone so far, you will have to tell me now, Aggie. You have succeeded in arousing my curiosity to such an extent that I won't permit you to leave here without revealing this dangerous plot."

Miss Greyson smiled briefly at the deliberately dramatic choice of words but said soberly, "That's just what it would be, I fear—a plot. Do you recall a few moments ago I said I thought the position I had planned to take before Mr. Dobson proposed would be ideal for you?"

"Yes, of course, but would they accept me in your place?" Virginia looked doubtful.

"No, never!" The reply came without the least hesitation. "The position is primarily that of a companion and chaperon to a young lady of seventeen. Naturally her parent would not consider a girl of one and twenty for a position of such responsibility."

"Well, then?"

This time there was a pause before Miss Greyson continued slowly, "I had not yet met Sir Reginald Brewster when Hugh offered for me last week. He engaged me on Lady Mallory's recommendation subject to an interview that met with our mutual satisfaction. So much has happened since then that I have not had the opportunity to write to him to cancel the arrangement." Her voice trailed off and the two women stared consideringly at each other.

Virginia broke the silence after a charged moment.

"Does he know your age?"

"Yes."

Another silence, shorter this time.

"Does he know what you look like?"

"No, there was no description in Lady Mallory's letter to Sir Reginald. She was kind enough to allow me to read it before she posted it off to Essex."

"Essex?"

"Yes, a small village, Templedene, about twenty miles from London."

"I have never been to London or Essex." Then as the pause lengthened, "Would there be any chance, do you think, of meeting a mutual acquaintance of Lady Mallory's in Sir Reginald's household?"

"Lady Mallory is not personally acquainted with Sir Reginald. His wife was a connection of her cousin's. The cousin wrote that he was seeking a suitable female to take charge of his daughter until her comeout, which has been delayed for some reason or other. I have never met the cousin."

"Ahhh . . ." Virginia's eyes gleamed with satisfaction as she jumped up and crossed the room to stare critically into the mirror over the fireplace. "That leaves only the problem of my age, or rather my lack of age, to be overcome. Do you have any suggestion, Aggie?"

It had taken several hours of experimentation to achieve a disguise that satisfied Miss Greyson's criteria. It had been a simple enough matter to render Virginia fairly plain-looking by concealing her main assets. The wealth of chestnut hair could be screwed back and hidden underneath a pointedly unattractive cap, and the green of her eyes could be neutralized behind thick spectacles that also deprived the world of an unrestricted view of her rather spectacular black lashes. Unfortunately the spectacles also deprived Virginia of her accustomed view of the world,

37

and learning to walk or sew when she was wearing them was not the least of the problems confronting her in her new identity. The real difficulty in effecting this new identity, however, was to create the impression of added years. At close quarters theatrical makeup could be detected at once, so was not to be considered. It was Miss Greyson who finally hit upon the idea of dulling her friend's glowing complexion with a thin dusting of gray powder. The same applied to hair and eyebrows completed the process and added ten years to her age. In fact, she had complained to Aggie that her disguise made her look much older than the real Agnes Greyson, Virginia remembered as she reviewed the events that had launched her into her new life.

A little smile lightened her serious expression as she recalled Aggie's dogged insistence that she must err always on the side of caution. For the scheduled interview in a hotel in Bath she had had the benefit of her brisk friend's advice and criticism of her performance. Bolstered by a creditable disguise and the desperation necessary to embue her playacting with conviction, she had succeeded in impressing Sir Reginald with her capabilities for the position of companion to one daughter and governess to the other, and in January had embarked on her new life. She had told her aunt that she was paying an extended visit to a girlhood friend residing outside London and had tried not to be wounded by the relief her relative had been unable to conceal.

Reviewing the months of her association with the Brewster family, Virginia could now see that the move had been her salvation. Before coming here she had been so plunged into grief and despair that nothing less than urgent necessity could have prompted any action of any kind from her. Life amongst the youngsters at Fairhill demanded constant alertness on her part and left little time for brooding. She had avoided analyzing her feelings up to now, preferring to coast along from day to day, concentrating only on the daily routine or, at most, on the next event or activity scheduled.

She wasn't really happy—somehow it was impossible to envision a time when she might know real happiness again, but she was grateful not to be actively miserable. There was a certain satisfaction in performing her role in the household, and definitely an increasing pleasure in the warm relationships she was developing with the various members of the family. She had not realized the extent of her involvement until Mr. Kirkland's arrival with its implicit threat of disruption. Naturally she could not expect to remain here forever—even Olivia would have no further use for a governess in two or three years, but for the moment there was sanctuary at Fairhill, and she was determined to do everything in her power to maintain her position in this pleasant, normal family.

Ideally this meant removing the threat in the person of Mr. Kirkland, but Miss Spicer was no air dreamer, and it was perfectly plain that he had every intention of pursuing his acquaintance with the lovely Juliet. She had been uneasy from the moment of intercepting the glances exchanged between those two tonight, and now as she tossed and turned on the formerly comfortable bed, she tried to think of some way to prevent the incipient friendship from ripening. It was understandable that she should be concerned about possible developments from the standpoint of her own vulnerable position, but there was something else teasing at the edges of her memory. The nearly full moon, which had moved into view through an opening between the curtains she had drawn too hastily hours ago, had descended a few degrees before, on the fuzzy threshold of sleep, she was jerked awake by a sudden, word-perfect recollection of Mr. Kirkland's final statement on the occasion of that original meeting in Bath. He had denied any wish to get to know Miss Virginia Spicer better, declaring on a note of laughter, *"I infinitely prefer to concentrate my efforts on improving my acquaintance with heiresses."*

Juliet was a very considerable heiress. To Virginia's certain knowledge, she had inherited her mother's marriage portion, and Sir Reginald made no secret of his generous intentions with regard to dowering his two daughters. Oh, Lord! Was her charge to be the object of fortune hunters before she even made her bow to society? How could she alert Sir Reginald to the danger without disclosing her source of information?

Suddenly she was too warm and agitated to lie still. Thrusting the blanket aside, she grabbed her pillow and pummeled it vigorously before turning it over. Ah, that felt much cooler, at least for the moment. In a logical manner she attempted to rein in her galloping imagination. Surely a man could not be condemned on the slight evidence of a joking remark? Where was her sense of fair play? The scene she had overheard had been played out in a spirit of pure fun, at least on the part of Randall and Mr. Kirkland (Ned's reaction could be discounted).

She had no knowledge of Mr. Kirkland's financial standing; for anything she knew to the contrary, he might be rolling in riches. And even if he were comparatively poor, it still did not necessarily follow that he would seek to make his fortune by contracting an advantageous marriage. And further, even if this should be his intention, Sir Reginald was eminently capable of protecting his daughter's interest without aid from an ignorant governess. Besides, unless she was vastly mistaken, nothing less than an earldom would impress Sir Reginald, who was all too conscious of his own plebian origins. The baronetcy had been created by George III as a reward for the financial support that Sir Reginald's father, a wealthy mill owner, had provided during the war with the American colonies. On the soothing thought that no mere "mister" would find favor with her employer as a suitor for his daughter, she drifted into sleep at last.

CHAPTER THREE

It was with a deep reluctance that Virginia dragged herself out of bed the following morning, after what had seemed little more than a teasing nap. As she stared gloomily into the mirror, the thought crossed her mind that she looked Miss Greyson's age today before doing a thing to her face. She grimaced wryly at the shadows under her eyes and proceeded to plait the long hair with fingers that over the past few months had, of necessity, acquired deftness. Mornings were a problem under the best of circumstances because it was vital that she become Miss Agnes Greyson, aged one and thirty, before she set her eyes on another soul. She knew her habit of sleeping behind a locked door and declining all personal maid services was considered eccentric by the household, if indeed they did not harbor the suspicion that she wished to conceal some deformity. But this had been a potential hazard that she had reckoned with before she arrived, and she had been quite firm on the point. At her request warm water was left on a stand outside her door each morning. What she would do if one of the girls should need her services during the night was a horrible prospect she had never allowed herself to dwell on, but so far they had slept undisturbed and so had she. Fortunately she was an early riser who required no calls.

She rushed through the familiar routine this morning,

applying the fine gray powder to the front of her hair before tying on the ugly cap. It was amazing how a judicious rubbing of the stuff on the outline of her mouth could thin the finely modeled lips, and her arched black brows all but disappeared under the same treatment. She shrugged into the depressing brown cotton gown, plunked the spectacles on her nose, and turned away from her image with a slight shudder of aversion. In the beginning of this masquerade the sight of her new self had been vaguely reassuring. As long as she looked like this, she was safe from discovery. With the coming of the good weather, however, her reflection as Miss Greyson had gradually taken on a slightly distasteful aspect, *which was nonsensical!* "This is now *you;* make the best of it," she told herself firmly.

With this piece of good advice hopefully assimilated, she twitched her dress into line and proceeded briskly downstairs to the breakfast parlor. Here everything was blessedly normal. Bertram and Olivia, who were early birds, were attacking their food with the enthusiasm of youth. Mr. Ryding was drinking his coffee, but he set the cup back in its saucer and rose with a smile as Virginia entered the room soundlessly. She waved him back and also Bertram, who had started to execute a similar movement.

"Good morning everyone," she said in her brisk Miss Greyson voice, flashing a brief all-embracing smile at the occupants of the breakfast room, including Penniestone, who had entered almost on her heels to take her order. "Just coffee this morning, please, Penniestone." The words were meant for the butler, but Olivia, whose sharp eyes and ears missed nothing, particularly anything one might hope she'd miss, looked up from her porridge and studied her governess frankly.

44

"Don't you feel well, Miss Greyson? You look sort of . . . limp this morning." Sympathy and curiosity were equally blended in Olivia's query.

Virginia produced a mechanical smile. "I have a touch of the headache today, that is all, Olivia."

"A headache? Oh, pray, Aggie, not *today*! Had you forgotten we are engaged to ride with Sir Malcolm this morning?"

Virginia smiled warmly at the woebegone figure in the doorway. "Do not fret, my dear Juliet. I shall manage an easy ride, which this promises to be, and the fresh air will no doubt prove beneficial. I did not look to see you down so early, but do come in and have some breakfast." She patted the seat beside her invitingly, and Juliet drifted in, absently accepting Penniestone's assistance in serving her. There was an abstracted expression on her lovely face that turned swiftly to consternation when she glanced down at the heaped plate in front of her.

"Goodness," she protested faintly, "I don't want all this. You know I never eat meat in the morning, Penniestone. One egg and some toast will do nicely."

"Try the roast beef, Juliet, it's good," her brother urged.

The large blue eyes fixed on the young man who was helping himself to another slice of rare beef though she ignored the suggestion. "I was just thinking, Bertram. If you and Mr. Ryding mean to join the party Aggie need not come. She could lie down and rest her head."

"No, I thank you," came the prompt reply. "Watching you playing off your airs for the benefit of that Mr. Kirkland while we amble around the Manor's boundaries at a slow walk is not my idea of sport. Chris and I are for a good gallop in the wood, aren't we, Chris?"

"How can you be so disobliging, Bertram?" his sister complained. "And uncivil, too, for I am persuaded Sir

45

Malcolm meant his invitation for you as well." The blue eyes, full of entreaty, sought those of Mr. Ryding. "Do you not agree, sir, that it would be extremely uncivil of Bertram to go off on his own under the circumstances?"

"I *was* under the impression that the invitation included everyone," the tutor admitted. He smiled persuasively at Bertram. "No doubt Mr. Kirkland will be glad of a gallop or two during the excursion. I believe he mentioned he was trying the paces of a new hack."

"Oh, very well," Bertram assented, "if you would like to go, I suppose I must."

"*There*, Aggie!" Juliet faced her chaperon with the triumphant smile of one who has just accomplished something for another's good at great personal cost. "Now you may stay here and take care of that headache. You should have let Mrs. Murchison make you that tisane last night. Shall I order it for you now?"

"No, thank you, my dear," Virginia said firmly, concealing the amused comprehension she was experiencing at Juliet's eagerness to escape her chaperon's eye. "I am touched by your solicitude, but I promise you no such drastic measures will be necessary. It is a mild headache and will no doubt disappear in an hour or so."

"I do not wish to go riding either, Miss Greyson," Olivia piped up. "You and I can walk in the gardens for a time."

"That sounds a very nice program for the morning," agreed her governess, refilling her cup from the silver coffee pot. As she turned to pour some for Juliet a second later, she noted with amusement that that young lady's avowed disinclination for a hearty breakfast had not prevented her from cleaning her plate. Nursing her cup between her hands, she frowned slightly at the dark brew. Perhaps she should not have allowed Juliet to maneuver her into remaining at home while she carried on an unmonitored flirtation with Mr. Kirkland, but after a nearly sleepless night the opportunity to postpone her next meeting with a possible nemesis had been too tempting to renounce.

It was no more than a postponement of the inevitable, of course, but a few quiet hours in which to reforge her courage and gather the necessary resolution to face the man with all flags flying would be most welcome. And, indeed, her presence in the riding party was not likely to cause a significant delay in the getting-acquainted process between two persons who were obviously attracted to one another. She could better use her time in deciding how to go about driving a spoke in his wheel.

When the riding party returned several hours later, Virginia was able to greet her charge with complete self-possession. A quiet stroll in the delightful shrubbery at Fairhill had done much to restore her equilibrium, and Olivia, when not forced to compete for the attention of her governess, had proved to be a pleasant companion. She was no nearer the formation of a policy to discourage Mr. Kirkland's attentions to Juliet than ever, but she felt more capable of dealing with whatever situation might arise.

Over a late luncheon with her sister and chaperon Juliet was full of the delights the morning had offered. Mr. Kirkland was the most attentive of escorts, the most charming of conversationalists, and, in short, the epitome of all the manly virtues. Virginia listened to a reconstruction of his conversation with an attentive expression that masked a growing sense of forboding. He was certainly wasting no time in ingratiating himself with the girl!

"Mr. Kirkland was most sorry to hear you were indisposed this morning, Aggie dear," Juliet was saying brightly. "He sent you his regrets that you were unable to join

47

us and his earnest hopes that you will soon be restored to perfect health."

"How very . . . civil of Mr. Kirkland," Virginia murmured, "to express an interest, however false it must be deemed, in having the company of a middle-aged chaperon in addition to that of a lovely young girl."

"No, really, Aggie," Juliet continued earnestly, "he was most interested in you, said I was fortunate to have the influence and company of such an intelligent and charming woman. He talked about you for several minutes most admiringly."

Her companion was so perverse as to remain completely ungratified by Mr. Kirkland's approbation. Indeed, if her complexion were not already so pallid, someone more observant than Juliet might have detected a slight loss of color at this flattering report.

"Why should Mr. Kirkland talk about me?" she inquired with a touch of sharpness.

Juliet was casual. "Oh, he simply wondered how long you had been with the family and where you were from originally—you know the sort of thing—simply trying to get to know all of us."

"I . . . see. And what did you tell him?"

The young girl looked faintly surprised by the question. "Why, what should I tell him? I explained that Papa had been looking for a companion for me until my comeout and that Lady Mallory had recommended you."

"Did you mention Bath?" Virginia asked, striving for a casual tone herself while she kept her hands loosely clasped by a strong effort of will.

"I did, naturally. Mr. Kirkland said he has a wide acquaintance in Bath himself. He mentioned some names, but I don't recall them. He wondered if you might perhaps have met there, though he was unacquainted with Lady

Mallory." She laughed merrily. "I told him impossible, for you would not have forgotten someone like him, would you, Aggie?"

"No," Virginia agreed in hollow accents, "one would not be likely to forget Mr. Kirkland once met."

Over the next several days the one boon Virginia would have wished granted by a good fairy would have been the opportunity to forget Mr. Kirkland. It seemed every time she turned around he was calling on some pretext or other, sometimes with Sir Malcolm in tow, but just as often by himself. Scarcely a day went by that she was spared the unwelcome sight of his handsome, inquisitive face bending politely over her hand before he turned his attention to Juliet. He delivered the London newspapers to the family with Lady Wrenthorpe's compliments and obligingly collected Amelia after visits with her friend.

Virginia had herself well in hand now and was able to greet him with a cool civility on each occasion and to reply to his conversational overtures with a bland assurance that echoed his own. He was a witty and entertaining conversationalist, but thanks to her unconventional upbringing, Virginia had been at home in the company of gentlemen since she was sixteen. If he hoped to disconcert her or trap her into admitting to a prior meeting, she was determined to disappoint him. At their first encounter after that morning ride she had evaded, he had smilingly inquired whether they might have met in Bath. Virginia endured the searching stare that succeeded the smile with outward equanimity as she calmly denied a meeting, and she answered his subsequent queries as to possible mutual acquaintances with apparent willingness, not even blinking when Randall Briggs's name was mentioned.

"I'm afraid Lady Mallory has not been socially active

in recent years," she explained sweetly. "She does not often go into town."

"Surely, being a longtime resident of the area, she would be acquainted with the Spicer family, whom I understand to be a prominent local family, would she not?"

"W-why, yes, the Mallorys and Spicers are friends of long standing. Are *you* well acquainted with the Spicers?" she asked, making a quick recovery.

"I've met only one member of the family, a Miss Virginia Spicer, a moderately attractive female with rather too much height in her manner. Would you say that was a fair description of the young lady, Miss Greyson?"

"I am not sufficiently acquainted with Miss Spicer to pass an opinion on her manner, sir," Virginia replied repressively, striving to keep a certain natural stiffness out of her own manner.

"Ah, just so, ma'am. Would you concur with my judgment that Miss Spicer is a reasonably attractive young woman?" Mr. Kirkland persisted smoothly.

"As to that, sir, I found her much like any other young woman of that age." Virginia had regained her balance now and spoke with admirable disinterest.

"Oh, ungenerous, Miss Greyson!" exclaimed Mr. Kirkland with a mocking smile. "Why, I have it on the authority of my own observation that Miss Spicer is considered something quite out of the common style in those parts."

"Then she stands in no great need of my approval to swell the ranks of her admirers," avowed Virginia with spirit, wondering all the while how she came to be in the ludicrous position of appearing to disapprove of herself. It was with relief that she welcomed the timely appearance of her charge in the doorway. "Here is Miss Brewster now. Juliet, my dear, we are indebted to Mr. Kirkland as kind

Lady Wrenthorpe's messenger for conveying the London papers to us."

She subsided with gratitude as Juliet's exuberant thanks engaged all Mr. Kirkland's attention thereafter. The gentleman's manners were such that he did indeed attempt to keep the discussion general, but at this point Virginia was pleased to abet Juliet's efforts to maintain control of the conversation by retiring, in spirit at least. She kept her glance on her fingers, which were busy with a delicate piece of embroidery, while her pulses steadied down to their normal pace and her brain reviewed the scene just enacted.

On the whole she felt she had given nothing away, but on the other hand she would never dare take her oath that Mr. Kirkland's suspicions regarding a previous meeting had been entirely laid to rest. The wretched man was as persistent as an ant with a huge crumb in front of it. Though inadequate to the task himself, he *would* take it to his destination by whatever means suggested themselves. Unless her acting ability was sadly deficient, she must have convinced him that she recalled no meeting. If something about her appearance still teased at his memory, surely he would now conclude that he had perhaps glimpsed her on some occasion at Bath without having been formally presented. Good manners alone would demand that he abandon his cross-questioning tactics in future.

Over the next several days events seemed to bear out this theory. Mr. Kirkland, though always courteous to the unobtrusive governess, directed his considerable charm of manner almost exclusively toward Juliet. He dangled after her elegantly, paying charming compliments that brought a glow of mingled triumph and pleasure to the young girl's sparkling countenance, but to do him credit, which Virginia did, however reluctantly, he never went a step beyond the line of what was permissible in his behavior toward such an unfledged girl as Juliet. His visits, though frequent, were of short duration, and word came back through the usual country sources that he joined Sir Malcolm in paying courtesy calls at other homes in the vicinity. In fact, a more popular visitor had never graced the neighborhood of Templedene.

Such was the situation a sennight after Mr. Kirkland's arrival when the Brewster household was enlivened by the anticipated return of the master from an unusually protracted stay in London. Sir Reginald was a man of varied business interests that frequently took him to the city, but though he had maintained a suite of rooms in St. James's Street for a number of years, he preferred to keep his residence in the country.

Just recently he had entered into negotiations to purchase a suitable town house from which to launch his daughters into society. The late Lady Brewster had been quite well connected, and had she lived, no doubt the family would have spent part of every year in town as a matter of course. The early years of her marriage having resulted in several confinements in rapid succession, however, Lady Brewster's constitution, never robust, was wholly undermined. She did not again achieve a sufficient degree of health to undergo the rigors of the London social season and, in fact, was dead before Olivia had attained her second birthday. Sir Reginald's social ambitions suffered a total eclipse at the demise of his wife, and he was content to keep his family in the comfortable house in Essex, where he had formed pleasant friendships with a number of the local gentry.

Sir Reginald was a fond, indulgent parent whose appearance after an absence was always greeted with delight by all his children, but his daughters at least were espe-cially eager for his return on this occasion, since he had sent word a few days past that he had brought his search for a town house to a successful conclusion. Both girls were agog with curiosity as to the location and style of their future residence. No more than mildly interested in the new house, Virginia was nevertheless as eager to wel-come Sir Reginald as his daughters at the moment. It would be a decided relief to turn the responsibility for the fast blooming friendship between Juliet and Sir Malcolm Wrenthorpe's guest over to her father.

After a deal of mental wrestling with her conscience she had determined that it would be an act of supererogation on her part to confide her own doubts and suspicions of Mr. Kirkland's purpose to Sir Reginald. If ever a man were capable of protecting his daughter's interests, that man was Sir Reginald Brewster. With a sense of rescue animating her features, she greeted her employer with unusual warmth on entering the breakfast parlor the morning following his return to Fairhill.

Sir Reginald smiled at her in a kindly fashion. "Come in, come in, Miss Greyson. You are looking particularly well today."

For a second Virginia stood very still, all expression wiped from her face while she tried frantically to recall whether she might have neglected to apply the gray pow-der, then she relaxed and slipped into her chair. Goodness, what a way to react to a mild compliment! Since the advent of Simon Kirkland, she had lost all her hard-gained confidence in her role as middle-aged companion. Taking herself to task mentally as a coward, she pretended an interest she did not feel in Penniestone's movements, until she was able to make some unexceptional remark in the brisk voice she had cultivated for her new position.

Mr. Ryding and Bertram, back from their morning ride, joined the early pair within a few moments, and the talk turned to seasonal changes in the area since Sir Reginald had last been home. Virginia allowed it to wash over her as she made a covert appraisal of her employer in the light of the new role he would have to assume, sooner than he might have expected, of protector of his nubile daughter's interest. She saw a man who carried his five and forty years with the ease of splendid health. Except for a sprinkling of gray in the front of his crisp brown hair and a slight thickening of his waistline, Sir Reginald could not have changed appreciably from the days of his youth. His eyes were the same clear gray as his son's and younger daughter's, though they did not share the same ingenuousness of expression. Without being precisely handsome, his blunt features were arranged to form a pleasant whole, and his smile revealed his genial nature.

Bertram had something of his sire's cast of countenance, but his was a finer-honed version. The senior Brewster was an impressive figure, not much above middle height, but with the massive shoulders and strongly muscled thighs of an athlete, the type of man who would always appear more to advantage in riding clothes than in a drawing room. Although he certainly looked the complete gentleman, the master of Fairhill was more comfortable in the masculine company of the hunting and sporting country gentry than amongst their ladies making small talk over the tea cups.

In the dozen years that followed his wife's early demise, the only continuous feminine companionship he had enjoyed (and he might have taken exception to the verb employed) had been provided by an elderly aunt, who had made her home with him for the sake of his motherless children until eight months previously, when she had de-

54

parted for Harrowgate to nurse her ailing sister. This event had been the spur to Virginia's own inclusion in the household.

On the whole she liked Sir Reginald very much. If she found his conversation uninspiring and his tastes to be confined almost entirely to sporting pursuits, the same could be said of a great many men in his position and, when balanced against the warm gratitude he had several times expressed for her beneficial influence over his daughters, were hardly to be reckoned as serious flaws in an employer. He might not aspire to a reputation as a wit, awake on every suit and au courant with all the trends and spicy gossip of the tonnish world, but Virginia was persuaded that intellectual superiority would avail Mr. Kirkland nothing if in the pursuit of *his* interest he ran up against what Sir Reginald perceived to be in the interest of the Brewster family.

She sat back with her second cup of coffee, more than satisfied with the results of her silent survey. She was suddenly most desirous of being among those present when Sir Reginald met his daughter's newest admirer.

As is so often the case, the historic first meeting between antagonists did not at all measure up to the drama with which the interested parties had invested the event. Virginia was aware that in amongst a volley of questions concerning the pertinent details of the new town house, Juliet was acquainting her father with all the latest local news since Sir Reginald had been away, and foremost among snippets about the number of kittens produced by the kitchen cat and the youngest stable boy's latest peccadilloes were rhapsodic descriptions of the Wrenthorpes' distinguished guest and his behavior on several occasions.

The governess was moved to admiration by her employer's calm and interested reception of each tidbit. There could be no doubt that Sir Reginald had assimilated the importance to his daughter of this visitor—she had seen the assessing look that crept into his eyes as Juliet waxed eloquent on Mr. Kirkland's manifest attractions—but the master of Fairhill, widowed at a young age, had made a conscientious effort to be both father and mother to his offspring, and he knew better than to interrupt the flow of excited chatter with parental questions.

Juliet came away from the interview confirmed in her belief that her Papa was the most understanding parent in the world, and one moreover who never failed to enter into his children's most pressing concerns, while her companion breathed a sigh of relief that the burden of protecting the lovely innocent was no longer on her shoulders alone.

Sir Malcolm brought his visitor to call upon Sir Reginald on the day following his return to Fairhill. The females of the household were not privileged to witness this initial meeting, which took place in Sir Reginald's study, but it was obvious that the occasion was distinguished by the utmost cordiality on all sides. Penniestone reported to Cooper, Sir Reginald's valet, that the best Madeira had been ordered sent up, and the second footman, who was stationed in the hall outside the study, confirmed that on several occasions bursts of merriment had penetrated the double doors of solid oak. Juliet later confided to her companion that she had known Papa would appreciate the multitude of virtues that distinguished Mr. Kirkland from the plodding provincials who had hitherto paid court to her.

In any event, relations between the two households continued in a harmonious fashion, and Virginia had ceased to expect any dramatic disclosures when a note was delivered to Sir Reginald inviting the inhabitants of Fairhill to a dinner party celebrating the return to the Manor of the elder daughter of the family and her husband from an extended stay on their estates in Northumberland.

CHAPTER FOUR

"And we are all bidden to attend, Aggie, even Bertram and Mr. Ryding, and Olivia is to come too to keep Mellie company," Juliet declared, waving the sheet of cream-colored paper under her companion's nose. She had entered the small room the females of the family used as a private sitting room with more haste than elegance, animated by the desire to be the bearer of such pleasant news before Olivia should steal a march on her. "Arabella Wrenthorpe that was—she is Lady Teasdale now—is a most good-natured girl with very easy manners. It will be delightful to see her again."

"Is she quite young then, Lady Teasdale?" inquired Virginia with interest.

"Three years older than I am, and she has been married for almost a year. I was one of her bridesmaids last September. It was the greatest fun imaginable. There were over two hundred guests, and I wore the loveliest gown of celestial blue crepe over a white underdress with a wreath of white roses in my hair."

Virginia smiled in sympathy with Juliet's enthusiasm. "I was a member of a wedding party last year also. It was a spring wedding, however, and we wore varying shades of yellow and ivory," she went on in a reminiscent vein, then broke off abruptly at the odd look on the younger

59

girl's face. "It was a very quiet wedding," she finished awkwardly. "The bride was a g-woman I had known all my life, almost a sister one might say." Her color rose as Juliet continued to stare at her companion with ill-concealed amazement, and she hastened to change the subject. "Do tell me what dress you favor for the Wrenthorpe dinner party."

Thankfully, this red herring proved successful, and Virginia was treated to a critical appraisal of Juliet's extensive wardrobe that lasted for the next ten minutes. She did not interrupt the recitation or try to reply beyond a smile or a murmured agreement when Juliet asked her opinion on various possibilities, having guessed correctly that these queries were posed in a strictly rhetorical sense, the young girl being totally absorbed in conducting a debate in her own mind.

Virginia was grateful for the breathing space in which to reassemble her shattered confidence. Never before had she made such a gaffe in her dealings with the Brewster girls. Naturally Juliet would stare to hear her middle-aged companion declare that she had served as a bridesmaid no longer than a twelve month ago. She was all the more shaken because she had honestly believed that over the last few months she had created another self who was totally separate from the former Virginia Spicer and who dealt with the concerns of the young Brewsters on an entirely different level than Virginia Spicer could have done at age twenty-one.

What unhappy influence could have prompted staid Miss Agnes Greyson to commence exchanging girlish confidences with a seventeen year old? If, as would seem evident, she had not succeeded in burying her former identity for the duration of her employment at Fairhill, she had best set about accomplishing this task post haste lest the employment in question come to an abrupt and painful end. Meanwhile she must trust to the self-preoccupation of the very young to keep Juliet's powers of observation dulled. For this reason she was more than willing to repair to Juliet's bedchamber to continue the one-sided discussion about the all-important choice of a gown for Friday's dinner party.

As usual when crossing the threshold of the young girl's room, Virginia experienced an aesthetic satisfaction that the setting complimented its exquisite occupant so perfectly. It was a corner room, and the sheer white curtains beneath the chintz draperies at the two large windows allowed abundant sunshine to create an impression of brightness and freshness. This was further enhanced by the sparkling white bedcovering with its ample folds. The posts of the single bed were thin and gracefully turned and supported a ruffled canopy of the same blue and rose floral-patterned chintz that hung at the windows. A deep blue carpet covered the central portion of the large square area. In this room all the furniture was of a pale satinwood that shone with frequent polishing. There was a particularly attractive small escritoire near one window that held a blue and white Chinese vase, now filled with crimson roses whose aroma poured out to greet them. A carved washstand was tenanted by a bowl and pitcher formed from the same blue flowered white porcelain.

After a pleasurable appraisal of the charming apartment, Virginia dropped into a dainty cane-backed chair with a blue velvet seat and prepared to give her attention to Juliet, who was dragging gowns willy-nilly out of a huge French armoire and holding them up against her body for a brief inspection in the long mirror next to the washstand before whirling to display each to her companion.

The return of Sir Reginald and the fairly casual treatment of herself by Mr. Kirkland in the past week had succeeded in soothing Virginia's jumpy nerves. She was easily able to simulate enough interest in the proceedings to satisfy Juliet. They considered the merits of a lavender dress in a soft cotton, self-trimmed with ruching at the hem, dismissed the claims of a yellow sprigged muslin, despite its flattering color, on the grounds that it was liable to emphasize the wearer's extreme youth, and finally settled on a rose pink confection with tiny puffed sleeves tied up with knots of flowers and a décolleté low enough to draw attention to the pale perfection of Juliet's throat and shoulders.

On the night of the party her maid threaded a narrow velvet ribbon of the same deep rose as the sash around the high waist of the gown through an artless arrangement of loose curls that flattered the girl's fresh beauty. As Juliet tucked a handkerchief into the netted reticule that she slipped over her wrist and accepted a delicate fan fashioned of carved ivory sticks and cream-colored silk, Virginia, who had come to supervise the final moments of her charge's toilette, expelled a long breath of pure admiration. Really, the child had never looked lovelier. The deep blue eyes that were quite brilliant enough at any time to suit the taste of the most particular critic had taken on an added sparkle tonight, revealing eager anticipation of a rare treat.

"You look delightful, my dear," she said simply. "Your father will be pleased with his lovely daughter tonight."

"Thank you, Aggie. You look very becoming also." Juliet was being sweetly earnest. "You should wear that style of dress more often. It gives you an air of . . ." She searched for a word. "Of elegant simplicity." She put her head on one side and studied her companion with eyes that held a tiny gleam of something that might have been curiosity.

Virginia acknowledged the well-meant compliment with a polite little smile, but she was a trifle uneasy over her own appearance, which had presented something of a problem tonight. Her wardrobe was a problem at any time since she had had almost no money with which to provide herself with the sort of garments likely to be worn by a middle-aged governess back in January when she was preparing to enter employment with the Brewster family. Naturally, none of her own dresses were suitable for her prospective situation. With Agnes Greyson's generous participation in the short time remaining before her own marriage, she had been able to make three daytime dresses in the drab colors and modest style they had deemed advisable to project Virginia's new image.

She had exchanged her smart green wool pelisse with its fur cuffs and collar for a slightly shabby black one that Agnes had worn for two years, pleading that she wished her friend to accept it as a wedding gift when the older woman had demurred. She had insisted on making her a present of a very fine Norwich silk shawl that had cost every penny of fifty guineas also. When Agnes had protested that she must pack her nicer things away for future use in the event the position did not last, Virginia had declined with all the determination of one burning her bridges behind her, declaring with simulated lightness that all her clothes would be out of fashion by the time she might need them again. Only the very real distress on her friend's generally placid countenance had caused her to relent to the extent of leaving a small trunk of her nicest possessions in Miss Greyson's care.

It had been an economic necessity to attempt to alter a couple of her less-striking gowns for evening wear. She

63

had included the one she was wearing tonight in the belief that the plainly made dove gray silk would be more suitable for a woman past her youth than some of her other gowns. Unfortunately, subsequent appraisal of herself in the dress when safely established at Fairhill had revealed that not only did its simple lines and perfect fit emphasize her excellent figure, but these same qualities rendered any alterations impossible. With few enough changes at her disposal for the occasional local gatherings to which she accompanied Juliet, she had even considered whether she might lessen the attractiveness of the gown by adding some sort of irrelevant trimming, but apart from her lack of creativity when it came to fashion designing, the disadvantage of the figure-molding aspect of the gray silk would still remain. Regretfully she had relegated the dress to the back of the wardrobe until tonight, when for reasons she did not stop to analyze she had dithered over her simple toilette until it was almost time to check on Juliet, at which time she had thrust aside her well-worn gowns and unhesitatingly emerged with the gray silk in her hands. It had been a matter of two minutes to don the gown.

She had whisked herself out of her bedchamber without so much as a glance at the results, but Juliet's unaccustomed praise had, too late, caused doubt of the wisdom of her impetuous decision to undermine the calm detachment, which she had cultivated as an actress perfects a role each time she plays it. Now as she helped Polly to dispose a gauzy scarf over Juliet's shoulders, she told herself reassuringly that figures did not reveal age, faces did; and she had taken the usual precautions with the gray powder. A somewhat more elaborate but equally unattractive lace cap totally concealed her rich chestnut tresses and her spectacles, as always, destroyed any other claims her features might have to be considered even passable. Faced with the impossibility of altering things at this point, she dismissed her qualms with a brisk shake of her head.

"Come, my dear, it is time we proceeded to the saloon. Your papa will be wondering what is happening up here. I hope Olivia is nearly ready."

"Oh, Livvy was ready ages ago. She looked in for a moment before you arrived." Juliet smiled her thanks at Polly and followed Miss Greyson through the door the maid had opened.

As they descended the wide staircase together, the young girl eyed her companion consideringly and returned unerringly to the subject Virginia wished to avoid.

"Is that a new gown, Aggie?"

"No, I've had it this year or more. Here, let me adjust this scarf a trifle for you, so it will drape more gracefully in back."

Juliet halted obediently and stood still while this maneuver was performed. "There, that's better."

They resumed their descent with Virginia trying unsuccessfully to speed their progress. Juliet was quite content to dawdle.

"I do not recall seeing it before. Why have you not worn it ere this? It's by far the most becoming of your gowns."

Virginia sighed silently but managed to keep her voice pleasant and casual as she explained, "I prefer gowns with long sleeves except in the summer heat." She was certainly not sorry to arrive at that moment at the doors to the main saloon, standing open to reveal the three men of the party within. Hearing their voices, Olivia had darted toward the doors as the ladies entered.

"What took you so long, Juliet? I could understand it taking you forever if you had a lot of handicaps to overcome, but *you* should be able to dress in fifteen minutes, hairstyle and all."

65

This forthright speech, uttered in an impatient tone, brought forth spontaneous laughter from everyone save Juliet, who blushed in adorable confusion. Virginia had ample opportunity to observe the reactions of the three gentlemen in the room since they were, to a man, absorbed in staring at her companion. Bertram's mischievous smile flashed briefly before disappearing from sight as he bowed low before his sister in mock homage, but it was the sight of the identical expression adorning the faces of the two elder men that caused Virginia to grip her lower lip firmly between her teeth to prevent an instinctive protest. *Oh, no, not that complication, please!* Her head swiveled instinctively toward Sir Reginald to ascertain whether he was aware of Mr. Ryding's reaction, and her tension eased somewhat, since it was obvious that Sir Reginald's attention was still concentrated on his lovely daughter, whose hand he now raised to his lips in a gallant gesture.

Glancing again at Mr. Ryding, Virginia was relieved to see nothing save polite admiration on his face as he added his quiet compliments to his employer's. She could almost have convinced herself that she had imagined the tutor had stared at Juliet in a tender and *proprietory* fashion at first, were it not for a slight betraying rise of color in his cheeks when he became aware of the older woman's regard. His face was carefully expressionless now as he wished Miss Greyson a civil good evening, and she experienced a surge of pity for his hopeless state mixed with a new respect for his self-control.

As the party prepared to depart, she derived what consolation she might from the conviction that Juliet had been distracted by her brother's farcical gesture before she had had time to observe the effect her beauty had had on her brother's tutor. *That* would have been tantamount to putting a loaded gun in a child's hands, she reflected

66

grimly. Juliet was enough of a coquette without providing her with additional ammunition.

At least her flirtation with Mr. Kirkland was not likely to have unfortunate repercussions with respect to Bertram and his tutor. Some instinct assured Virginia that Mr. Ryding would never allow his partiality to become apparent, no matter how many suitors flocked around Juliet. She refused to speculate about his strength of character, however, should Juliet show signs of returning his affection. Instead she focused her attention upon the evening ahead of them.

She had been to the Manor on several previous occasions. Lady Wrenthorpe had languished for lack of young companionship following the marriage and subsequent departure of her elder daughter. She had shown herself more than willing to offer her hospitality and chaperonage to Juliet during the period before Miss Greyson had joined the Brewster household and had continued to welcome the young girl and her new companion to the Manor. Indeed, she pressed invitations on Juliet to regard the Manor as a second home.

If Miss Greyson suspected that Lady Wrenthorpe hoped by this practice to throw the well-dowered girl across her son's path more frequently, she was careful to keep her suspicions to herself since Sir Reginald obviously valued the friendship of his neighbors.

She rather enjoyed visiting the Manor, which had a marvelous situation on a gentle hill amidst tangled romantic gardens that had long since ceased to be controlled by a diminished outdoor staff. There was a very fine stand of trees that formed the boundary between the Brewster and Wrenthorpe properties. By road the houses were more than two miles apart, but the young people of both families were accustomed to cutting through the woods for easier access.

The sun was descending as the Brewster carriage entered the straight drive flanked by massive rhododendrons, and its dying rays gave a red-gold glow to the noble pile of weathered gray stone that formed the principal wing of the house and lighted fires in the mullioned windows. This entrance led into a great hall hung with antique armor and weapons, a chamber that was as uncomfortable as it was impressive. It featured an enormous stone fireplace that could hold several good-sized tree trunks but was incapable of combating the drafts that whistled through the place in winter. The handsome oak staircase that branched off after a single-flight led to a newer wing on the right where the family apartments were located.

The Fairhill party, minus Olivia who had followed a footman to Amelia's bedchamber, was escorted into this wing at a snail's pace by Dunston, the venerable silver-haired butler of Thorpe Manor, whom Virginia privately considered a likely candidate for the distinction of the oldest butler in captivity. In the course of their pilgrimage she had several times to restrain the impulse to assist his progress with a supporting hand on his shriveled arm. No one else in the quietly chattering party seemed in the least concerned that this effort might prove to be his last in this mortal sphere, nor did the hesitant rasp of his audible breathing apparently inspire the others with a compelling urge to complete each tentative inhalation for him.

Evidently the doddering Dunston was such a familiar institution in the neighborhood that no one save a stranger took notice of him, but Virginia heaved a sigh of relief when his heroic exertions were crowned by success in the attainment of the archway to the large drawing room humming with half-realized vocal tones that ranged from snatches of shrill soprano to rumbling bass echoes. A quick glance at the girl by her side revealed that Juliet's spirit was on tiptoe with excitement, her lovely face alight with anticipation of pleasure.

Although Dunston's quavery announcement of the late-comers scarcely rose above the level of conversation in the large apartment, their arrival did not go unnoticed. There seemed to Virginia, who had expected a more or less intimate gathering of the two families, to be crowds of people stationed about the room, but her startled senses had no time to identify the components of each group before the pattern was disturbed as several elements surged forward to engulf the Fairhill party. Behind them the groups quivered from reaction to this wrenching apart, then reformed into new patterns.

"Sir Reginald, this is indeed a pleasure!"

"Dearest Juliet, at last!"

A younger, more vivid version of the blond woman approaching Sir Reginald with extended fingers flew past Lady Wrenthorpe to throw her arms about Miss Brewster with a squeal of delight, while the rest of the company looked on with varying degrees of affectionate tolerance.

Lady Teasdale—for Virginia did not require Juliet's answering squeak of *"Bella!"* to identify the young woman embracing her charge—was obviously a tiny bundle of nervous energy with a petite but perfect figure and her mother's huge, rather light-blue eyes and small-boned features. It took several minutes of combined efforts on the part of her parent and brother to quash the one-sided conversation between the young women and restore enough order to permit general introductions to be made. Miss Greyson and Mr. Ryding were presented to Lord Teasdale, a slightly built young man of moderate height some half dozen years older than his wife, as fair as she but not nearly so loquacious. Virginia liked his candid gray eyes and quiet manner at once and could not but approve of the way he brought his animated, wildly chattering bride to a halt by the simple expedient of raising one light brown eyebrow in her direction whenever she tended to become carried away by enthusiasm.

After the first impression of vast multitudes, it was a relief to discover that the other people in the room were members of one family already known to her, with the exception of a young man, the son of the family, newly down from Cambridge for the long vacation. Mr. Alistair Penrose was a good-looking youth of nineteen or so whose facade of bored sophistication cracked apart at his first real look at Juliet, whom he had not seen for nearly a year. He abandoned his two sisters in mid-sentence and hastened to station himself next to Juliet, to whom he turned after greeting Sir Reginald and making his bow to Miss Greyson and Mr. Ryding.

"Your very obedient servant, Miss Brewster," he declared warmly, with a light in his brown eyes that was familiar to Miss Greyson.

"Why so formal all of a sudden, Staro?" asked Bertram with his friendly grin. "Has Cambridge made you so high in the instep you've forgotten your old friends?"

"I'd like an answer to that too, Staro," Juliet inserted with a provocative upward glance that belied demurely pouting lips. "Have you become too grand to address me by my given name?"

Virginia knew an instant's pity for the furious red that swept over Mr. Penrose's fair skin as he heartily shook Bertram's hand, but it was emotion wasted as the young man recovered quickly.

"No, *you* have," he said, addressing the dark-haired girl, his voice and countenance eloquently expressive of

70

the most fervent admiration, "or if not grand exactly, at least so grown-up I daren't call you Juliet—at least not without permission."

"Well, you have it," that young lady declared promptly, responding to the invitation in his tones with an enchanting smile for him, before turning the smile toward Mr. Kirkland, who had been standing at Sir Malcolm's side throughout the exchange wearing a faint smile of his own. She greeted the older man with the somewhat conscious assurance of a woman who knows her beauty to be unrivaled in present company, and the smile playing around the man's lips deepened as he bowed with easy grace.

While turning to greet Mr. and Mrs. Penrose and their two daughters, Virginia almost bumped into a solid gentleman of whose presence she had been in happy ignorance until that moment, obscured as he must have been by the slimmer but even larger figure of Mr. Kirkland.

"Ah, Miss Greyson, what a delightful surprise to meet you here!" he boomed, shaking her somewhat reluctantly proffered hand with a vigorous pumping action that should have drawn water from the deepest well. "And to see you in such fine looks too, delightful, delightful!"

The thick lips of the Reverend Adolphus Elliott gave the appearance of smacking as if each word he uttered were a tasty morsel to be appreciated individually. Over his shoulder the eyes of the two women in the Brewster party met briefly. Mr. Kirkland noted with interest that Miss Brewster's sparkling twin sapphires were brimful of mischief, and he directed a penetrating glance to the wooden countenance of the governess. As usual, the opaque spectacles glittered mockingly at him, frustrating his efforts to read her expression, but he wondered if the thin mouth was more than ordinarily compressed in the second before her left hand rose to her face to allow the middle finger to settle the spectacles more securely on the bridge of her nose in a gesture that had become familiar to him in the last fortnight.

Thanks to the carrying quality of the minister's trained baritone, the attention of all present was momentarily diverted to the woman least likely to appreciate the distinction. It required all the resolution Virginia could command not to shrink or blush during the interval —mercifully brief—when her points were assessed, for the most part she knew, with indifferent kindness and instantly dismissed with polite murmurs of agreement.

She was uneasily aware, however, that such welcome dismissal was not unanimous. Unless she was vastly mistaken, Lady Wrenthorpe's discerning eye had estimated the cost of her silk gown within five guineas; Mrs. Penrose, with two daughters to settle, had raised a small lorgnette to her myopic eyes for a detailed view of the woman who called herself Juliet Brewster's companion; and Mr. Simon Kirkland's bold gaze had stripped her naked and taken her measurements in the process. Too late the folly of allowing feminine vanity to overrule her intelligence impressed itself sharply upon her quivering spirit. An angel from heaven could not have been more appreciated at that moment than Dunston, whose tottering approach signaled that dinner was served.

They sat down sixteen to one of Lady Wrenthorpe's renowned turtle soup dinners. Virginia was comfortably ensconced between Mr. Ryding and the senior Penrose, who had a droll sense of humor and kept her well entertained. On the other side of the table Juliet had not been best pleased to find herself partnered by her brother, with Mr. Alistair Penrose on her left hand; but an incipient pout was quelled by a steady look from her chaperon, and by dint of ruthlessly ignoring poor Bertram's claims on her attention, she contrived to amuse herself quite satisfactorily with the lively conversation of the returned scholar. In the pauses while he exchanged a few words with his younger sister, a girl of the same age as Miss Brewster but seemingly much less mature due to an inhibiting shyness, Juliet exchanged meaningful glances across the table with Mr. Kirkland, who did his duty by Lady Teasdale and the elder Miss Penrose with an experienced charm of manner. By the time Lady Wrenthorpe led the women back into the main drawing room, leaving the gentlemen to the peaceful enjoyment of their port, Virginia had relaxed enough to give the guard that kept constant watch over her tongue a metaphorical kick as she joined the two elder ladies in trivial conversation while the young girls plied Lady Teasdale with eager questions concerning her new way of life. During the course of the conversation Lady Wrenthorpe made a point of complimenting Miss Greyson on her attractive gown, but Virginia had had the entire dinner hour to decide how to handle this situation.

"Yes, it is a pretty dress, isn't it?" she agreed. "Though to be perfectly truthful, not quite to my taste. But since it was a gift from my former employer, naturally I feel compelled to express my appreciation by wearing it on occasion. So kind of her, you know. Actually, except for the warmest of days, I much prefer a dress with sleeves—so much more practical, don't you agree?" She smiled vaguely at the two matrons who hastened to concur, though Virginia was well aware that ladies of fashion would clothe themselves in the skimpiest of materials and barest of styles with total disregard for comfort and practicality while the fashion for such styles lasted.

Mrs. Penrose quickly changed the subject, and Virginia

was content to sit and give the appearance of listening to a catalogue of that lady's latest symptoms. From then on an occasional murmur of sympathy was sufficient on her part as the elder ladies vied with each other in producing evidence of the delicate state of their health. Lady Wrenthorpe was recounting the details of a particularly debilitating bilious attack and the radiant bride was deep in a vivid description of the sweeping renovations being carried out on the drafty old house her husband had inherited in Northumberland, when the gentlemen reappeared, having cut short their after-dinner drinking in favor of feminine company.

Lady Wrenthorpe, Sir Reginald, and the senior Penroses decided to make up a table for a rubber of casino at one end of the room, and Sir Malcolm pressed the younger ladies to give the rest of the company some music. After a blushing disclaimer, the younger of the two Misses Penrose was persuaded to sing while her sister accompanied her at the pianoforte. Virginia, who had seen at a glance how matters were shaping once the older party drew away, could only applaud Sir Malcolm's social skill. Mr. Alistair Penrose had made a beeline for a seat near Miss Brewster, and it was clear that he had every intention of monopolizing her ear. Lady Teasdale had claimed Mr. Kirkland's attention and that of her husband for the moment, leaving the sisters to be entertained by young Bertram and his tutor. Mr. Ryding embarked on a desultory conversation with Miss Emily Penrose, but Bertram had neither the inclination nor the resourcefulness to drag more than monosyllables out of Miss Alice Penrose, whom he had ignored and stigmatized as chickenhearted throughout their mutual childhood.

Most irksome of all to Miss Greyson's way of thinking was the celerity with which Mr. Elliott had occupied the place next to herself on the sofa, relinquished by Lady Wrenthorpe when the card players departed. For sufficient reasons she ably seconded Sir Malcolm's efforts to organize a musical interlude.

And the evening did turn out to be most enjoyable for those involved. Once she opened her mouth to sing, Miss Alice Penrose could no longer be recognized as the tongue-tied girl with scarcely a word to say for herself, and that only when goaded. Her pure lilting soprano once released was a joy to hear, and there was no mistaking the sincerity of her audience when they pleaded for more songs. When she finally declared she couldn't sing another note and accepted the hearty applause with which her listeners rewarded her with shy smiles and modestly downcast eyes, she looked like another girl from the timorous creature who had sat silent through dinner.

Not unnaturally, the other young ladies felt disinclined to subject themselves to comparison with Alice's performance, but the moment was saved when Miss Greyson had the happy notion of inviting Bertram and Juliet to render a duet or two. Neither suffered from any pangs of shyness under normal circumstances, and they were easily persuaded to extend the musical session, only demanding that Miss Greyson should play for them so she might drown out any wrong notes. Bertram's clear tenor blended beautifully with his sister's small but well-trained voice, and their selections were enthusiastically received. Lady Teasdale was summoned to join them in a rollicking country song, and she then cajoled her reluctant spouse into joining her in a sentimental ballad. Throughout this portion of the impromptu program Virginia had remained at the pianoforte, and she consented to accompany the young couple once they had agreed on a song. Their voices were perfectly attuned for the expression of romantic sentiments.

At one point during their rendering of a popular ballad she watched the newly wedded pair exchange a long, intimate look that excluded the rest of the world, and she was unaccountably assailed by a wave of desolation that almost froze her fingers in their controlled movements. How deeply in love they were and how very unlikely it was that *she* should ever know such reciprocal emotion. The poignancy of the moment ebbed and her fingers continued to perform with automatic skill, but the lighthearted mood of the evening was shattered for Virginia.

She would have risen from the instrument when Lord and Lady Teasdale laughingly declined to repeat their triumph, but Mr. Kirkland, who had been the leading voice in making specific requests during the musicale, now begged the pleasure of a solo on the pianoforte by Miss Greyson. She cast a startled glance at his face, looking for the faint mockery that was generally present during his dealings with her and failing to find it. At her slight hesitation the Reverend Mr. Elliott and Sir Malcolm chimed in with vociferous support of Mr. Kirkland's request, and she sat down again, not unwilling to comply. The somber loneliness of her present mood demanded release in some form, and she embarked on a demanding composition by Mozart, the execution of which soothed her sore spirit to some degree, enough at any rate so that when the polite applause ceased she was able to bring the musicale to a jolly conclusion by launching into a couple of lively numbers to be sung by the entire company. By this time the card game had ended and more voices were added to swell the quite creditable chorus.

Mr. Kirkland, sitting to the right and slightly behind the pianoforte, had been offered an unobstructed view of the musician's back throughout the evening. Being a true music lover, his attention was focused primarily on the performances, but over the course of an hour or so he had ample opportunity to study Miss Greyson as his idle gaze fell on her straight back from time to time. He had marked her appearance in that gray thing earlier in the evening in a reflexive masculine assessment. She had a much better figure than he would have guessed, he was thinking now as he eyed the seated musician thoughtfully, equal to or perhaps even superior to that of any other female in the room. Viewed from the back, one would place her in the same age category, too.

In fact, he mused later, pursuing this theme as the party partook of tea before breaking up, from the neck down she appeared no older than Arabella Teasdale, and the smooth white skin revealed by the low-cut dress rivaled that of the beautiful Miss Brewster. Rare, too, such dazzlingly white skin. No wonder the reverend was showing signs of interest. Beauty of features wasn't everything; Miss Greyson was intelligent and conversable, and the reserved manner that was as plain as her face struck him as being assumed. For the right man he'd wager there was fire beneath that prim exterior. He grinned at the idea that the minister might very well share his suspicions. Mr. Elliott could not have been much above forty. Though he seemed a bit prosy, no man who enjoyed food and drink to such an extent could fail to appreciate Miss Greyson's concealed charms.

The object of his speculations, glancing up casually from the delicate Meissen teacup in her hand, encountered the dark eyes of Mr. Kirkland fixed in an unwinking stare on her mouth. For a second her fingers tightened around the handle of the cup, and then she set it back on its saucer with painstaking precision. When next she looked in his

77

direction, Mr. Kirkland was exuding charm for the benefit of the two Miss Penroses.

Miss Juliet Brewster was also aware of Mr. Kirkland's actions in this direction. Though she continued to pursue a mild flirtation with her childhood friend, she had been alert with a knowledge deep under her skin of Mr. Kirkland's every move during a long evening that somehow had failed to fulfill its promise, though she was hard put to explain why this was so. Everyone had complimented her on being in great beauty tonight, it had been delightful to see Arabella Wrenthorpe again, and she knew herself to outshine the two Penrose girls, even though the excellence of Alice's singing must be admitted. Yet somehow the evening had not been entirely successful.

She had not been seated near Mr. Kirkland at dinner, and despite the occasional exchange of glances, he had not sought her out when the gentlemen rejoined the ladies. Granted that she had been occupied with Staro Penrose, a man in love would not have let such an impediment stand in his way. Her lovely mouth took on a petulant curve as the time came to make their adieux, and then at the last moment Mr. Kirkland singled her out for an especially warm farewell. His eyes were openly admiring as he begged permission to call upon her the next day with Lady Teasdale. Juliet's spirits bounded upward, but she tossed her head slightly and agreed to his proposal in deliberately cool tones.

Miss Greyson, watching the byplay, was forced to acknowledge Mr. Kirkland's address. He had contrived to make himself agreeable to each lady in the course of the evening. Not only was he the perfect guest, but she would not be surprised to learn that the elder Miss Penrose had experienced a flutter in the region of her heart after sitting beside him at dinner. He was definitely a man of the town, experienced in the art of handling women. And here was Juliet after watching this performance still determined to bring him to his knees. No more than her charge did she believe a legitimate suitor would be deterred from the object of his choice by the attentions of another man. There was, of course, the possibility that Mr. Kirkland had it in mind to subdue the tendency of an acknowledged beauty to captivate the heart of every eligible male who came within her orbit before he made his intentions known.

For the first time since their initial meeting Miss Greyson wondered if she had underestimated the danger to her companion in Mr. Kirkland's acquaintance. Somehow, being courted by a fortune hunter who stood no chance of being accepted by her father seemed infinitely preferable to having Juliet's unfledged emotions played with by an experienced heartbreaker.

Of necessity the gentlemen provided the lion's share of the talk in the carriage that returned the Brewster party to Fairhill presently, since Olivia was spending the night at Thorpe Manor with Amelia and each of the other two ladies was engrossed in her own thoughts to the virtual exclusion of rational conversation.

CHAPTER FIVE

The following afternoon Miss Greyson, soberly and unfashionably clad in her usual mid-brown cotton, entered the small saloon after enduring a less than successful lesson on the harp with Olivia. Though hardworking and gifted at the pianoforte, Olivia had of late been seized with a sudden, inexplicable aversion to the harp, and her subsequent reluctance to perform on that instrument found expression in rendering the weekly session of instruction hideous for her unfortunate teacher.

The latter would have been grateful for a short period of solitude in which to allow her clanging nerves and the persistent pounding sensation in her temples to subside before being obliged to rejoin the human race. During the lesson just concluded, however, a message had been sent to her in the nursery where the harp had been relegated at the urgent request of almost the entire household, summoning Miss Greyson to join Juliet in receiving Lady Teasdale for tea. After a brief detour to her room to renew the gray powder that tended to wear off on warm days, she had hurried downstairs and greeted the several occupants of the sunny room in a composed fashion.

"There you are, Aggie dear, just in time for tea," greeted Juliet from behind the shining silver tea service, "and I daresay it will be welcome if the noises I heard coming from the nursery earlier were an indication of how Livvy's lesson progressed." She handed the cup she had been filling to Mr. Kirkland, who presented it to Miss Greyson with a bow before resuming his seat beside Juliet on the emerald brocade sofa. Lord Teasdale had accompanied his wife to Fairhill and now offered the sugar basin and milk to the governess with a courteous smile. She prepared her tea and took a grateful sip.

"How well I recall those loathsome harp lessons Mama insisted upon," Lady Teasdale said with a moue of distaste. "They nearly drove Miss Martinson into an early grave, to say nothing of ruining all my fingernails, and all for naught since I never achieved the least proficiency at it."

"I beg you won't enlighten Olivia about the possible danger to her nails, Lady Teasdale," Miss Greyson pleaded with a rueful smile. "It is about the only excuse she hasn't offered for discontinuing her lessons."

"That's because Livvy bites her nails anyway," Juliet chimed in, then quickly changed the subject. "Aggie, Bella has had the most marvelous idea! We are going to put on a play—not just a casual play reading of an evening, but a real production! Sir Malcolm has offered us the use of the old ballroom at the Manor, and we'll have costumes and rehearsals and everything of the most professional. Can you conceive of a more delightful way to spend the summer?"

"No indeed, most delightful." Miss Greyson, conscious of four pairs of eyes fixed on her face, conjured up a faint murmur of agreement, then added hesitantly, "Does Sir Reginald—that is, I assume your papa would have no objections to your taking part in local theatricals?"

"Oh, no, not in the least," Juliet assured her companion. "How could he when Lady Wrenthorpe has sanctioned our enterprise?"

"Mama is prodigiously fond of the play," Lady Teasdale cut in, relieving Miss Greyson of the necessity of replying to this blithe assumption on Juliet's part. "In fact, she has declared her willingness to undertake a role herself, provided a small part can be found that would not necessitate her learning too many lines."

"Indeed? I trust then that such a role will be found. Have you decided upon a play?"

The gentlemen, who had remained silent until now, explained that this very point had been the subject of discussion just before Miss Greyson's entrance upon the scene.

"Miss Brewster seems to favor Shakespeare," Lord Teasdale remarked with a charming smile in Juliet's direction.

"Oh?" Miss Greyson's eyes sought enlightenment from her charge. "Just Shakespeare in general or a particular play?"

"Well, I thought *Romeo and Juliet* might be fun to do," replied the young girl with a mixture of self-consciousness and defiance.

Oh, dear, of course she sees herself as her namesake, thought Miss Greyson with dismay, but she was spared the obligation of commenting by Lady Teasdale who declared dismissively, *"Oh, Shakespeare!* Such fusty stuff! What we want is something more modern and entertaining."

"The Bard can be quite entertaining when done in a competent fashion," Mr. Kirkland responded, with what Miss Greyson had to acknowledge was welcome diplomacy, "but we don't have the Globe theater at our disposal,

I'm afraid, nor a cast of hundreds to reproduce the true spirit of his plays."

"How about *The Beggar's Opera*?" suggested Lord Teasdale. "That continues to be popular after nearly one hundred years."

"Yes, of course!" exclaimed his wife. "You'd love it, Juliet. A bit *warm*, of course, but so amusing. We saw it last winter in town."

Miss Greyson, recalling the ribald nature of the lyrics of some of the songs from this perennial favorite, felt sure Sir Reginald would have a rooted objection to his daughter's witnessing a production of the opera-burlesque, let alone taking part in that production!

"I don't believe *The Beggar's Opera* would be quite suitable for an amateur production," she began tentatively, trying not to see the mutinous expression on Juliet's face.

It was with real gratitude that she gave way to Mr. Kirkland, who concurred smoothly, "Most unsuitable for amateurs in fact. There are sixty-nine songs in that work sung by any number of the large cast. I really doubt we are up to such high flights. No, we must choose a play with a reasonably small number of players and one that does not demand too much in the way of stage settings."

"Comedy or tragedy?" inquired Lord Teasdale.

"Oh, comedy to be sure," replied his wife. "If we expect our friends and neighbors to sit through *amateur* efforts" —with a pointed glance at Mr. Kirkland—"we must at the least insure that the lines we speak are entertaining, even if the performances leave something to be desired. Besides, it's summer," she added with a seeming irrelevance that was yet perfectly comprehensible to her audience.

"We may even surprise ourselves," murmured Mr. Kirkland with a bland expression.

"What do you think of *The Way of the World*?" offered Lord Teasdale. "Congreve has generally been well received everywhere."

Mr. Kirkland appeared to consider. "Certainly Congreve is both witty and amusing, and there are some memorable scenes in this play that are a joy to the actors, but the plot is sadly deficient in construction. Throughout the first four acts he sets everyone at odds with everyone else, and then, with all schemes foiled and everyone embroiled in conflict, provides a resolution in the fifth act for which there has been absolutely no preparation. In short, despite its undeniable attractions for the players, it is a confusing play for the audience."

With an apologetic glance at Juliet, Miss Greyson pointed out that most of the female roles in the play were generally enacted by women of somewhat more mature years. "Would *School for Scandal* be a good choice, do you think, or are there too few female roles perhaps to make it an attractive proposition?" She made the suggestion in a tentative manner and then sat back to await developments.

Mr. Kirkland was looking at the governess with something akin to respect. "There are only four feminine characters, admittedly, but one of them—Maria—is perfect for the debut of a young actress." He sketched a smiling bow in Juliet's direction. "The roles of Lady Teazle and Lady Sneerwell have long been considered prime parts, and though shorter, that of Mrs. Candour is a good one also. Would there be bitter disappointment amongst the local aspirants, do you think, under the circumstances?" His questioning glance roved from lady to lady.

Miss Greyson remained prudently silent, but neither

Lady Teasdale nor Miss Brewster seemed to regard a scarcity of female parts as a handicap to the selection of Sheridan's celebrated play, quite the contrary in fact, if one might conjecture that their expressions were a true reflection of their thoughts on the matter. Juliet was not familiar with the plot, but Lady Teasdale's eyes had taken on a determined gleam at the mention of the role of Lady Teazle. The younger girl glowed with satisfaction because Mr. Kirkland had practically selected a role for her personally.

"Would Miss Penrose and Miss Alice feel slighted if not invited to participate since their menfolk will undoubtedly be among the players?" inquired Lord Teasdale in a spirit of fairness that caused his wife to purse her lips and raise an eyebrow in Juliet's direction.

That young lady gave a trill of laughter. "Alice would expire of fright if asked to speak a line in public, and Emily does not even care for play readings, but Mrs. Penrose might be interested in taking a role."

"I can see her as the definitive Lady Sneerwell," commented Mr. Kirkland softly, preserving a sublimely innocent countenance under a lambent look from the governess.

"On the other side of the coin, there are quite a vast number of male roles. Would this pose a problem in casting?" Miss Greyson addressed her query to Lady Teasdale, who might be presumed to know the likely possibilities in the locality, but it was Mr. Kirkland who answered.

"If memory serves, there are eight or ten speaking parts, if not more. With the three of us at the Manor and young Penrose and Mr. Penrose, who confessed to me last night that he had ever a penchant for acting, we shall require as many again to complete our cast. Perhaps the Reverend

Mr. Elliott would be willing to participate in a spirit of neighborliness." He flicked a sly glance at Miss Greyson, which that lady affected not to see, and turned to the lovely girl at his side. "Do you think Sir Reginald would care to take part, Miss Brewster?"

Juliet giggled enchantingly. "Most emphatically *not*! I'd dearly love to be present when you ask him though. Of course there is Bertram—and Mr. Ryding."

Mr. Kirkland grinned in response to the mischief on Juliet's face, looking young and carefree and altogether unlike the personification of a hardened rake, with which character Miss Greyson had been attempting to endow him in her mind. "Oh, well, doubtless there are cronies enough in the area that Malcolm can enlist to join our cast. He and I will be in London for a day or two early next week so we shall engage ourselves to procure the necessary number of scripts."

"Famous!" pronounced Lady Teasdale with satisfaction. "By the end of next week we should be well under way."

The instigation of a theatrical enterprise in the locale caused the pace of life at Fairhill to increase pleasurably over the next few weeks. When Virginia had arrived at Fairhill in the damp depths of late January, the household had consisted of Sir Reginald, who was more often absent than present, and his two daughters. Though not officially out, Juliet was old enough to act as her father's hostess for the few quiet dinners with local families that constituted the entire social life of the family since the departure of Sir Reginald's aunt. Virginia was in no mood for the active social round she had been accustomed to in Bath, but it was a relief to be able to turn her back on her own grief and devote her attention to the moderate activities of the two girls she had come to supervise. The subsequent arrival from Eton of Bertram in need of a convalescent period had provided another interest in their circumscribed lives, and then in late April the advent of Mr. Ryding had signaled a slight acceleration in the tempo of life at Fairhill.

As the months passed and the queer numb despair that had settled over her like a smothering blanket after the death of her father gradually receded, Virginia had become increasingly swept up in the affairs of the young Brewsters. The alarm and fear sparked by the arrival of Mr. Kirkland had acted as a shock to her system, jolting her senses into renewed receptiveness. This was not an unmixed blessing, however. All personal feelings had been submerged in her grief for the loss of her father's affection and companionship, but now she began to experience anew the demands of her own nature. In a way her position became more difficult because now she must remind herself on occasion that she was only an employee, that she had no right to a personal life and the ordinary satisfactions of other females of her age and background. She was emerging from her own purgatory of the emotions, but there was no going back to her former life.

The theatrical undertaking served to point up the gap that now existed between her past and future. It had been there, of course, from the moment she had engaged herself as a governess and companion, but during those first months she had been too numb to care. The first inkling, had she but recognized it, that she was undergoing a disconcerting change in her attitude, had been that curious reluctance to appear at the Manor in one of her drab Miss Greyson gowns. And she had given in to temptation in the form of a gray silk creation that had ensured her a most uncomfortable evening. In all likelihood no lasting harm had been done, though there was no denying the curiosity, momentary but real on Juliet's part, and she had been only too conscious of the speculative nature of several glances she had intercepted from Mr. Kirkland, whom she had dubbed her own personal nemesis.

At least the discomforts of that evening had served to put her on her guard when the subject of amateur dramatics had arisen the following day. She had been careful to display no particular enthusiasm, though her role of chaperon demanded that she safeguard the eager Juliet from any unwise selection of the work to be performed. To this end she had been compelled to reveal some knowledge of popular plays. When the trio from the Manor had departed that afternoon, Mr. Kirkland had managed, in the flurry of good-byes, to speak a few words to her ear alone, complimenting her on her wide acquaintance with theatrical productions. Calling upon her own dramatic ability, she had infused her voice with what she hoped was the correct degree of polite unconcern as she remarked casually that her former employer had been a keen follower of theatrical activity in Bath.

"How fortunate for you," Mr. Kirkland had purred, and added in the same dulcet tones, "but did not you say earlier that Lady Mallory had been a very infrequent visitor to Bath in recent years?"

Drat the man and his memory! She had recovered quickly to say sweetly, "Very infrequent, sir. The only attraction that could lure Lady Mallory into town was the arrival of a new play." She had given him a limpid look from behind her spectacles and turned to shake hands with Lord Teasdale. Not for anything would she have revealed that her knowledge of *The School for Scandal* was as recent as the previous summer, when she had played the role of Lady Teazle in an amateur production of similar scope to that being attempted at the Manor.

That little passage at arms dictated the most circumspect behavior on Virginia's part with regard to the venture into dramatics. She walked a thin line between supporting Juliet in her enthusiasm and manifesting any noticeable personal interest. Though urged on by her charge, she was resolute in refusing to try out for a role, offering her services instead as a general prompter and helper at rehearsals. It had not escaped her notice that Lady Teasdale had failed to second Juliet's pleas that her companion should plunge into acting; she had no intention of forgetting her place.

A copy of the play had been unearthed in the library at the Manor, nestled among the works of Hugh Kelly and keeping company with Goldsmith's *She Stoops to Conquer*. Lady Wrenthorpe gave way to nostalgia as she recalled the time she and the late Sir Jeremy had played Lady Betty and Lord Winworth in Kelly's *False Delicacy* during a Christmas visit to one of her family connections in Hampshire. She was inclined to favor a revival of this comedy of misunderstood affections and misdirected courtships over the livelier *School for Scandal*, pointing out that none of the roles were those of persons of mean character, as in the latter play.

This opinion was greeted with less than proper filial respect by her son and elder daughter, who were vociferous in declaiming their preference for playing characters who verged on the villainous. When appealed to for support by an avowedly scandalized Lady Wrenthorpe, Mr. Kirkland also aligned himself against his hostess, with profuse apologies to all moralists and persons of nice sensibilities, on the grounds that villains were more fun to play, even if virtue triumphed in the end and some of the best lines went occasionally to purer characters. In fact, he informed Lady Wrenthorpe, he would infinitely prefer to play Joseph Surface, the venial elder brother masquerading as a model of propriety, than the more appealing Charles, who though a ruined spendthrift, is basically an honest and generous character. Lady Wrenthorpe subsided with a laugh, and eventually declared her willingness to undertake the small role of Mrs. Candour, a sanctimonious gossip. Nothing would prevail upon her to consider the larger part of Lady Sneerwell, but through Mr. Penrose's efforts, his wife was persuaded to tackle this role long beloved of actresses.

Lady Wrenthorpe's copy of the play found its way to Fairhill during the time Sir Malcolm and Mr. Kirkland were in London. Juliet seized it eagerly and shut herself up in her bedchamber, abandoning all her household duties until she had finished reading it. She emerged from her seclusion with a discontented air that left her companion unsurprised. Though Maria was a pivotal character in the play, being sought after by the two brothers, the role was actually a small one. She was on stage a good deal but had relatively few lines.

Juliet, with grandiose ideas of her talents, could not be expected to be content with this state of affairs. Miss Greyson was called upon to exercise the utmost tact, mixed with a judicious amount of flattery, to cajole the disappointed young girl into accepting the situation with a good grace. She pointed out that the play had already been decided on and laid stress on the fact that there was no other suitable role for a very young lady except that of Lady Teazle, which called for an experienced actress. With some cunning she led Juliet gently toward the realization that she would be totally involved in all the pleasurable aspects of taking part in a drama, and would undoubtedly be much admired as Maria without chancing a notable failure as did Lady Teasdale, who would very likely play the demanding role of Lady Teazle. As she expanded on this theme, she had the satisfaction of seeing the light of battle die out of the girl's eyes, to be replaced by an expression of extreme thoughtfulness. Juliet was well aware of the imbalance between male and female roles in this play and was not slow to grasp the possibilities latent in the situation so delicately hinted at by her duenna. She would be the only unattached female amongst a dozen men, which was a condition much more to her liking than remaining at home to work on her embroidery for the next month.

When the young girl eventually left her companion, her spirits had undergone a remarkable change for the better. To Miss Greyson it was an immense relief to have been spared the necessity of coercing Juliet into acceptance by reminding her that a refusal to participate after having expressed a marked degree of enthusiasm for the project initially would leave a very negative impression of her sportsmanship with her neighbors. In dealing with the headstrong Brewster girls, she had learned that it frequently proved more efficacious and infinitely less wearing on her nerves to induce them to do the correct thing by cajolery, rather than attempting to appeal to their sense of what was right and proper. If the rightness of her own actions in this maneuvering troubled her conscience (as it did on occasion), well, the unvarnished truth was that she could ill afford such a nice conscience, situated as she was in a position that depended to a large extent on maintaining the goodwill of her charges.

In one quarter cajolery, this time as practiced by Juliet, was less than successful. Much to his sister's chagrin Bertram remained completely unreceptive to the idea of displaying his histrionic talents before his friends and neighbors. In the first place, he argued reasonably, he didn't know that he *had* any histrionic talents to display and didn't much care if he didn't, and in the second place he had better things to do with his time in full summer than waste it indoors rehearsing a play. As for addling his brain by memorizing pages full of prosy nonsense, what did Juliet take him for anyway?

And there matters would have remained had not Mr. Ryding exercised a little of his quiet influence over his young friend. He pointed out that there were minor roles that would allow Bertram to enjoy the experience of participating in such an endeavor while not entailing a lot of dogged memorization. He further pointed out to the reluctant thespian that the company was in desperate need of male players to swell their ranks and it would be nothing less than a betrayal of friendship to refuse to take part. The rehersals would most likely take up only an hour or so in the afternoons, and even that might not be required daily if Bertram were to play one of the servants who made only one or two appearances in the course of the drama.

Under the combined onslaught of his sister's and tutor's urgings, Bertram's resistance was overcome. Like his sister he commandeered the copy of the play and read it through, counting the speeches of the various characters as she had done, but with the exact opposite end in mind. The result of this perusal was a tentative agreement to portray the servant Tripp, who appeared in just three scenes, and his acceptance valid on condition that Mr. Ryding likewise confine his contribution to a small role so as to suffer the minimum disruption of their other activities.

With this Juliet had to be content. Olivia, who like Amelia was deemed too young to participate, was far from happy to be excluded from the most interesting event of the summer, but conceded that the discontinuance of the despised harp lessons during the period of preparation of the play went a long way toward reconciling her to the exclusion. Besides, Miss Greyson had promised that she and Mellie might watch rehersals once the cast had established a good working schedule.

The next several weeks were devoted almost exclusively to the production of *School for Scandal*. Mr. Kirkland, as the person with the most experience of amateur dramatics, was named director of the entire production, and he proved a stern taskmaster, running his rehersals along strictly businesslike lines, alternately bullying and flattering his principals to obtain their best efforts. Given the mentality and motivation of amateurs, the office of director was no sinecure, at times requiring the judgment of a Solomon, at others the mediation skills of a diplomat, and, thanks to the temperamental nature of some members of the cast, always the patience of Job.

Miss Greyson, who had offered her assistance in a spirit of compromise with little expectation of being called upon to do more than help rehearse Juliet at home, found herself ruthlessly pressed into daily service. Mr. Kirkland, displaying a hitherto unsuspected talent for extracting the last drop of effort from his associates, took every advantage of her promise of assistance to use her as prompter, assembler of stage props, mover of furniture as required, and a stand-in for any member of the cast who chanced to be absent when the director desired to rehearse a scene. She also proved invaluable in soothing ruffled feelings or lacerated pride on those occasions when the director, in a surcharge of creative agony, forgot that he was not dealing with professionals.

Mr. Kirkland's businesslike approach was admirably

suited to drawing the best efforts from the masculine members of the cast, and proved reasonably successful with Lady Teasdale, who combined a real flair for acting with a toughness of mind that enabled her to accept intelligent criticism and profit by it without suffering a loss of self-esteem. Unfortunately for the smooth conduct of the rehearsals, the other three ladies were endowed with more delicate sensibilities, and their ability to accept criticism was in inverse proportion to the degree of sensibility obtaining. Lady Wrenthorpe, who had done some acting in her younger days, delivered her speeches with creditable aplomb, but had some difficulty in moving about the stage with a like degree of confidence. She was also a bit slow to learn her lines, and since her scenes involved several other persons, they required a good deal of rehearsal time. Miss Greyson, noting that her ladyship's nervousness increased and her performance deteriorated with each repetition, suggested in an undertone that Mr. Kirkland go on to another scene while she rehearsed Lady Wrenthorpe apart. This suggestion met with instant approbation on all sides.

Juliet, on the other hand, was word perfect in her part in short order, but she had acquired little in the way of stage presence by the end of the first week of rehearsals and still declaimed her lines in a stiff little voice almost totally devoid of animation.

"Juliet, my dear, try to project your lines more. I can barely distinguish your words," Miss Greyson called from midway down the ballroom one afternoon when the rehearsal had been underway for an hour or so.

They had been working on the second act. The first scene between Sir Peter Teazle, newly married at age fifty, and his very young wife had gone superlatively well. Mr. Penrose as Sir Peter was a natural actor, and he brought a superb sense of comic perplexity to the character of the old bachelor, who was confounded by the demands and intransigence of his new bride. He was the only member of the cast to excel Lady Teasdale, who played the young wife, and their scenes together were certainly the most electric in the play thus far.

The next scene, involving more than half a dozen players at different times, was not nearly so advanced and needed a lot of work just on the timing alone. The day was warm and the members of the cast were learning that acting could be as dull a way of spending time as any other activity that demanded patience and practice. Mr. Kirkland had become a trifle caustic in his remarks in the last half hour and wore the air of one determined to preserve his patience whatever the cost. Miss Greyson had intervened before he could explain for the fourth time that Juliet must speak to the audience, not just to the person next to her on the stage. With trembling lip the young girl turned her back on the director and addressed her companion sharply: "I am speaking as loudly as I can, Aggie, without shouting."

"There, love," came the cheerful reply, "that's better. Turn slightly away from Joseph when you deliver your line and keep that tone in your voice and it will reach me. Remember, you are distressed at the character assassination that has been going on."

The exchange between Joseph and Maria was repeated, but with no discernible improvement on Juliet's part. Mr. Kirkland called a halt and approached the girl, who was looking at him with a slightly hostile anxiety.

"I'd like to try an experiment, Miss Brewster, if you will bear with me," he explained in a carefully reasonable tone. "Let Miss Greyson read your lines in this scene while you stand back at the far wall. Try to get an idea of the amount of projection necessary to make the speeches comprehensible from here, then repeat the lines to us from the back. Will you do this for me?" He flashed her a smile that Miss Greyson thought privately ought to be declared an unfair weapon, and succeeded in winning a faint response from Juliet as she went to do his bidding.

"Fine . . . excellent, Miss Greyson, thank you," said Mr. Kirkland warmly when the dialogue in question had been repeated. He turned to address Juliet. "Did you have any difficulty understanding any of that, Miss Brewster?"

"None at all," came the cold, distinct reply.

"Good. Now I will give you Joseph's lines and you reply from there."

Juliet complied somewhat reluctantly with this request, and the short scene was repeated once more with the actors at opposite ends of the room.

"That was much better, Miss Brewster. Do you feel now that you are able to gauge the amount of projection necessary?"

"I feel like I am shrieking my lines," the young girl declared with a disgruntled expression as she approached the stage.

Once again that devastating smile came into play as the director assured her cheerfully that no one else thought she was shrieking and that it would soon become second nature to her. If he had stopped just there and gone on to rehearse the next scene matters would have proceeded smoothly, but as he confessed to Miss Greyson later, some ill-judged desire for perfection must have prompted his next remarks. "Now that we have overcome the main problem, we shall be able to concentrate on getting some feeling into Maria's lines. Did you attend to Miss Greyson's reading of the part? That is just the feeling I am looking for from you."

"But why from me, Mr. Kirkland?" Juliet replied sweetly, opening her eyes to their widest. "If Miss Greyson's performance is so vastly superior, surely she should be playing the role."

Virginia groaned inwardly. *That's thrown the cat in amongst the pigeons. How could he be so stupid?* Aloud she said at her most brisk, as befitted a governess, "Don't be nonsensical, my dear Juliet. I am far beyond the age of portraying a young girl like Maria. The role is perfect for you and with time you will be perfect in the role. Now stop treating us all to a fit of the sulks and try that scene once more."

After one fulminating glance at Mr. Kirkland, who had been staring at Juliet in utter consternation, she descended from the stage and walked purposefully to the rear wall. "Let's start with Joseph's first words to Maria." Her own words were brimming with a confidence she was a long way from feeling at that moment, as she tried to ignore the trembling in her knees. If only Mr. Kirkland had the wit to seize the opportunity to proceed with the scene, disaster might yet be avoided.

He had. Joseph's words rang out clearly in the ballroom, and hesitantly at first came Maria's reply. Both Mr. Kirkland and Miss Greyson might be forgiven for their fulsome praise of Juliet's performance at the end of the exchange. It might be more than the improvement actually warranted, but in the opinion of both was no more than was called for after the tensions of the past half hour. Miss Greyson at least breathed a sigh of relief when Lady Teazle entered the stage on cue and the rehearsal progressed without further incident.

It had become the custom for those members of the cast who were not pressed for time to remain at the Manor for tea and refreshments after the play rehersals. On the afternoon in question Juliet was foiled in her intention to abjure the social hour and walk home immediately by a sudden rain squall that blew up with almost no warning. After a few compelling words spoken in private by her companion, she was persuaded to put a good face on the situation and take tea with the others, but no words of Miss Greyson's were sufficient to prevent her from turning a deliberate cold shoulder on Mr. Kirkland's attempts to charm her out of the sullens.

Without appearing to do so, Miss Greyson was bending her whole attention upon the byplay from a chair too far removed for her to overhear the actual dialogue. She thought dispassionately that Juliet's tactics revealed her extreme youth, but she could still sympathize with the child's mortification. Obviously it would be to Mr. Kirkland's advantage to heal the breach, yet she was inclined to acquit him of acting merely from a sense of expediency. She would take her oath that he had been stunned earlier today by the girl's behavior and was now sincere in his desire to soothe away any hurt he might have inflicted on her, inadvertant though it was.

Perhaps Juliet's ease in masculine company had concealed her basic immaturity of character from a man who was already dazzled by her beauty. She seemed bent on revealing it now, her companion noted with a sense of helplessness. She could not maneuver herself into a position to deflect Juliet's snubs, and the wretched chit refused to meet her eyes. Fortunately Mr. Kirkland decided to cut his losses and retire from the fray before the girl's behavior became obvious to everyone in the room. He bowed politely and sauntered over to sit beside Lady Wrenthorpe, who was chatting with Mr. Penrose.

Miss Greyson had to conceal a smile at the look of frustration on Juliet's face as she glowered at his retreating back before beginning an animated conversation with Lord Teasdale. On the way home later, the young girl treated her companion with a touch of reserve which Miss Greyson thought it prudent not to recognize. Luckily for all concerned, Juliet's moods never lasted long, and she was her sunny self again within twenty-four hours.

The play rehearsals plodded along during a spell of uncomfortably warm weather. Juliet's performance improved steadily. If she was not endowed with the acting talent that distinguished Lady Teasdale and Mr. Penrose, at least she was adequate to the part and, as Miss Greyson had recognized, was physically correct for the role. It having been necessary to draw upon a limited supply of volunteers in the area, the same unhappily could not be said of all the roles. Mr. Kirkland would have preferred Sir Malcolm or Mr. Ryding in the part of Charles Surface, the reformed wastrel in love with Maria, but for reasons of their own, both men insisted on playing smaller parts. Sir Malcolm undertook the role of the scandal monger, Sir Benjamin Backbite, and Mr. Ryding that of Careless, the friend of Charles Surface. The role of Charles went to Mr. Alistair Penrose, who was willing and fairly competent, but a trifle young to be entirely convincing. The least successful piece of casting of all was that of Mrs. Penrose as Lady Sneerwell, the reputation-wrecking widow whose machinations were intended to prevent the marriage of Charles and Maria and to secure Charles for herself.

Though Lady Sneerwell was undoubtedly intended to be somewhat older than Maria and Lady Teazle, Mrs. Penrose looked every day of her forty-two years. This would not have been so noticeable had not the object of her affections been played by her own son! Even these handicaps might have been overcome had Mrs. Penrose been able to bring some talent and enthusiasm to the role, but she found it even more difficult than Lady Wrenthorpe to commit whole scenes to memory and had no idea of how to acquit herself on a stage. After three solid weeks of daily rehearsals her original supply of enthusiasm for the venture was sadly depleted.

Miss Greyson feared very little impetus would be needed to have her cut her stick, as the slangy Bertram would phrase it, and that impetus was provided one afternoon in the form of a politely worded request from Mr. Kirkland to repeat a scene for the fifth time. Mrs. Penrose threw up her hands and declared herself unable to continue devoting most of her waking hours and all of her energy to the preparation of a play, situated as she was with a family that was in grave danger of being neglected and tenants who were accustomed to receiving her helpful attentions. She went on in this vein for several minutes, displaying more animation than she ever had in her stage role. The pleas of her husband and the rest of the cast, who urged and cajoled her to see the project through to its conclusion, left her unmoved from her determination to resign. Noticeably silent among the petitioners, however, was the voice of Mr. Kirkland, and the reason for this became apparent when, all entreaties having failed, Mrs. Penrose had taken her leave of the company in a spirit of relief apparently untinged with compunction for its plight.

Miss Greyson, staring worriedly at the door through which that lady had just vanished, turned a concerned face to Mr. Kirkland and voiced the thoughts of all.

"What is to be done?"

"I should think that would be obvious," he replied calmly. "*You* must take over the role of Lady Sneerwell."

CHAPTER SIX

"Oh, no! No, I could not! I am sorry but it would be impossible." Her words were quite controlled but there was a hint of panic in her eyes.

"Why impossible? You already know the lines; it's my guess you know everyone's lines at this point, and you've done bits and pieces of it at various times. Nothing could be simpler."

Virginia stared at him in horror while a chorus of agreement and encouragement rang out from the other actors, led by Mr. Elliott who was playing Sir Oliver Surface in a pompous but acceptable fashion. He complimented her on her modesty and urged her to make a sacrifice for the sake of all the hard work thus far expended by the entire cast. She turned a shoulder on the minister and glared at Mr. Kirkland in silent indictment for the discomfort she was suffering from the tug of war going on in her own breast. Each time Mrs. Penrose had murdered a line or missed a cue she had longed to jump up on the stage and take over, but now she feared for her primary role of Miss Greyson should she ever step out of character, and this was a reason she could never offer in explanation! She bit her lip in vexation and repeated her refusal, knowing her excuses sounded lame yet unable to justify her reluctance.

Mr. Kirkland made no reply to her protests, allowing

the combined entreaties of the large cast to speak for him while he continued to smile at her in a reassuring fashion that utterly failed in its purpose. Juliet's voice sounded clearly and clinched matters once and for all.

"Aggie, you simply *must* take the part. The performance is in less than a sennight. How could we find someone else at this late date?"

This of course was unanswerable. Making only the proviso that she should immediately step down if another suitable candidate for the role could be found, Virginia gave in with as good a grace as she could muster and concentrated on concealing from everyone her uneasiness at this turn of events.

Once she stepped on the stage and actually assumed the role, the danger was, as she had foreseen, that she would lose herself in the enjoyment of acting again. It was indeed a stroke of good fortune that the part of Lady Sneerwell called for a woman past her youth, and one who need not be physically attractive. If she were careful it might serve to reinforce her main characterization upon which her employment continued to depend.

With the addition of a competent actress in a key role the rehearsals took on a new spirit. Everyone's performance was improved by the change, and Mr. Kirkland's charming smile, which had been in abeyance over the last fortnight, was once again in evidence as the play began to take shape. There were minor upheavals still to come, of course. Sir Malcolm was absent in London for a couple of days and Bertram was dragooned into reading his lines, when he would much rather have been fishing the stream; the screen that played such a significant part in the last acts, when Lady Teazle was forced to conceal herself in Joseph's house, could not be trusted not to overturn at the wrong moment and must be replaced; and Mr. Elliott suffered a stomach upset that might have kept him from performing had not a soothing elixir produced by Mr. Penrose proved of immediate benefit. These were the unexpected disasters that one learned to expect in any theatrical venture and merely contributed to the rising sense of excitement amongst the players.

For the first time since her father died, Virginia was conscious of a small thrill of anticipation on rising each morning. Once this had been her normal approach to each new day, but that was in another existence. At the moment she was deriving a good deal more satisfaction from this new existence than she had dreamed possible back in January. Her duties had never been onerous—quite the reverse—and life at Fairhill marched at a considerably slower pace than she had been accustomed to in Bath, though the pace had certainly speeded up just lately. She had no complaints on that score, however, for she seemed to have much more energy of late to cope with the increased demands on her time.

In fact, once the basic change in her circumstances was accepted, she really had no serious complaints about her present routine. The only fly in the ointment, and that a harmless one, was the deepening partiality of the Reverend Mr. Elliott for her society. Surely she could dismiss any notion that the ambitious cleric was seriously trying to fix his interest with a penniless nobody who could bring him neither material goods nor an entrée into the best society, and who could not be considered to possess a degree of physical attraction to cause a man with an inflated idea of his own worth to count the world well lost for love. Once said, however, she could not quite reconcile this plausible theory with the extreme particularity that distinguished his conduct toward herself, the result being that a considerable portion of her mental energy was expended in finding ways to elude his attentions without evoking any speculative interest from the rest of the large cast, who seemed to represent a significant portion of the genteel families of the area. Although nothing she could not cope with, the ridiculous situation did detract somewhat from her enjoyment of a pleasant spell of summer activity.

She was brooding over Mr. Elliott's irritating habit of conducting her to a chair with a hand under her elbow—for all the world as though she were infirm—as she waited in the main hall at Fairhill for Juliet to retrieve the fan she had left behind in her bedchamber. It was three days before the scheduled performance of the play, and the ladies were about to walk to the Manor for a full rehearsal. At the sound of a swishing skirt from the stairway, Miss Greyson settled her plain straw hat more firmly on her head and produced a smile for Juliet's benefit, but not, apparently, quite quickly enough.

"Goodness, Aggie, why the gloomy expression just now? It's a beautiful day, the play is going well, and we have plenty of time to walk to the Manor. I wasn't gone above a minute or two." She laughed up at her preceptress and slipped a hand within her arm to draw her toward the door. "Cheer up. By this time Saturday we shall all be famous for miles around."

Virginia dismissed Mr. Elliott from her thoughts and allowed herself to respond to the infectious gaiety of the younger girl.

"For a second I could not remember my lines in the last scene," she offered, seizing the first thing that came to mind for an explanation of her doleful expression. "I expect to have nightmares of forgetting lines from now until after the performance."

"Fustian! You know you are word perfect in the part.

106

One would imagine that you had trodden the boards all your life." Juliet suited her steps to the slightly longer stride of her companion as they headed around toward the wood behind the stables. "Have you ever acted before, Aggie?"

Did she detect a hint of something deeper than idle curiosity in Juliet's question? "Just play readings during the winter evenings," she answered with apparent willingness, keeping her gaze on her feet in their brown half boots as the walking became a trifle rougher at the edge of the trees. "Do you object to coming straight home after rehearsal today, my dear? Olivia is feeling so out of things after three days in bed with that wretched cold, poor lamb. I promised to come back and drink tea with her this afternoon to celebrate her being allowed downstairs for an hour or two."

"It's your company Livvy wishes, not mine," laughed Juliet, "but I am perfectly willing to return directly home. There are one or two things I should see to myself."

The ladies exchanged inconsequential conversation as they walked at a steady pace along the well-defined path between the two estates, enjoying the earth scents and the slightly cooler air among the trees. It was going to be a hot afternoon for a full rehearsal, Virginia mused as they left the cool greenness behind after fifteen minutes and were immediately conscious of an oppressive stillness settling over them for the short distance to the back of the Manor where the ballroom had been added as a separate wing. The sky had a rather brassy look, and not a petal stirred in the rose garden as they walked through it and stepped onto the terrace and through the open doors into the relative dimness of the makeshift theater.

"Are we so early then?" Juliet exclaimed in some surprise when no sounds accosted their ears.

In the interval it took for their eyes to adjust to the comparative gloom of the ballroom, they were able to confirm that they were the only persons present, but before Miss Greyson had even focused on the face of the small watch pinned to her dress, Amelia came hurrying in from the direction of the main corridor. It was easy to see that the normally quiet child was in the grip of some strong emotion for her soft brown eyes were eager and her pale little face glowed with unusual color. Big with news, surmised Virginia as she smiled at the girl who paused to greet her very correctly before pouncing on Juliet.

"Is Livvy still feeling poorly, Juliet?"

"She is much better but cannot leave the house as yet. Where is everyone today, Mellie?"

"In the green saloon. We have guests."

Juliet raised questioning brows and Miss Greyson waited for some amplification of this simple statement, wondering why she must deliberately clear her brow of the frown that seemed determined to settle there.

"Malcolm came home last night—"

"Thank goodness!" interrupted Juliet. "Now we can have a proper rehearsal. But why is no one here, Mellie?"

"The others are in the green saloon meeting our guests." Amelia took a deep rapturous breath and plunged: "Oh, Juliet, she is so beautiful—like a princess!"

"Who is?" demanded Miss Brewster with a sudden scowl. Miss Greyson's index finger rubbed slowly along her forehead while her intent gaze never left Amelia's excited face.

"Lady Eugenia," Amelia said reverently, and fell silent in apparent contemplation of that lady's regal beauty.

"You said guests, Amelia?" Miss Greyson probed gently as Juliet seemed unable for the moment to find anything to say.

108

"Yes, ma'am, Lady Eugenia Phillips and her brother, Lord Hampton. Malcolm brought them back from London with him last night. They are friends of Bella's and are going to make us a visit. You must come and meet them before the rehearsal. Mother sent me to fetch anyone who came directly to the ballroom."

Amelia turned and ushered the others out of the room, her bright, wholly uncharacteristic chatter filling the few moments that were necessary to accomplish the trip. As far as Miss Greyson could tell, her conversation was entirely devoted to detailing the manifold attractions of Lady Eugenia Phillips, but she was only half listening, being more involved with speculating about Juliet's instant hostility to the unknown guest. If she were a cat, her ears would be back and her tail would be twitching, she thought with distinct unease. Juliet was in general the most gregarious creature alive, but her fur was certainly bristling at the announcement of the presence of a real diamond in their midst. Heretofore she had known herself unrivaled with regard to beauty, so she could afford to be generous in her attitude toward other females.

But at this point in her ruminations Miss Greyson took herself to task for being herself less than generous to Juliet in considering jealousy of a potential rival as the most likely explanation of the girl's frozen resentment. Juliet might simply be afraid that the advent of guests at this particular moment might have repercussions with respect to their play. She tried to assure herself that Juliet's manners were too good to permit her to reveal any prejudice she might harbor, but she wished all the same that she might snatch a private word with her charge before they entered the saloon. With something of the sort in mind, she fell back a pace and put out a tentative hand to stay Juliet's steps, but Mellie turned at that instant and paused in the doorway, waiting to accompany them inside. Miss Greyson had to be content with delivering a warning look at the unreceptive countenance of her companion before she stepped into the crowded apartment.

One comprehensive glance informed her that almost all the players were present, and the only apparent stranger was a tall blond man talking earnestly with Lord Teasdale in a corner, but she did not make the mistake of assuming the beauteous Lady Eugenia was absent. A cluster of men whose expressions ranged from politely admiring to blatantly fatuous testified to the concealed presence of the beauty in their midst. None of these gentlemen had noticed their entrance, an occurrence unparalleled in Juliet's short but triumphant career. Miss Greyson placed a firm hand on the girl's waist and guided her over to the green plush sofa where Lady Wrenthorpe was listening patiently to what appeared to be a monologue by Mr. Penrose.

The latest arrivals had barely had time to greet their hostess when Lady Teasdale burst out of the crowd surrounding her friend and pulled the latter, laughingly protesting, toward Juliet and Miss Greyson. She made the women known to each other and beckoned Lord Hampton to her side for the same purpose. In short order Miss Greyson felt herself thoroughly appraised by two pairs of shrewd blue eyes. She responded to their charming acknowledgments of the introduction in brisk, clear tones.

Juliet greeted Lord Hampton with a hint of shyness in her manner, and for the first time in her knowledge of the girl, Miss Greyson saw that she was plainly more interested in a member of her own sex than in a gentleman. She was studying Lady Eugenia with the same frank interest with which Lord Hampton was regarding herself, but her polite regard held none of the admiration displayed by that gentleman.

110

His sister's obvious assets were certain to provoke admiration from anyone not already prejudiced in her disfavor. She was of a good height and carried herself well, her golden head balanced gracefully on a lovely long neck. Her shining blond tresses were gathered in a modish arrangement atop her head and confined with a yellow ribbon that matched a stunning day dress of dotted muslin, tucked and French pleated to display to advantage a slim but nicely curved figure. She possessed the long narrow hands and feet demanded of fashionable beauties. Her eyes were also long and narrow, and they were fringed by gold-tipped lashes several shades darker than her hair, insuring that no one could ever describe this fair lady as insipid despite her pale coloring. She looked beautiful, intelligent, exquisitely groomed, and regally poised.

Juliet responded with cool civility to the lady's low-voiced, slightly gushing charm and visibly stiffened when Lady Eugenia turned to her friend and remarked impulsively: "I declare, Bella, if Miss Brewster is not the prettiest child imaginable, you may call me the greatest goosecap in all England.

"Don't you agree, Peter?" she demanded playfully of her brother, who corrected, "In my humble opinion Miss Brewster is the loveliest young woman in England." His smile for Juliet caused that young lady to drop her eyes while a soft flush spread over her cheeks. On her companion it had a quite different effect. All of her protective instincts, alerted once needlessly in the case of Mr. Kirkland, as she had long since admitted, rushed to the fore once more as she decided that she neither liked nor trusted Lord Hampton.

"Do you make a long stay in Essex, Lady Eugenia?" she inquired more to divert attention from the earl than to acquire knowledge.

"Dear Lady Wrenthorpe has very kindly insisted that we remain for some few weeks in this lovely country—a delightful prospect after the heat and smoke of London."

Some of the gentlemen had drifted over to listen to the conversation, and it was plain that this piece of news met with unanimous and vocal approval. Lady Eugenia's ready smile flashed over her face as those intelligent blue eyes noted the undisguised enthusiasm of Mr. Alistair Penrose and two of Sir Malcolm's friends and the more restrained pleasure displayed by Mr. Kirkland and Sir Malcolm.

"I'm glad I came," she declared with a prim mouth and a saucy upward glance from under her lashes. "Everyone is so friendly in the country."

"Should we not be starting our rehearsal soon?" asked Juliet rather abruptly of Mr. Kirkland.

That gentleman smiled at her with a tolerance that Miss Greyson hoped her charge would be unable to interpret, and agreed equably that, pleasant though the social interlude had been, they had best get down to business before the day grew any hotter.

As the general exodus toward the ballroom began, the wistful but very distinct voice of Lady Eugenia was heard to declare her extreme partiality for theatricals. "If I promise to sit as quietly as a mouse, would I be permitted to sit in a corner and watch the rehersal?"

She directed this plea and a melting look at Mr. Kirkland, who said with a benevolent smile, "My dear Lady Eugenia, of course you may. Mellie often watches the rehearsals. You'll keep Lady Eugenia company, won't you, chicken?" Virginia could only hope the greater warmth in the smile the man gave the child was equally discernible to Juliet, who was almost pawing the ground in her eagerness to be away.

112

"I should adore to watch with Mellie," Lady Eugenia said sweetly. "What play are you doing?" She had fallen into step with Mr. Kirkland and reacted to his reply with an exaggerated start of surprise that Virginia was convinced was assumed.

"But what an *uncanny* coincidence! I played Lady Sneerwell in *School for Scandal* only last May. Such a delicious role! I'd adore to do it again. What a pity we didn't arrive sooner!"

A premonition that was almost a certainty flashed across Virginia's mind. She made a vague comment on the heat to Sir Malcolm at her side, determined to ignore the conversation less than a yard away from her, yet she was almost resigned to her fate when Lady Teasdale's voice squealed: "Eugenia, you can play the role! Miss Greyson has been helping us out because our first Lady Sneerwell defected, but she would much prefer to remain behind the scenes, would you not, Miss Greyson?"

Virginia's eyes had been on Sir Malcolm at the beginning of this speech and had not missed the quick expression of pleasure or the uneasiness that replaced it almost instantaneously before she turned a controlled face toward an expectant Lady Eugenia.

"Lady Teasdale is perfectly correct, ma'am. I assumed the role only because there was no time left for someone else to learn it. If you can be ready with just two rehersals . . ." She allowed herself that much fight, the challenge of a question in her voice before falling silent. It was out of her hands now.

Mr. Kirkland, whose expression held neither pleasure nor uneasiness, stated flatly that he did not believe any change of players at the last moment would be conducive to the success of the play. Virginia had not been able to prevent her glance from seeking his or her chilled senses from deriving some comfort from his support, impersonal though it might be, but she had no illusions about who would emerge victorious. Lady Teasdale, despite her appealing manner, possessed a will of iron and was long practiced in manipulating the behavior of her mother, brother, and husband. Mr. Kirkland was a guest in her brother's home. The outcome was never in doubt.

In a spirit of detachment she was even able to admire the wistful hesitation Lady Eugenia infused into her tones as she stated that two rehersals would be ample, but of course she would not dream of taking the role if the substitution might endanger the success of the production. Encountering a quickly repressed flash of irritation in Mr. Kirkland's dark eyes, Virginia decided to go down with all flags flying. Avoiding his gaze, she proceeded to offer her immediate assistance to Lady Eugenia in acquainting her with as many of the stage directions in the various scenes as could be managed before the rehearsal should get underway. The cast had been milling about them during the entire exchange and they were now the last to enter the ballroom. Juliet, who had been far ahead, rushed up to her companion and burst into speech.

"What is all this about giving up the role of Lady Sneerwell, Aggie? You cannot be serious?"

"Oh, but I am, my dear. You know I accepted the part only on the condition that I might step down if a suitable candidate appeared. Lady Eugenia has played the role before so she must be considered eminently suitable." She added the last as a warning to Juliet, but that damsel was too indignant to be silenced immediately.

"But, Aggie, you have worked so hard on this play, helping everyone. You should have the pleasure of acting yourself. It isn't fair!" declared Juliet in the eternal cry of youth.

"Hush, my dear, it's what I want," Virginia said firmly, but the cold lump that had settled near her throat melted somewhat at the warmth of Juliet's support. Unquestionably the child had taken Lady Eugenia in instant dislike, but that could not wholly account for her championing of her companion, and the latter was more grateful than she could say.

"The child is very fond of you, Miss Greyson—you are most fortunate," said a thoughtful voice at her side, bringing her back to the present with a bang.

"Yes. Shall we begin, Lady Eugenia?" Safely Miss Greyson again, Virginia picked up the script she had left on the stage earlier and the rehearsal began.

Two hours later Miss Greyson could agree with Mr. Kirkland that it had gone quite well. The last-minute substitution had had less of a detrimental effect on the performance than he had feared. As usual the director had relied on the assistance of Miss Greyson, who seemed always to know just what he wished to accomplish. It was indeed fortunate that he had found such an able assistant, because at one point this project had seemed doomed to earn the ridicule of the countryside for its reward. She made a better Lady Sneerwell than did Lady Eugenia, but the latter was adequate and would be even better could she be prevailed upon to play down her physical attractiveness. He was not such a fool as to suggest that to a woman of Lady Eugenia's stamp, however, he thought with grim amusement as he walked over to Miss Greyson at the end of reheral and said with some concern, "You are looking very weary, Miss Greyson. It was really too hot for rehearsing today. A cup of tea will help to restore your usual energy."

Virginia forced a smile in response to the genuine kindness in the director's regard, for he had not exaggerated the matter. She was drooping with fatigue, but much as she longed for a cup of tea at the moment, she was ten times more anxious to get right away from the Manor.

"Thank you, sir, for the kind thought," she replied lightly, "but I promised Olivia to go straight home today to drink tea with her, and I think I must not disappoint the poor child. She has been feeling sadly put upon to be forced to miss the full rehearsal." She looked around for Juliet as the members of the cast began to drift away in twos and threes and raised her voice. "Oh, Juliet, are you ready? We should be leaving now."

Juliet sauntered over to the pair by the stage, but her eyes did not quite meet those of her companion. "I think I will change my mind and stay here for tea after all unless you object, Aggie. In fact, I think you should remain too and drive home later. The sky is beginning to look frightfully gray."

Her companion rested a thoughtful glance on the innocent countenance of Miss Brewster. Obviously Juliet had no intention of leaving a clear field for Lady Eugenia in which to practice her arts of fascination. No matter, someone would see that she reached home safely. "Yes, we are in for a wetting, but not, I think, in the next few minutes. I am persuaded there is ample time for me to walk back before it starts. I do not like to disappoint Olivia."

"No need for that, ma'am. I shall be happy to drive you to Fairhill, right now if you wish it, or later," Mr. Kirkland promptly offered.

Virginia tried hard to conceal her irritation at their well-meant interference with her determination to achieve some privacy and said firmly, "I would not dream of taking you away at such a moment, sir, and I must confess I am looking forward to a brisk walk to blow the cobwebs from my brain. I shall see you later then, Juliet." She

116

smiled at them both and slipped out the door before either could offer any additional reasons to delay her.

It was a palpable relief to be away from the crowd for a few minutes. The path in amongst the trees was quite dark by the time she entered it, for the sky was getting blacker by the moment. Neither circumstance caused her an instant's unease. After nearly a month of play rehearsals she knew the way to Fairhill blindfolded, and in her present mood she rather welcomed a battle with the elements. At least the elements were impartial, showering down on rich and poor alike.

Back at the Manor a couple of hours ago she had once again been made to recognize the gap that existed between these people and herself simply because she found it necessary to earn her own living. Lady Teasdale and Lady Eugenia had had no thoughts of wounding another human being by their action with regard to her role in the play; in fact, they did not see her as someone whose feelings needed to be considered, should she dare step out of her allotted place. Only a fierce flaming resentment at such an attitude had enabled her to call upon the requisite pride to conceal her disappointment. Not for the world would she have displayed the least vulnerability before either woman.

It had been a grueling interlude in the airless theater, but she prided herself that she had carried it off successfully. Juliet might suspect the truth, but Lady Wrenthorpe and the men had been fooled. Lady Eugenia and Lady Teasdale, of course, had not given the matter a thought. But now she was alone and she could admit that she *had* been hurt and she *was* disappointed not to be acting in the play after all. Once admitted, she must now forget the incident completely. Such occurrences were part and parcel of her new situation in life, and it was clearly her own

117

fault that, knowing this and accepting it, she must still allow herself to indulge such useless regrets. She forced her attention to her surroundings.

The first drops of rain were pattering about in the leaves above her head as she reached the halfway point in her walk, but very few actually landed on the ground for several minutes. She increased her pace, aware all at once that the wind had been rising steadily and now presented itself as a worthy opponent in that battle she had rashly claimed to welcome.

In the next five minutes she was given her wish as the heavens opened and spilled out the bath water of the gods. The trees afforded little protection now and in three minutes she was thoroughly wet. Actually it *was* rather exhilarating once she had removed her rain-spattered spectacles so she could see where she was heading. The wind continued to whip her skirts and tug at her hat, which gave occupation to both her hands. A sudden picture of the appearance she must present crossed her mind's eye and she laughed aloud.

His head down against a spatter of wind-delivered rain, it was her laughter that Mr. Kirkland was aware of first as he rode along the path on his rescue mission. He raised his head in astonishment and spied a few yards ahead the bedraggled but unbowed figure of Miss Greyson at the same time she became aware of hoofbeats. In another few seconds he was at her side, looking down into her rain-washed face. Before he could confirm the astounding impression that her expression had been one of wild exhilaration, it had melted into contrition as she rushed into speech: "Oh, you should not have come after me. I am fine, *really*!"

He ignored this piece of nonsense. "Why were you laughing?" he asked, watching intently as she lifted the hand not holding her hat to sweep a wet lock of hair out of her eyes and back under the sodden cap.

"Suddenly I had a picture of what a sight I must be. Please turn back. There isn't much farther to go, and I cannot possibly get any wetter." She had been gentling the neck of the big bay, who was apparently averse to standing about in the rain, so she missed the sharp escalation of two black brows. "Thank you very much for coming to rescue me, sir," she added with a belated but conscientious effort to sound properly appreciative.

"Stop arguing and get up here!" he commanded, reaching down a strong brown hand to her.

She hesitated for an instant, not best pleased to be ordered about so abruptly, but one glimpse of the ominous set to his mouth decided her against making an independent stand. She put her foot on his custom-made boot as he indicated and vaulted up in front of him, not at all grateful to have her solitude cut short. They proceeded in silence while the rain continued to pelt them both. Mr. Kirkland had brought a shawl to protect her, but there was no point in mentioning that now.

Even had the wind and rain not made conversation virtually impossible, it is unlikely that either party would have sought any communication in the next few moments. Still in the grip of a reckless elation, Virginia had temporarily forgotten her companion and her discomfort in favor of watching the wild swaying of the branches as the rain turned the leaves inside out.

The same explanation could not be advanced for Mr. Kirkland's silence, for his thoughts were very much on his passenger, and a pretty turmoil they represented at the moment! He controlled the nervous horse with absent-minded expertness and guided him out of the wood before speaking abruptly in a voice pitched to compete with the wind before realizing that the wind had diminished as quickly as it had arisen, and with it most of the rain.

"I wanted to tell you that I am really sorry about what happened this afternoon." He felt the woman in front of him start at the sudden boom of his voice above her ear.

"You are very kind," she replied in a colorless tone, "but it does not signify. Lady Eugenia will do very well in the role." She was aware of his impatient movement behind her shoulder.

"She'll do well enough, though she's not as good as you. That's not what I meant and you know it. I'm sorry for your disappointment. I wish there were something I could do about it."

"You are quite mistaken, sir," came the quick, firm rejection of his sympathy. "There was no disappointment. You may recall my unwillingness to undertake the role initially."

"Gammon, my good woman!" Then as she stiffened in annoyance at this unacceptable form of address, "Oh, very well, *my dear Miss Greyson,* I should say—you may have convinced the others that you cared naught about being coolly displaced like that, but don't try to cozen *me* into believing you were not disappointed, or Miss Brewster," he added thoughtfully.

She was thankful that he couldn't see her face in case it reflected the comfort these words gave her, and seized the opportunity to change the direction of the uncomfortable conversation. Her light laugh was an acting triumph. "Juliet was imagining herself in what she mistakenly believed to be my shoes, but she is a fiercely loyal little soul once she gives her friendship."

"Yes, she is a good child, her airs and vanity notwithstanding."

This unloverlike assessment, uttered so carelessly, was

going to provide Miss Greyson with food for thought when she could attain some privacy, but Mr. Kirkland was not diverted from his original point as his next words proved. "Not that her championship was entirely disinterested, of course. Miss Brewster recognizes competition when she sees it." He ignored her gasp of indignation. "I was speaking of you, and however much you might protest to the contrary, I *know* you enjoyed participating in this play. Why, you've become almost a different person since this project began. Sometimes one would swear you were no older than Miss Brewster or Lady Teasdale. And I repeat, I am sorry that matters turned out this way."

This time her gasp was one of pure fright, and it was accompanied by an involuntary shrinking that she could only hope he would put down to her sodden condition. They were almost abreast of the rear of the house, thank heavens. As he turned to go around to the front, she squealed, "Please, not the front. Just leave me at the side entrance so I may slip upstairs and change without being seen."

In less than a minute she had jumped down from the huge horse without giving him time to dismount and assist her. She stood there, disheveled but erect, looking him straight in the eye. "Thank you, sir, for . . . for everything." Before he could begin to frame a response, she had opened the door and vanished inside.

The man on the horse remained where he was for another thirty seconds, his unseeing eyes riveted to the door through which she had disappeared. There was a slight scowl furrowing his brow, and although a restless motion of his horse's head caused him to remove his glance and adjust his hold on the reins, the scowl remained as he set off slowly to retrace his steps. The rain had ceased entirely now, but he was as little aware of the reality of this as of the path along which the big bay picked his way daintily.

His thoughts, disjointed as they were, stayed with the woman he had just left. A very surprising person, Miss Agnes Greyson! For someone who should pass almost unnoticed in the world by virtue of her appearance and position, she seemed to have made an unexpected impact. And how had this come about? Certainly *he* had found Miss Greyson of interest right from the inauspicious beginning of their acquaintance, but that was because he had received the direct impression, never explained to his satisfaction, that she had recognized him.

When he had tried to question her about possible mutual acquaintances in Bath, she had not been forthcoming. Short of demanding to know why she might have lied about a prior acquaintance—a question clearly barred by convention—he was stymied, since a thorough search of his memory had provided no clue. That first impression had faded or had been pushed into the background over the next two weeks, when most of his time had been devoted to improving his acquaintance with the beautiful Miss Brewster.

A somewhat wry smile stretched his lips at this point in his reflections. Juliet Brewster was very likely the most highly finished work of nature he had been privileged to encounter in his decade on the social scene, and there was no denying he'd been vastly taken with her looks. The grin incorporated a trace of satisfaction as he recalled that he had managed to see a great deal of Juliet, despite the unobtrusive but careful surveillance of her duenna. Obviously she had marked him as a rake or fortune hunter, and her attitude had added spice to the chase.

The reminiscent smile reversed itself and became a frown of perplexity. When had the chase ceased and the realization dawned that, despite her powerful physical appeal, Juliet was a child still and would probably bore him stiff within a month of taking the vows? He did not really know the answer to this, but somehow, once encumbered with the responsibility for an amateur theatrical production, his steady pursuit of the fair Miss Brewster had gradually stilled to a halt. He still enjoyed her company and derived amusement from abetting her youthful attempts at flirtation, but any idea that he might have met the woman whom he would willingly marry had gradually receded.

The smile appeared briefly, self-mocking now. When he became embroiled with a project he was as single-sighted as a horse with blinkers. It was not a gross exaggeration to say the play had become his raison d'être in the last month, and it had slowly been borne in upon him that the only other person to feel something of this was Miss Greyson. The initial inspiration had been Arabella Teasdale's, but after ample opportunity for observation he could say with conviction that her main concern was her own performance. There was no reason why this should not be so, of course, but he could appreciate the difference in Miss Greyson's attitude. He'd turned it to good use also.

Miss Greyson had been invaluable to him, and though he had not gotten around to thinking about it, he had come to consider her as a friend. That was why the events of this afternoon had left him so furious at his own inability to prevent her from being hurt. Despite the best performance she'd ever given, designed to show everyone the contrary, he had remained firmly convinced that she *was* hurt and upset. He had not joined the others for tea, but had remained in the ballroom pondering his next move when the blackness of the sky roused him to action. It had really confounded him to come upon her absolutely drenched and laughing about it, when he had persuaded himself he was going to the rescue of a poor, suffering creature. She had neither wanted nor needed rescue, but he had had no intention of accepting a dismissal at her hands and had compelled her acceptance of a ride. And what had that availed him? She had firmly rejected his expression of sympathy, but he had made it; that was the important thing.

On second thought perhaps she had not rejected his sympathy quite so definitely as it had appeared on the surface. Her eyes when she had thanked him had been more expressive than her simple words. It was the first time he had ever seen her without her spectacles, and though it had not registered at the time, he recalled now that they were lovely eyes, green in color, set at a slightly tilted angle and outlined with long black eyelashes that had been matted together in wet clumps.

A sudden jerk on the reins caused the bay to stop obediently. Anyone venturing on the wet path in the next few minutes could have been excused for wondering if an equestrian statue had suddenly been deposited there. Mr. Kirkland sat as unmoving as a statue while his brain vaulted to a lightning conclusion, rejected it with equal speed, and then advanced on it anew with all due deliberation.

He had seen those eyes before! Or eyes very like those! They belonged to a hoity-toity miss who queened it over all the other young ladies in Bath. And *that* was impossible of course! The fact that Miss Virginia Spicer, the rage of Bath society, and Miss Agnes Greyson, governess-companion on the shady side of thirty, had similar green eyes could be nothing more than coincidence. True green eyes were rare but not unique; coincidence must be the answer. How could it be otherwise? The difference in their respective circumstances alone made the line his thoughts were taking utterly ridiculous.

He had met Miss Spicer just once, but she had been dressed in the height of fashion and was obviously used to moving in the best circles of Bath. Everything about her had indicated wealth and assurance. Miss Greyson, on the other hand, was obliged to earn her own living, and the kindest thing that could be said about her appearance was that it was always neat—until today! Also the difference in their ages must be a full ten years or more. Nor, with the exception of the eyes, was the coloring of the two women the same. Miss Spicer was very nearly a redhead, and her skin he recalled in perfect detail as being very fine and dazzlingly white. Miss Greyson's complexion had a rather unhealthy look, sort of grayish like her name.

His brow grew furrowed as he tried to recall the color of her hair. Now that he thought about it, her hair was always completely covered by a cap except for a bit in the front that didn't seem to have a definite color.

On the point of allowing the restless motions of the bay to dictate the resumption of his progress toward the Manor, he slumped again in the saddle and stared at a spot on the path midway between the horse's ears while a question nagged at his consciousness. *Why* had he never noticed the color of Miss Greyson's eyes before this? He had been meeting her on an almost daily basis for five or six weeks. Surely spectacles could not disguise the color of the wearer's eyes. With great difficulty he conjured up a mental picture of Miss Greyson's face, but it was a blurred image. Perhaps that was the reason he had not noticed her eyes. Except for the spectacles, there was nothing definite about her face, no feature that stood out. Because of the grayish tone of her skin the whole effect was indeterminate.

But not today!

His pulses quickened and excitement spread through his body as he visualized the woman who had just left him with her rain-washed face lifted to thank him. He was positive her skin had been pure white and her brows a well-defined black above those black-fringed green eyes! For some reason of her own Miss Agnes Greyson was in the habit of altering her coloring with some kind of grayish powder or paint. He had still not gotten a good look at her hair, but women could change their hair color also.

None of this necessarily meant she was another person. He must avoid jumping to unsupported conclusions just because a wild hunch was hammering at his pulses. There was still the vital matter of an age difference of a decade to be accounted for. According to Juliet Brewster, Miss Greyson was thirty-one years old, older than himself in fact. *But was she?* With mounting excitement he recalled that straight back and elegant figure at the pianoforte several weeks before, recalled that he had thought then that she looked no older than Arabella Teasdale from the neck down. Then today she had mounted Russet, who stood seventeen hands high, with the agility and swift grace of a girl.

Small wonder she had gasped and shivered when he had tried to express his sympathy with some complimentary remark about her youthfulness. It was fear of discovery, not a chill, that had caused that reaction! Incredible as it seemed, Miss Agnes Greyson and Miss Virginia Spicer were one and the same!

At this point he was no longer listening to any warnings of caution. Against the argument that this masquerade could make no sense, therefore it was impossible, had to be set the most important fact of all, the one thing that convinced him the two women were one person. In the instant of meeting Miss Agnes Greyson had recognized someone who should have been a stranger; ergo, Miss Agnes Greyson was Miss Virginia Spicer! He knew it in his bones. He'd stake his life on it!

During the next two minutes while he allowed Russet to head for home and oats, he permitted himself the pleasure of self-congratulation on solving a mystery. But in a remarkably short time it dawned on him that the solution of one mystery had merely led to the discovery of another. The question of why Miss Virginia Spicer had taken on a new name and identity was infinitely interesting, but by the time he had reached the Manor's stables he had to admit that this puzzle would not prove quite so easy to resolve.

He could always ask Miss Spicer, of course, and most certainly would resort to this tack if necessary, but only as a last resort. For the present he whiled away the remainder of the short ride in idle speculation. Since Miss Spicer was a nubile female, his first thought was *cherchez l'homme*, but a brief consideration of her appearance as Miss Greyson caused him to discard that notion with a cynical smile. What man could she hope to entrap looking like that? It might be the opposite case of course—she might be running away from some man, but that seemed equally farfetched. A girl in Miss Spicer's circumstances was scarcely likely to be unprotected; in fact, he could name at least two unattached males who would welcome the opportunity to leap to her aid.

One could also run away from the law or from some unhappy situation. Wives ran away from husbands; murderers ran away from the Bow Street Runners. Both situations seemed about as plausible as the plot of most comedies, but with nothing to go on, he was permitting full rein to his imagination. It was even conceivable that this impersonation might be for the benefit of a friend, but he found his imagination quite inadequate to the task of deciding in what way and for what reason.

One decision he had already taken by the time he left Russet in charge of his groom, however. The performance of *School for Scandal* was scheduled for Saturday. Once the play was safely over, he would be taking a trip. Mr. Randall Briggs of Bath was about to have the honor of another visit from his brother's school friend, and this time the conversation would not be confined to current political strategies or the prospects for hunting in the fall!

CHAPTER SEVEN

There was an expectant little stir in the dark theater and then Charles Surface sent the screen crashing down.
Charles: "Lady Teazle, by all that's wonderful!"
Sir Peter: "Lady Teazle, by all that's damnable!"

From her seat in the middle of the audience Virginia could feel the positive response of the crowd. The play was going over well; in fact, from about ten minutes into the first act she had found herself relaxing her clenched hands and sitting back in her chair to enjoy the performance. Somewhat to her own surprise her enjoyment of the play was unclouded by personal regret. Thanks in part to the partiality of her young companion and the unsentimental empathy of Mr. Kirkland, her wounded sensibilities had revived wonderfully after her wild walk in the rain, and she was able to appreciate the relative unimportance of the incident that had so upset her.

She had, moreover, managed to gain her own bedchamber without meeting any member of the household, which had spared her a number of horrified questions and tongue clackings, not to mention favorite panaceas to ward off chills. It had been a matter of a couple of minutes to peel off her sodden clothing and rub her cool damp skin dry. Fortunately the day had been so warm there was no possibility of taking a chill. Alive to the lateness of the hour and the impatient nature of her younger charge, her movements had been swift and efficient as she arrayed herself in whatever came to hand, but a necessary pause in front of the mirror for the purpose of sweeping her damp hair out of sight beneath a dry cap had given her a jolt. A spasm of alarm had contorted her features and widened her eyes.

Her spectacles—where were her spectacles? She almost dived for the discarded pile of wet garments and pounced on the brown gown. When she lifted it the spectacles fell out of the pocket and she put them on with fingers that were none too steady. How could she have forgotten the most important part of her disguise in the presence of the one person who could challenge her identity? The rain was no excuse and neither was her state of mind when Mr. Kirkland had arrived to rescue her. There was no extenuating circumstance important enough to excuse such arrant stupidity. She had closed her eyes and made a concerted effort to recall his expression when they had parted. Nothing at all out of the way, a bit more serious than usual, the good-natured mockery that characterized his response to the female of the species for once not present. But nothing else surely. He had long since ceased to have any suspicions of her.

Comforted by this sensible reassurance, she had checked her image in the mirror once more before going to join Olivia and had received another disagreeable shock. She still looked wrong somehow! In an instant she had the reason. Her skin, glowing from the brisk rubbing, was entirely free of the gray powder. With trembling fingers, she had corrected the condition quickly, not quite daring this time to examine Mr. Kirkland's probable reaction to her earlier appearance with absolute impartiality. He would have noticed nothing amiss; it was too rainy, and in any case she had been seated with her back to him for very nearly the entire time they had been together. He would have ascribed any change in her appearance to the wetting she had received. After all, he had never seen Virginia Spicer in a drenched condition either; there was no reason to make any connection between the two women.

She had gone down to Olivia, not altogether comforted by her rationalization, but determined to put the matter out of her mind. And she had succeeded fairly well, thanks to the last-minute bustle caused by the imminence of the performance. Now seated in the audience, flanked by an enraptured Olivia and a proud Sir Reginald, she conceded wryly that the real test of her resolution was yet to come, since she had not yet come face to face with Mr. Kirkland following their wet ride to Fairhill. She had taken the coward's way out and allowed herself to be persuaded by a fussy Juliet that her experience with the storm might have dangerous repercussions (presumably in the region of her chest) if she did not stay quietly at home the next day to recruit her strength with chamomile tea and rest. Juliet would make her excuses in a manner guaranteed to wring sympathy from an ogre, the girl had promised her companion, overriding the latter's feeble protests that she was scarcely at death's door or even deserving of any sympathy.

The day had dragged by, her initial relief at being spared an encounter with Mr. Kirkland gradually overtaken by a nagging awareness that she was shirking her duty in withholding her help at that last crucial rehearsal. And when Juliet returned from the Manor, another dimension was added to her uneasiness. The young girl had had little to say beyond assuring her companion that Mr.

131

Kirkland had not been unduly concerned about the series of minor disasters that had plagued the final rehearsal.

There had been something about Juliet's demeanor that triggered Miss Greyson's curiosity, however, an aura of smugness, for want of a better word. Gentle probing in the most likely direction had elicited no tidings of any circumstance that was apt to remove Lady Eugenia from the stage on the morrow or from the vicinity in the immediate future, nor had her performance as Lady Sneerwell been noticeably deficient. Mystified but still pursuing, Virginia had abandoned that trail in favor of a casual inquiry as to whether Mr. Kirkland had been especially pleased with Juliet's performance that day. Mr. Kirkland had assured her a week since that he had every confidence that her portrayal of Maria would have just the correct balance, the girl had reported blithely.

Her companion had been obliged to restrain her imagination for want of a clue. Then a postprandial discussion of Juliet's choice of gown for the dancing that would take place in the ballroom after the play had produced the startling information that Juliet was in the expectation of hearing something of a particular nature from Mr. Kirkland during the social part of the evening. A combination of cowardice and dismay had kept Virginia silent after a swift look at the lovely, abstracted face informed her that Juliet was unaware of the revelation she had just made. It was a habit of hers when pondering a decision of some importance to consider the alternatives in the presence of another person, who might be invited to offer suggestions or comments. It had not taken Virginia long to discover that the young girl scarcely heard any remarks that might be forthcoming in such a situation because essentially she was conducting the discussion with herself.

During the epilogue of the play, delivered by a triumphant Lady Teasdale, last night's revelation returned to Virginia's mind, as it had during every unoccupied moment of her day, and left it as troubled as on the first hearing. Her instincts and her observations had arrived at the identical conclusion—that unless he were bent on concealing his feelings for some reason, Mr. Kirkland's interest in Juliet had actually dwindled, not been kindled over the past few weeks.

She cast a speculative glance at Sir Reginald, who was on his feet applauding enthusiastically as the cast took bow after bow. If Juliet's father were likely to forbid the match, a man of honor probably would strive to conceal his feelings, as Mr. Ryding had been doing; but he would certainly *not* make an assignation at a party to reveal his hopeless passion. If Juliet had misunderstood Mr. Kirkland, her disappointment would be keen, and her companion would be advised to keep a watchful eye on her tonight. All things considered, Miss Greyson was not looking forward to the rest of the evening as she accompanied Olivia, Amelia, and Sir Reginald to the main dining room, where a tempting array of cold foods awaited Sir Malcolm's guests.

The two youngest girls were being allowed up to watch the first half hour of the dancing before retiring to Amelia's quarters for the night. They were the first to congratulate the players as the cast joined the guests for refreshments. Olivia, who was meeting Lord Hampton and his sister for the first time, looked as bowled over by the latter's blond beauty as Mellie had been. Lady Eugenia, resplendent in a deep green dress sparkling with brilliants, entered the room with her hand on Mr. Kirkland's arm as she made a laughing remark for his ear alone. Within seconds the players were surrounded by admiring friends and relatives and drawn off into little groups, but as an entrance it had been eye-catching, and a quick check of Juliet's tightened mouth revealed that that young lady had not missed the intimate little gesture.

She was not allowed to dwell on the incident, Miss Greyson saw with satisfaction, as her family was soon superceded by the usual swarm of swains vying for her attention. Sir Reginald, at his daughter's side, gave way laughingly to an earnest youth whose sole desire seemed to be to see that Juliet took some refreshment after her arduous stint on the stage. Always receptive to flattering attention, the lovely brunette began to sparkle, and her companion was able to relax for the moment and turn her attention to the youngest ladies present.

Amelia had a governess of sorts, a timid mouse of a woman who never could have coped with the lively Arabella, but she was away at present visiting her aged parents in Bristol. Virginia could place no dependence on the indolent Lady Wrenthorpe when it came to supervising her younger daughter and her guest, although in fairness it must be admitted that Amelia alone would require little supervision.

Olivia, however, was a horse of another color. Always more enterprising, she was quite capable of cajoling some of the younger gentlemen into inviting her to dance. Even though the company consisted mainly of local families well known to the Brewsters, such behavior in a girl of fourteen would not be overlooked by the straitlaced matrons sitting around the edges of the ballroom.

It did not come to quite such a pass before the thirty minutes grace period was up, but the general hilarity from the corner where the voluble Olivia and her shadow were holding court was beginning to attract the attention of those nearest them when Miss Greyson glided into the

134

group and explained with a smile that the young ladies must make their adieux. Olivia's face fell ludicrously.

"Just ten more minutes, please, Miss Greyson! Bertram says the orchestra is going to play a waltz. I've never seen the waltz danced and neither has Mellie."

Virginia was not proof against the eager appeal that was echoed in Amelia's brown eyes. "Very well. If they play it immediately you may see the first waltz. Ah," she said as the orchestra swung into one of the fast German pieces, "you are in luck."

Most of the young men rushed off to secure partners for the dance that was still regarded by some old-fashioned persons as slightly scandalous, though it had the seal of approval of the highest sticklers in London. Miss Greyson shepherded the two girls to seats near an exit, but her eyes were on Juliet's sapphire-blue figure. She could not help seeing the anticipatory glance the girl sent in Mr. Kirkland's direction at the first strains of the waltz or his obvious unawareness of the unspoken message. He bowed smilingly over Lady Teasdale's hand and led her onto the floor.

Four young men reached Juliet at the same moment and demanded her hand in chorus. Mr. Ryding, with whom she had been engaged in conversation, made a gesture of surrender and stepped back good-naturedly. Judging by the pantomime of the next few seconds, Miss Greyson guessed that he had advised Juliet she must choose blindfolded to be fair, for that young lady closed her eyes and twirled once around, extending her right hand toward the cluster of hopeful applicants. The quickest of them seized the hand and whirled her out onto the floor before the others could react.

Miss Greyson expelled a long breath. It had been a quick recovery, and she hoped only Mr. Ryding had been

135

cognizant of the naked shock on Juliet's face when Mr. Kirkland had casually invited Lady Teasdale to dance. Miss Greyson could not be positive from her angle, but she rather thought the tutor's position had shielded the girl from the eyes of the men approaching her. Her own eyes searched out Mr. Ryding, and she was reassured by the quick smile he sent her way. Thankfully she returned her attention to the two girls beside her. Their excitement and pleasure was contagious, and she had always loved waltz music.

She would have enjoyed the next few moments had not Mr. Elliott's rotund form advanced on her position just then. His smooth, porcine countenance was shiny as he beamed hugely on spotting her, the thick lips below a broad retroussé nose stretched widely, forcing his receding chin even farther into his neckcloth. He dropped onto the chair beside the governess.

"My dear Miss Greyson, what a delightful surprise to find you recovered. We sadly missed your helpful presence yesterday at rehearsal. Indeed, I had formed the intention of calling on you to see how you did after your terrible experience in the storm, but Miss Brewster explained that you were keeping to your bed as a precaution against developing a serious chill."

Bless Juliet! Miss Greyson was formulating a tactful reply when Olivia blurted, "But Miss Greyson was not— *ouch!*" The youngster turned a surprised face to her governess who removed her foot from contact with the child's ankle.

"I beg your pardon, Olivia, so clumsy of me! The music is ending, girls, time to go, I'm afraid." She bestowed a polite smile on the reverend as she pulled Olivia to her feet. "You must excuse me for the moment, Mr. Elliott.

The girls are going to retire now. Say good night to Mr. Elliott, Olivia, Amelia."

Amelia dropped a curtsy to the minister, who had risen to his feet with the apparent intention of escorting them to the door of the ballroom. Olivia followed suit somewhat hastily and said helpfully, "You need not come with us, Miss Greyson. Betty will be waiting to attend to us upstairs."

A firm hand on her waist propelled her inexorably toward the door. "I promised your father I'd see you settled, my dear. You will excuse me, sir?"

"Of course, dear lady, of course, but only temporarily. We shall have a long coze when you return. And my sister will be pleased to renew her acquaintance with you." He wished the girls a courtly good night, and Miss Greyson was at last able to escape with her charges.

Olivia was protesting that she had not meant to spoil her governess's evening, and Mellie also apologized for taking her away from the ballroom. Miss Greyson smothered their protests with tactful platitudes while she speculated on how long she might safely remain away from the party without seeming to abandon Juliet. If she had only her own inclinations to consider, she'd stay upstairs with Olivia and Mellie and be better entertained by their impressions of the evening. At the thought of the inhibiting effect her presence would have on the girls' conversation, a smile chased away the harassed expression acquired some moments earlier.

She dawdled as long as she could without arousing curiosity, pausing to assist Olivia with the buttons down the back of her peach-colored dress and to inquire for Betty's sister, who had been a maid at Fairhill until her recent marriage. However, in very short order her presence in the nursery wing was clearly superfluous, so she bade the two girls a pleasant good night and withdrew.

Her progress back to the ballroom was at a funereal pace, unlike her mental processes, which galloped over the events of the evening. She was decidedly uneasy about Juliet, who was in a dangerous mood thanks to what she would regard as affronts to her position as reigning belle in the neighborhood. Fortunately only one very close to the young girl would be likely to recognize that she had been furious at the apparent intimacy with Mr. Kirkland that Lady Eugenia had established in the minds of the guests by her entrance on his arm earlier, and that his failure to request the first waltz with Juliet had utterly rocked the girl off her heels.

That the entrance had been cleverly contrived by Lady Eugenia was perfectly apparent to Virginia, but Juliet was too inexperienced to be able to see much beneath the surface. It might be unjustified, but rightly or wrongly she had been expecting Mr. Kirkland to single her out for special attention tonight. By the time Virginia had left the room, he had allowed over an hour to go by without approaching Juliet.

So far the girl had done nothing to attract unwelcome attention, contenting herself with flirting openly with the men who surrounded her. But Virginia would not have cared to wager a large sum against the chance of some noticeable behavior staged to show the world how little she regarded being ignored by Mr. Kirkland. She could only cling to the fervent hope that that gentleman would not let much more time elapse before he invited Juliet to dance.

She knew she did not stand upon sufficiently cordial terms with him herself to suggest this, and in any case was desirous of avoiding his society tonight for her own sake.

138

Despite her rationalizations there was a nagging little fear that something about her appearance in the storm might have aroused his dormant suspicions concerning a prior meeting. A tactful approach to Mr. Kirkland on Juliet's behalf was not to be considered.

Her thoughts shifted to the unwelcome presence of Mr. Elliott. With a wry grimace she dismissed the ludicrous idea of Miss Elliott's purported interest in improving their acquaintance. The only time the two ladies had exchanged more than civil bows after church services was a month ago when Mr. Elliott had brought his sister to call at Fairhill, and it would take an extraordinarily unobservant person to deduce that the labored exchange of banalities on that occasion indicated a desire on the part of either of the ladies to further the acquaintance.

Miss Elliott appeared to be a year or two shy of forty; she was short, plump, and physically unprepossessing except for small, snapping black eyes that darted around continually, seeming never to rest on the person she was addressing. She had been keeping house for her brother for some dozen years, and Miss Greyson had a shrewd notion that her sweetly acid tongue would be swift to take preventative action should she even suspect that another woman might be contemplating supplanting her in that role. It would behoove her to avoid Miss Elliott's company whenever possible.

If only she could avoid her brother as well! As she approached the entrance to the ballroom on lagging feet, she steeled herself to endure the company of the minister, whom she was half convinced would be lying in wait for her return.

But it was not Mr. Elliott who pounced on her as she crossed the threshold.

"Well met, Miss Greyson! They are just striking up for

139

another waltz. May I have the pleasure?" Mr. Kirkland stood squarely in her path, smiling at her with a gleam of mockery in his dark eyes.

By a stern effort of will Virginia concealed her uneasiness at this confrontation and summoned up a creditable smile. "I am sorry, sir, but I don't dance. Thank you, though, for your kind invitation." She made a slight movement as if to step around him and proceed into the room, but by an even slighter movement he halted her progress. She could not now enter without physically removing him from her path.

"Now I would have guessed that you would be an excellent dancer, Miss Greyson. You move with such grace and youthful precision."

Really, the man had a talent for making a compliment sound like a threat, she thought with the beginnings of indignation, but she managed to reply evenly: "A governess does not expect to be seen on a dance floor, Mr. Kirkland. There are several young ladies whom you should rather honor with your invitation, if you will forgive the suggestion."

"Oh, yes, Miss Greyson, I will forgive it if you will forgive my not accepting it for the moment. I find I am in need of a breathing spell after all. Shall we find a spot in which to relax?" He offered his arm, and after an infinitesimal hesitation she placed her fingers lightly on the blue sleeve above his wrist and allowed him to escort her to a semiprivate area near some potted palms. All her instincts urged flight, but there was nothing she could do without appearing rude. She kept her eyes on the dancers and waited for him to speak.

"You have not congratulated me on a successful performance, Miss Greyson. Is it a case of saying nothing if your

140

conscience will not permit you to praise untruthfully?" This provocation brought her face around to his.

"Of course not! You know without my telling you what a remarkable achievement that performance was in the face of such a wide range of temperaments and abilities. If I seemed slow to offer my felicitations, it was because you were surrounded by admirers earlier."

"And just now?"

"Just now," she said with some asperity, "you were too intent on embarrassing the governess with your invitation to dance to be in the mood to receive admiring comments." She noted that he made no attempt to deny the charge. Indeed, the little smile that curved what should have been a nice mouth took on a rather unpleasant aspect in concert with the hard-eyed stare she was being subjected to. Her eyes went back to the floor though she saw nothing. She could only pray her tenseness was not evident in every part of her body as she concentrated on keeping her hands relaxed in a loose clasp in her lap.

It seemed he wasn't yet done with baiting her. "How did you feel about watching the play from the audience when you had expected to be part of it?"

"I told you before that I accepted the role only because the situation at the time was desperate. It was a relief to relinquish it."

"And I told *you* before," he said, mimicking her flat delivery, "that I did not believe you, Miss . . . Greyson."

"That is regrettable but will not keep me awake tonight," she replied tartly.

His sudden laughter sounded genuine, but she kept her eyes upon the twirling performers on the dance floor. The orchestra was playing another waltz with great verve. She was searching for Juliet among the dancers and his next words were slow to register.

"I am going away for a few days—to Bath."

"Indeed? Then I must wish you good-bye and a safe journey." The polite sentiment was forced out between stiff lips. It would be nice if he contrived to break a leg en route, she thought wistfully. That would solve her own problem and Juliet's. The child would soon forget him if he vanished from the scene for a time.

"You have many friends in Bath, have you not, Miss Greyson? I would be most happy to be the bearer of greetings from you. Do you have any messages I might deliver?"

"I think not, thank you."

"Not even to Lady Mallory?" he persisted. "I would be most happy to call upon her. I am persuaded she will be thrilled to learn at firsthand just how indispensible you have become in your new post, Miss Greyson."

Virginia's heart had skipped a beat at the mention of Lady Mallory. Now it was racing so that she felt suffocated, but she must say something to stop him! "I . . . I have written to Lady Mallory on several occasions. It will be quite unnecessary for you to visit her."

"But I *insist* on doing this little favor for you. Think of all the time and effort you expended helping me to get this play in trim. What is Lady Mallory's direction?"

"There is no point in giving it to you, sir, I'm afraid. The last letter I received from Lady Mallory was full of plans for a sojourn in Scotland. She will be away for six weeks at least." Desperation had provided inspiration and Virginia faced him, outwardly calm.

"Ah? A pity, but not entirely unexpected."

She returned her gaze to the floor, refusing to be goaded into further speech on that subject. There was Juliet dancing with Lord Hampton, surely for the second time. A new worry made a place for itself in her poor brain. She must speak to Juliet when this marathon dance ended and make certain she did not accept a third invitation from him. Every nerve in her body was quivering from recent abrasive contact with the obnoxious creature at her side, but she concentrated on Juliet. However, when Mr. Kirkland announced in a pleased voice that Mr. Elliott was heading their way, Virginia's control snapped.

"I beg you will excuse me, sir. I am excessively thirsty; it's so warm in here." She rose swiftly to her feet, murmured something about getting a drink, and clamped her tongue between her teeth to prevent it from uttering a plea that he not tell Mr. Elliott where she had gone. In the mood he was in that would be sufficient to have him set the minister on her trail immediately.

Five minutes later when Mr. Elliott cornered her at the buffet table where she was gulping down a glass of lemonade, she did not need his reference to Mr. Kirkland to inform her to whom she owed this second meeting.

"Recruiting your spirits with the fruit of the vine, Miss Greyson?" he boomed in a heavy handed attempt at levity.

"Lowering my temperature with the fruit of the lemon tree," she corrected, a touch of lemon juice in her tones as she stared blandly back at him. "You are looking a trifle warm, sir. May I pour you a glass?"

He stayed her movement toward the ladle in the silver punch bowl with an upraised hand. "A trifle sweet for my taste, dear lady. I shall try our host's champagne." He accepted a glass from the waiter and sampled it judiciously. "Yes, very nice indeed, very refreshing." Noticing the waiter's sardonic expression, Virginia wondered if he had done some earlier sampling. She moved back toward the ballroom with little expectation that he would allow her to go unescorted, but she was intent on speaking with Juliet, who had been avoiding her all evening. He must have swallowed his champagne in one gulp because he was at her side in a few seconds.

"You must allow me to tell you how greatly I admire your sacrifice, dear Miss Greyson. Such unselfishness, such nobility of character is too rare indeed. You are an example to us all."

Virginia stared. How much champagne had the man drunk? His smooth-skinned face was shinier and redder than usual, but that could be due to the heat in the ball-room. He appeared perfectly steady on his feet. "I beg your pardon, sir, I fear I do not perfectly comprehend your meaning," she said, masking her uneasiness and speeding up her pace a trifle.

He reached for her hand. For a startled moment Virginia thought he intended to raise it to his lips, and she made an involuntary movement to escape. However, he contented himself with giving her hand an approving pat before releasing it once more. "How very like you to be so modest! Always hiding your light under a bushel as they say. We, the whole cast, I should say, were deeply sensible of the gracious manner in which you sacrificed your pleasure for another. You have earned the respect and admiration of us all."

Good heavens! So that was what he was talking about. She had so much on her mind at the moment that her disappointment over losing the role seemed to date from another era.

"You accord me too much undeserved credit, Mr. Elliott," she said with great firmness. "There was no nobility involved, I assure you, in giving up something that I had not wished for in the first place. Now, let us speak of something else, shall we? Do you and your sister intend to take a holiday this summer?"

Twenty minutes later she was still listening to a dissertation on the myriad difficulties involved in securing the services of a locum when a man of the cloth desired to leave his post temporarily. They were back in the ballroom, seated at the edge of the dance floor, from which vantage point Miss Greyson could at least keep her eye on Juliet. She had been immensely gratified to see her charge whirling in the arms of Mr. Simon Kirkland on her return. Judging from the mocking expression in Mr. Kirkland's eyes as they met hers briefly, he had expected it to annoy her, as he had everything he had said in that memorable tête-à-tête earlier. A pity he would never know that his invitation was just what she had been most desirous of all evening.

Virginia thought them the handsomest couple on the floor, even better-looking than Lord Hampton and his sister, who were circling the room with the ease of long practice, but a few moments' observation while she listened to Mr. Elliott with apparent interest revealed that Juliet displayed none of the radiance that had illuminated her beauty at the start of the evening. Obviously Mr. Kirkland's attentions had not been of a nature to satisfy her expectations.

At one point in the dance her step had faltered momentarily, and though she soon recovered her footing, there was a frozen look to her countenance that remained unchanged for the rest of the dance. It seemed to Miss Greyson that Mr. Kirkland's offer to return her to the company of her companion was rejected out of hand at the end of the number, for Juliet veered off alone in another direction, slipping away amongst those leaving the floor. When next Miss Greyson caught sight of her, she was dancing with Mr. Ryding, which served to allay her growing anxiety for the moment. But she was resolved to confront the girl when the music ended, even if it meant being uncivil to Mr. Elliott and stationing herself in Juliet's path to achieve her purpose.

She managed the feat without any dramatic maneuvers beyond a mendacious assurance to the minister that she would be delighted to have a cozy chat with Miss Elliott after seeing that Juliet took a few moments to cool off and refresh herself after the exertions of hours of dancing.

As it turned out, she perjured her soul to no good end, for Juliet put her off with a scintillating performance that produced a spate of words, revealed nothing of her thoughts, and did not deceive her companion for an instant. Miss Greyson was aware that, had she dared, the girl would have refused to accompany her to the dining room, but thankfully Juliet was too well mannered to create a scene in public. Her discontented mouth confirmed Miss Greyson in all her speculations about the girl's true reaction to the evening's events. Laugh she might, and flirt outrageously and dance continuously, but the gaiety was almost entirely spurious; Juliet was suffering a severe disappointment which she was gallantly attempting to conceal.

As was only to be expected, they were heavily escorted to the refreshment table. Private conversation would have proved difficult even had Juliet been willing, which she clearly was not. The best Miss Greyson could expect was that the child would sit out a dance or two and give her body a rest.

Even this hope was not to be realized. When they returned to the ballroom, Juliet exclaimed immediately, "Oh, they are playing another waltz!" Her innocently expectant glance fixed itself on one of her train, who waltzed her off before the others could frame a request.

Miss Greyson excused herself without the disappointed young men really noticing that she had left their company as they joined forces in apostrophizing their quick-footed colleague turned traitor. She headed purposefully for a chair in an unobtrusive area, only pausing once to congratulate Mr. Penrose on his performance and speak to his ladies for the sake of civility. Solitude was what she craved at the moment, a chance to relax her own taut nerves. Watching the play had been enjoyable, but the pleasures derived from the earlier part of the evening had long since been obliterated by succeeding events. She could bear the tedium of Mr. Elliott's conversation in small doses, but tonight she felt as though she were being hunted by the man. A quick reconnaissance of the room from under her lashes placed him among a quartet that included his sister, Lady Wrenthorpe, and another gentleman, unknown to Miss Greyson but already respected for the apparent ease with which he was holding his small audience engrossed in his conversation.

Safe for a few moments! She squandered them in a rather painful recollection of that alarming confrontation with Mr. Kirkland, which had pricked at the back of her consciousness ever since she had left him. It seemed to her to have had positively threatening overtones, although she sought to explain away her vague premonitions. If she did not set a guard on her fanciful brain, she would turn into one of those wretched creatures who convince themselves that people are persecuting them.

Resolutely she banished personal considerations. Her concern about Juliet was not imagination. Watching her circle the room, apparently in high gig, she could not refrain from wishing the evening were over and they were safely back at Fairhill. Guests would begin to leave within the hour, but Sir Reginald, who enjoyed a game of whist, was unlikely to be among the early departees. He had vanished from the ballroom hours ago after a duty dance with his hostess and one with his daughter, and was no doubt quite content to remain in the card room until the orchestra left off playing.

As if on cue the waltz music came to a flourishing stop. Miss Greyson located Juliet and her partner, but after her recent experience she had little expectation that the young man would be permitted to return the girl to her companion's side.

Nor was he. Juliet indicated she wished to speak with the Penrose girls before they took their departure. They stood talking for a few minutes while Mr. and Mrs. Penrose made their adieux to their hostess. Just as the music began anew and Miss Penrose and Miss Alice Penrose broke away from the group in response to an imperious signal from their mother, Miss Greyson was alerted by the simultaneous approach of Lord Hampton and Mr. Kirkland. Her hands clenched unknowingly on her reticule lying in her lap, then relaxed as common sense dispelled her instinctive alarm. Juliet knew better than to dance a third time with any one gentleman. It showed a degree of particularity that no young lady with any claim to a sense of decorum would care to demonstrate in the public eye.

Miss Greyson's eyes narrowed and her lips firmed as she watched the tableau about to be enacted. Lord Hampton made an elegant bow in front of Juliet just as Mr. Kirkland arrived at the side of Mr. Thomas Appleby, her former partner. How dare the earl place that child in an embarrassing position, Miss Greyson fumed from her corner, where she was powerless to smooth the situation. It was fortunate that Mr. Kirkland had read his intention and arrived to present Juliet with a valid excuse for declining Lord Hampton's invitation, since Mr. Appleby had already partnered her twice. A second later Miss Greyson's habitually straight back stiffened to a marked degree as her eyes swung from her charge, her hand on the earl's arm, gaily stepping into a set that was forming for a country dance, to the surprised face of Mr. Appleby, and thence to the inscrutable countenance of Mr. Kirkland. The latter met her accusing glance with raised eyebrows before shrugging slightly as he prepared to offer for another young lady close at hand. Mr. Appleby followed suit at once. At least their quick dispersal would do nothing to draw attention to Juliet.

Perhaps it was not too much to hope that the girl's indiscretion might go unnoticed so late in the evening. As Miss Greyson scanned the room, she was obliged to relinquish this forlorn hope, however. Her questing gaze found two turbaned matrons with their heads together and their eyes trailing Juliet's progress around the floor. If that was not sufficient to destroy any last shreds of her peace of mind, in the next instant her glance fell on her hostess in conversation with Mrs. Penrose, whose lingering farewells had enabled her to witness the gratifying spectacle of the vain Miss Brewster acting in a shameless fashion that she was happy to know neither of her girls would dream of imitating.

With a sinking feeling in her stomach Miss Greyson had no difficulty in interpreting the lady's sentiments as they appeared on her face. (And why could she not have been as expressive on the stage?) Mrs. Penrose, with two plain daughters to establish creditably, was the last person from whom to seek indulgence toward one who took the shine out of Emily and Alice without lifting her little finger. What an absolutely fitting end to as hideous an evening as she could remember, Miss Greyson thought bitterly. That was all that was wanted to fill her cup to the brim!

It was to overflow shortly. No sooner had she seen Mr. Alistair Penrose remove Juliet from Lord Hampton's company and relaxed her death clutch on her reticule somewhat, when Mr. Elliott appeared at her elbow to redeem her promise of a chat with his sister. Perforce she suffered herself to be led across the floor to a chair beside Miss Elliott, whose unwelcoming eyes belied her conventionally stretched lips.

Why, she's at least as furious with him as I am for contriving this meeting, Virginia realized all of a sudden, and her spirits which had reached rock bottom rebounded considerably as her sense of humor came out of hiding. She beguiled the tedium of the next half hour in supporting and amplifying each and every opinion Miss Elliott advanced on the performance, the music, the refreshments, and the company, projecting what she fondly trusted was animated interest on her features. When the minister's sister made an oblique reference to Juliet's misdemeanor, she replied without a blink, "Yes, that naughty girl! It was too bad of her to decide that because Lord Hampton is dear Lady Wrenthorpe's guest she might accord him extra civility without having a peal rung over her. I shall give her a severe scold presently." Her voice dripped odious archness.

After a threatening look from her brother the other woman had the grace to change the subject, but as she chose to extoll the performance of Lady Eugenia as Lady Sneerwell, there was little to choose from as far as Virginia was concerned. I am the most accomplished actress here tonight, she thought with grim satisfaction as she smiled into Miss Elliott's cold, opaque eyes and went her one better in praising the talents and accomplishments of the beautiful blond visitor. By the time Mr. Elliott, who had remained by the ladies' side throughout the cozy chat, indicated with regret that they must be taking their leave, his sister's feminine version of the family snout was pink and faintly twitching, and her large mouth was pursed with the effort it cost to conceal her frustration at having been unable to discomfort her opponent. She got to her feet with an agility that reflected her eagerness to be gone from present company, but despite a burning resentment that caused her ample bosom to swell to prodigious proportions inside her puce-colored gown, she dutifully seconded her brother's invitation to Miss Greyson for tea at the manse within a few days. Virginia smiled sweetly and accepted with a gushing alacrity that sent Mr. Elliott off wearing an expression of the most odious self-congratulation.

If the steely glint in Miss Elliott's little black eyes was anything to judge by, he would not long remain puffed up in his own conceit, however. For a moment watching them leave, Mr. Elliott almost hurrying to keep up with his stout sister's determined pace, Virginia's withers were wrung by a feeling of disinterested compassion at the uncomfortable ride home that was in store for him, but she resolutely banished pity and a twinge of guilt at her own behavior as she tried to decide whether to have a headache or some more interesting symptom when the date for the tea party arrived. A man who encouraged his sister to become such an impossible dragon was only reaping his just desserts!

Virginia was punished for her unkind thoughts later, however, for the drive home in the Brewster carriage was productive of a degree of discomfort that she might have foreseen in the circumstances. After a mildly successful evening of whist, Sir Reginald, to whose ears no breath of his daughter's indiscretion had been allowed to penetrate, was in a mellow mood as he gathered the members of his family together. The subdued manner of his lovely daughter did not immediately strike him during the flurry of leave-taking.

"Well, puss," he said genially as he handed her up into the chaise, "quite a triumphant evening for you, was it not? I'll be bound you experienced no lack of partners for the dancing."

His attractive rich chuckle grated on Miss Greyson's nerves tonight, though she could sympathize with his amazed consternation when Juliet burst out, "I have never spent a more wretched evening in my life!"

"Why, what's all this? You were a complete success in the play, and when I went into the card room you were being besieged by every young sprig in the county wishing to partner you. What can have happened?" Sir Reginald's honest countenance wore a look of such genuine concern that Miss Greyson could cheerfully have slapped her spoiled charge for her lack of control.

"Nothing *happened,* Papa," Juliet replied in a sullen tone, knowing she had gone too far, and unable to offer an explanation that would make sense to a gentleman somewhat stricken in years, or to any gentleman for that matter. "It is simply that an evening spent among such a dull set of persons could not help but be . . . disappointing," she finished somewhat lamely.

"You didn't find them such a dull set last week," put in Bertram with a rare and ill-timed percipience. "It's my belief that your nose is out of joint because Mr. Kirkland didn't pay as much attention to you as he did to Lady Eugenia. Just because you are so used to having all the silly gudgeons in the neighborhood making cakes of themselves over you don't mean you should expect a man of the world like Mr. Kirkland to dance attendance on a chit who ain't even out yet. I noticed he only danced with you once—probably just doing his duty and—"

"Bertram!" Mr. Ryding's quiet warning was drowned in Juliet's passionate protest. "That's not true, Bertram, it's not! He asked me a second time but I refused! I preferred to accept Lord Hampton, who is a much better dancer, and I think you are absolutely infamous to talk to me this way!" Juliet was dangerously close to tears, and her voice was shrill as she turned to her father for support. "Papa—are you going to allow him to speak so rudely to me?"

"Now that's quite enough, Bertram," Sir Reginald said gruffly. "Come now, puss, it's not worth crying about. I'd be mightily surprised to hear you were not the most sought-after young lady at that dance tonight."

"Juliet is overtired, Sir Reginald." Miss Greyson thought it high time to bring this appalling little tempest to a halt. Her quiet, confident tones continued: "She has been working very hard on the play all through this spell of hot weather, and the excitement of the performance followed by the dance has been a strain on her nerves."

At this point Mr. Ryding, who had been a silent and embarrassed spectator to the young people's squabble, spoke up in his pleasant way. "I hope you will accept my word for it, sir, that Miss Brewster was indeed the most sought-after young lady this evening, and deservedly so."

"There, puss, you see?"

Juliet's voice was now almost wholly suspended by tears, but she cast a grateful glance in Mr. Ryding's direction before subsiding deeper into her corner with a tiny sob. Miss Greyson could feel her tremble and acknowledged to herself a deeper concern than she wished to share with Juliet's father. The child was indeed overtired and overwrought as well. The strain of keeping up a pretense of enjoyment throughout the last half of the evening had culminated in this unfortunate scene. She needed a good

153

night's sleep and a period of inactivity to allow her to recover the tone of her spirits.

Juliet did not utter another syllable for the remainder of the drive. Bertram offered a few comments on the excellent sport he had enjoyed in Sir Malcolm's billiard room, but as these were received in an unencouraging manner by all within the chaise, he, too, lapsed into the general silence.

It was a decided relief to leave the chaise at the front door and ascend the shallow entrance steps. Sir Reginald kissed his daughter tenderly at the foot of the main staircase, and the ladies retired with all due speed. It would have been Hobson's choice to say who was the more thankful to seek out the sanctuary of her bedchamber, unless Miss Greyson received the edge because her offer to accompany Juliet to hers, prompted by a sense of duty and against her own inclination, was so firmly rejected.

CHAPTER EIGHT

In her dreams she was relentlessly pursued by a faceless form that no trick served to elude. Every corner turned, far from bringing her closer to safety, simply revealed another turning, and when a horse appeared fortuitously to carry her swiftly onward, a hopeful backward glance discovered that her pursuer was now mounted also. Each step had become a tremendous effort of will, and the distance between them was narrowing inexorably when Virginia came strugglingly awake to a golden summer morning.

Sunlight was streaming in the window that she had thrown open last night in a vain attempt to rid the room of a stifling airlessness, and the twittering of numerous birds drifted in on the sunbeams. She turned her head eagerly toward the sunlight, and relief flooded over her at having escaped the nightmare. But even as the stark details of the dream receded to a residue of nameless dread, the short-lived tide of well-being was submerged in a creeping sense of oppression.

Her eyes, under lids lowered to shield them from the sun's rays, stared fixedly at the bright patch on the polished floor while she concentrated on pinning down the reason for her vague depression. A half-opened fan lay in the sunny patch, the strong light making its stretched silk almost transparent. Evidently it had fallen off the bureau where she had tossed it on returning from the Manor last night.

Instant and total recall of the more embarrassing moments of that eventful evening sent her head back down on the pillow for a moment, but there would be no evading the consequences. She groaned and hauled herself out of bed, her mood entirely incompatible with the beautiful new day.

The routine of Miss Greyson's morning toilette was even more automatic than usual, for Virginia'a mind darted back and forth from analyzing the events of the previous evening to speculating upon the probable aftereffects. A swift summation of her own appearance after she had crammed her Sunday cap with its lace border over her braids left her unsurprised at the shadows beneath her eyes. After all, one couldn't spend the night fleeing the most determined pursuit and expect to look well rested the next morning.

She would not be amazed to find Juliet a bit off color today also. Though the girl was of a basically sanguine nature, last night's humiliation—or, to be more accurate, what she *saw* as a humiliation—had bitten deeply into her self-esteem. Somehow, though she *hoped*, Virginia had no real expectation that a girl, already accustomed at age seventeen to receiving the homage of nearly every male of her acquaintance, could put such an occurrence behind her without contemplating some sort of retaliation.

Though she joined the family for church services later, Virginia derived little spiritual benefit from the experience, being more concerned with a covert observation of her charge and intense speculation as to what path her reaction would take. She would have been better pleased to find Juliet subdued or even sulky, because these at least

156

would be honest reactions. But one glance at the young beauty all ready for church sufficed to warn Virginia that Miss Brewster was determined to reverse any impression of unhappiness she may have left on the minds of her family after the scene in the chaise last night.

Clad in a charming sprig muslin dress of a delectable shade of apricot that exactly matched the wide satin ribbon of her newest straw bonnet, set at a dashing angle atop her raven curls and tied daringly in a huge bow under one ear, Juliet was a picture to gladden the eyes of her anxious parent, who brightened at the sound of her voice as she scurried down the stairs to greet him with an enthusiastic kiss. She was in quite her best looks, too, if one disregarded a very slight suggestion of pink around her eyelids that was more than compensated for by the glowing color of her mouth and cheeks, aided somewhat, her unimpressionable duenna was persuaded, by a sparing use of forbidden cosmetics.

She was in tearing spirits, too, and kept them all entertained on the short drive to the church with a lively description of the series of small mishaps backstage that had beset the cast during last night's performance. Once or twice when she seemed to be coming to the end of a story, Bertram inserted a comment that set her off again. Sir Reginald and Mr. Ryding were kept in a ripple of laughter, but Miss Greyson was vastly relieved to enter the church and feel the enforced silence settle over them like a soothing hand. At this rate Juliet would be quite exhausted by lunchtime.

Miss Greyson had underestimated the strength of that young lady's determination, however. If anything, her performance after services was even more sparkling than during the drive from Fairhill. She charmed the Thorpe Manor contingent impartially, complimenting Lady Eugenia on her dress and Lady Teasdale on her hat, saying all that was proper to Lady Wrenthorpe and Sir Malcolm about last night's entertainment, and bestowing on Lord Hampton a particularly beguiling smile as they shook hands. During the interval when the two parties mingled in brief conversation outside the small stone church and the Brewsters received their youngest member from her overnight stay at the Manor, only Mr. Kirkland was denied the sunshine of Miss Brewster's regard.

The familiar sight of those broad shoulders, encased today in a form-fitting coat of olive superfine, had surprised Miss Greyson, who had understood him to be leaving for Bath immediately, until she recollected Lady Wrenthorpe's strong prejudice against traveling on the Lord's day. Mr. Kirkland would not lightly act contrary to the wishes of his kind hostess. Lady Wrenthorpe had more than once remarked that her son's friend was the perfect guest, undemanding, never above being pleased, considerate of his hostess's plans, and more than willing to participate in the family's activities.

Watching now as Juliet acknowledged his greeting with an unsmiling bow before turning to Lord Hampton with ostentatious speed, Miss Greyson wondered wryly if she and the lovely Miss Brewster were the only two females within a ten-mile radius who were not captivated by his practiced charm. She eyed him dispassionately as he stood talking to Bertram and Mr. Ryding. There was no denying that his appearance was impressive. Taller than the average with a fine athletic build, he was lean enough to show to advantage the well-cut coats he favored. There was never anything of the dandy about his attire, however, and those aspirants to fashion notoriety such as young Mr. Penrose would scarcely find anything worth adopting in the moderately stiff points of his snowy shirts that didn't reach high enough on his cheeks to impede his movements, or in the neatly tied but unobtrusive arrangement of his neckcloth, which was held in place by a tie pin of modest dimension. His waistcoats were invariably plain, and there was never more than one fob dangling beneath. A dark green signet ring was the only other jewelry Miss Greyson had ever noticed on his person, though he occasionally wore a quizzing glass suspended on a black ribbon from his neck. One glance sufficed to inform the world that his Hessian boots, undoubtedly made by Hoby, were the finest to be had, and many a gentleman's gentleman had gnashed his teeth in envy at the shine achieved on these by Mr. Kirkland's estimable Harrison. Neither bribery nor plying him with liquor in the hopes that he would divulge the secret whilst in his cups had ever caused one word on that subject to pass between the valet's lips.

Closer acquaintance with Mr. Kirkland had not altered Virginia's first impression that he was too boldly handsome for her taste, but to do him justice, the satirical light in his dark brown eyes could on occasion give way to the warmth of enthusiasm or kindness, and it must be admitted that his mouth was decidedly attractive when he forgot himself and broke into a spontaneous smile or laughed out suddenly. For the rest large white teeth and a hard square jaw saved his countenance from the idealized perfection of a classical sculpture. Miss Greyson approved the short hairstyle for his crisp dark locks instead of the picturesque wind-blown look so assiduously cultivated by the town smarts. As one who had never needed sessions on the backboard to encourage good posture, she also approved his erect military bearing. He looked up suddenly from the gloves of York tan he was drawing through his hands and caught her steady regard, returning it with a quizzing glance that rendered her acutely uncomfortable.

A period of reflection in the privacy of her room overnight had failed to banish the niggling suspicion that this sudden trip to Bath might have something to do with herself, preposterous though the idea seemed on the surface. This is how a criminal must feel, she thought with rueful humor, when he is still at large and unsure whether he is sought by the authorities. Her reverie was interrupted by an exclamation from Bertram.

"*Bath?* But *why?* Oh, I beg your pardon, sir, I just meant . . . this is a surprise. We had no idea you would be leaving us so soon."

Mr. Kirkland laughed and slapped the red-faced boy on the shoulder. "No offense taken, you young cawker. I have some personal business to attend to in Bath but—"

"We in the country cannot hope to compete with the delights offered by a city, Bertram. I am amazed we were able to keep Mr. Kirkland with us this long." Juliet must have been attending to the men's conversation with one ear, for she turned from her flirtatious interchange with Lord Hampton to interject before Mr. Kirkland could finish his explanation.

"My business should take no longer than a sennight or so. May I venture to hope that you will miss me while I'm away?" he asked, directing the full strength of his charming smile at the young girl.

Juliet's eyes opened to their widest. "Goodness, miss you in only a sennight? We shall scarcely have time to realize that you are gone before you'll be back, I daresay." She gave an indifferent laugh and turned once more to Lord Hampton.

"Ouch!" Mr. Kirkland winced theatrically. "Now that is depressing pretension with a vengeance." He made some innocuous comment to Mr. Ryding and Bertram, the one who had remained expressionless at the girl's

160

remark, and the other whose first wave of embarrassed color over his own gaffe had barely subsided before another took its place. They followed his lead and the moment passed.

Miss Greyson relaxed her clenched teeth, uncurled her fingers, and expelled a breath. Really, that child should be soundly smacked for such a breach of good manners. Perfectly able to appreciate the longing to give a setdown to the person who had wounded her pride that lay behind this cut, Miss Greyson nevertheless intended to deliver a pungent homily on the behavior demanded of a lady at the very first opportunity she could contrive to be private with Juliet. Mr. Kirkland had carried the incident off with a light touch, but Miss Greyson had seen the flicker of shock, quickly concealed, break over his face at Juliet's words. She was not surprised, therefore, to find him by her side as the members of the two households began to reenter their respective conveyances for the drive home.

"If it did not seem so totally inadequate to the occasion, I'd say I was being treated with a shade of reserve by Miss Brewster," he drawled in a low conversational tone that was at variance with the penetrating stare he fixed on Virginia. "Yet I am quite at a loss to know how I have offended. Can you enlighten my ignorance, Miss Greyson?"

The governess gave him one of her direct looks, which he returned forthrightly. After a moment she said wonderingly, "You really don't know why she is doing this, do you?"

Before he could reply beyond a slight negative shake of the head, Sir Reginald had come abreast of them to assist Miss Greyson into the carriage and the opportunity was lost. Thinking it over later, Virginia was more relieved than otherwise, for what could she have answered to a repetition of his question? Loyalty to Juliet forbade telling him the truth, and common sense warned that he was not the man to swallow some hoaxing tale, even if she were the woman to invent one.

Olivia's excited chatter and her sister's continued performance as the life of the party more than covered Virginia's silence on the return drive, for which she was grateful. Her own thoughts were in a perfect turmoil. It thoroughly annoyed her to find herself in reluctant sympathy with the detestable Mr. Kirkland, but such was the case. His surprise and chagrin at Juliet's treatment had been genuine. He could not know, therefore, that Juliet had been expecting to receive a declaration from him.

If she pursued that line to its logical conclusion, she was left with the certainty that Mr. Kirkland did not consider that his attentions toward Juliet had been so marked as to raise expectations on her part. Obviously he had indulged in a light flirtation, but Juliet flirted with more than one man. His behavior during the first two weeks of their acquaintance before the play was undertaken had been more intense, but Virginia had noticed signs of cooling on his part long since. Much as she disliked his brash personality, she had not met him almost daily for weeks without learning that he was a gentleman, so there could not have been promises made secretly in those early days on which Juliet might base her present disappointment. Young and inexperienced and, with ample reason, too confident of her powers of attraction, she had deluded herself into believing Mr. Kirkland's initial response to her beauty had ripened into a lasting attachment. This was Virginia's present reading of the situation.

But what if his surprise today had been counterfeit? If he *had* fostered in the breast of an inexperienced young girl expectations that he had no intention of honoring, could this trip to Bath not be seen in the light of an escape from the consequences of his actions? A man in this position would be almost compelled to pretend ignorance of his victim's reaction.

One could build up a consistent case for this explanation of recent events too, but somewhat reluctantly Virginia abandoned her theory. An honorable man would never behave thusly, and she was forced to concede that, whatever his faults, Mr. Kirkland was a man of honor. She had a healthy respect for Sir Malcolm's judgment, and he seemed to hold Mr. Kirkland in considerable esteem. Also a man of the world like Sir Reginald was perfectly complaisant about Mr. Kirkland's presence in his house, so that must be the definitive answer to her speculations.

Which left her with the delicate problem of how best to handle Juliet in the near future to insure that her behavior remained within the bounds of decorum and attracted no critical notice. Somehow, her uncomplicated life among the youngsters at Fairhill seemed to be receding ever further into the past.

CHAPTER NINE

In the woods the pungent aroma of decomposing vegetation mingled with the heady spiciness of the pines. Gently waving meadow grass nearby hinted at a breeze, but here the stillness was unbreached until a solitary rider appeared and set off down the well-marked path. Overhead leafy branches bisected the sky, revealing small, irregular segments of intense blue where they thinned. The air was pleasantly warm with none of the humidity that had oppressed the area lately. There could not have been a greater contrast to the day of his most recent ride through these woods, but except for an appreciative sniff on first encountering the woodland scents, the horseman's frowning preoccupation excluded all outside impressions. The perfect summer day was wasted on him.

Mr. Simon Kirkland had returned from Bath the previous evening with his suspicions confirmed and his attendant curiosity more or less satisfied, thanks to the garrulous Ned Fotheringham. Somewhat to his surprise Randall Briggs had proved reticent on the subject of his old friend, Miss Virginia Spicer. A casual inquiry extracted the unadorned statement that he had not seen Miss Spicer for several months. Gentle probing elicited nothing more than the information that Miss Spicer was believed to be paying an extended visit somewhere in the eastern shires. His friend's closed expression warned him that another topic of conversation was indicated if he wished to be thought no more than passingly curious.

Nor did the introduction of the name Agnes Greyson produce any information. Randall merely looked blank. He had offered to set an inquiry afoot if his visitor wished to contact such a person, at which point Mr. Kirkland had hastily retreated, disclaiming any personal desire to make the acquaintance of one whom he had understood to be employed as a governess in the household of Lady Mallory. He explained carelessly that he had met someone who claimed to be a relative of Miss Greyson, but he certainly did not plan to inconvenience himself or his host in order to pass along a casual greeting from a mere acquaintance to a person unknown to them both. Randall had admitted that his own acquaintance with Lady Mallory was of the slightest, and the subject had been allowed to drop.

It had taken time to arrange an occasion to pump his other contact, Mr. Ned Fotheringham, but his patience had been rewarded. He could not have said why he was so careful to arouse no curiosity on the part of his cronies, why he did not simply lay his own experience before them and openly request any information they might possess about Miss Spicer. That had actually been his original intention.

Perhaps he had had too much time on the journey to consider the situation from every possible angle, but the more he had compared the personality and circumstances of Miss Spicer at present with her behavior at their first meeting and recalled the admiration in which her friends held her, the less he believed she had embarked on this adventure for a lark of some sort. If there was a vital reason for her action, he could not jeopardize what might

166

even be her personal safety until he was in possession of all the facts.

Accordingly, he had claimed unspecified business dealings as the reason for his visit to Bath and had determinedly put up at the York House in George Street over Randall's strenuous objections, ostensibly so as not to inconvenience his friend. This way he could hope to conceal the fact that his business dealings consisted of finding ways to pass his time between meetings with his friends. In the end he was thankful he had taken what had struck him at odd moments as slightly theatrical precautions.

Through Ned, who did not share Randall's scruples about discussing his old friend's fortunes, he had learned the sorry story of Mr. Spicer's death and the subsequent revelations of his indebtedness. Like Randall, Ned believed Miss Spicer to be visiting friends outside of London and confided freely that he hoped for her sake it was to be a long visit. Lady Twistleton, her only relative, was a regular fusty mug, very high in the instep, and famed in the area for her abrasive personality, which was held responsible for a continuous parade of servants in and out of Langdon Hall. Mr. Kirkland had expressed his sympathy for Miss Spicer's bereavement and made delicate inquiries into her financial position.

"Not a groat!" Ned had responded with the relish often displayed by those to whose lot falls the task of conveying disagreeable tidings of a mutual friend. Rumor had it that even her mother's jewelry had gone to meet her father's debts.

Mr. Kirkland now knew the reason for Miss Spicer's employment, though he was as much in the dark as ever concerning her switch in identity. A tentative inquiry at the next meeting with Ned had shed some light on that

167

subject, though the whole story would have to come from Miss Spicer eventually.

"Miss Agnes G-Greyson? Yes, I am slightly acquainted with her, b-but she's M-Mrs. Denton or D-Dobson or some such now. Lives over in B-Bristol, I believe. Husband's a Methodist minister." He confirmed that the former Miss Greyson had indeed been in Lady Mallory's employment for several years and offered to discover her present direction if Simon wished to write or visit her.

Mr. Kirkland had thanked him politely and accepted this information in due course. Not wishing to lead Ned to make any connection between the two women, he had refrained from asking whether Miss Spicer and Miss Greyson were acquainted. He was amused but unsurprised to learn that Ned's information on the real Miss Greyson's present whereabouts had come from Lady Mallory, who seemed not to have journeyed to Scotland after all.

Miss Spicer deserved better than his silent tribute at the memory of her cool nerve under very trying conditions. He had certainly gone out of his way to discomfort her at that dance, and his ungentlemanly hectoring weighed heavily on his conscience.

After some hesitation he decided against paying the former Miss Greyson a visit. In his own mind he was convinced of her connivance in Miss Spicer's masquerade, and it would not do to alert her to his knowledge. She could send Miss Spicer warning by post before he could return to Essex, and heaven knew what the foolish girl might do if she feared discovery was imminent. She had little cause to trust him so far.

The return trip to Thorpe Manor was spent in pondering just what he should do with his new-found knowledge. That his thoughts were engaged with the very same sub-

168

ject on this short ride to Fairhill today was mute testimony to his state of mind. As the back lawns and kitchen garden of Fairhill came into view, he was no nearer to a decision than he had been on leaving Bath two days before.

Somehow, in all his speculation about Miss Spicer before finding out the truth, he had not chanced to consider just what he could do about changing her circumstances. Since piecing the story together, he had thought about little else, but to no good effect. Except to offer her money, which she would refuse even if a way could be found to keep his name out of it, there was no action in his power that could alter matters. With a view toward keeping things on the up and up as far as possible, he had mentioned to Randall in passing that Ned had acquainted him with the essentials of Miss Spicer's change in fortune. After an annoyed expletive directed at his gossiping neighbor that did him no disservice in the eyes of his friend, Randall had admitted that he wished Virginia had taken him into her confidence before departing so hastily without leaving her direction with any of her friends. The more he had considered her situation, the more he had felt he ought to offer for her. As one of her oldest friends, he had long had a great fondness for her and would as lief marry her as anyone else who had so far crossed his path.

With Miss Spicer's current location on the tip of his tongue, Mr. Kirkland had paused to reflect that it was surely none of his affair to reveal her hiding place even to one of her dearest friends if she had not chosen to do so herself. His initial relief at hearing what seemed to be an ideal solution did not survive the subsequent reflection that Miss Spicer might not care to avail herself of such a lukewarm offer even to escape severe financial difficulties. Evidently she had refused several offers in the past and might not be ready to trade her independence for security just yet.

On the other hand she could not enjoy denying her identity and pretending to be a dowdy middle-aged spinster, even if her position in the Brewster household was more or less congenial. Ought he to do something about this aspect of her situation at least—speak to Sir Reginald perhaps, or to Miss Spicer herself and acquaint her with the fact that Randall would like to contact her? Ought he to do nothing, leave the situation as he found it?

But how could he simply ride off in a fortnight as he had planned originally and leave her in this web of her own spinning? Suppose she were to be found out? She might disappear beyond the reach of those who could assist her, as she had once before. This last thought caused him to dismount with more speed than was necessary, earning him a startled look from the slow-witted stable boy who jumped forward to take the reins of his mount.

His footsteps were swift and purposeful as he headed around to the main entrance, but when Penniestone opened the door to him, he found himself asking for Miss Brewster.

"How do you do, sir? May I be so bold as to welcome you back?" Penniestone replied, taking his hat with the perfunctory smile he reserved for close friends of the family. "I regret that Miss Brewster is not at home at present, but Miss Greyson is in the main drawing room playing the pianoforte as she does each day. May I announce you, sir?"

The muted melodies of Bach had already reached his ears. Inclining his head, he allowed himself to be led to the drawing room door, but as the butler's hand touched the handle, he put his own on the dark sleeve and said impulsively, "No, do not disturb her performance by announcing me now, Penniestone. I'll enjoy listening until she finishes this selection."

The butler nodded in agreement and went off to his pantry, where he had been polishing silver, leaving the caller to make a quiet entrance into the room. Once inside Mr. Kirkland remained standing near the door, savoring the sounds of "Jesu, Joy of Man's Desiring" played by one who appreciated its beauty. Her back was to him and she remained unaware of his presence, so absorbed was she in the music she was creating.

When she turned her head slightly, he was permitted a glimpse of the lovely clear line of throat and neck and was astounded that her disguise had not been penetrated long since. She was a capable actress, of course, and was careful to maintain a brisk, rather flat delivery, eliminating girlish mannerisms from her voice. But at times her movements betrayed her youth.

Although he had met Miss Spicer only once in her own character and that briefly, he would be willing to describe her with the utmost confidence as a vibrant, physical individual who delighted in a variety of active pursuits. He had been riding with Miss Brewster in company with Miss Greyson on one occasion and had observed in passing that the older woman appeared to be controlling, very admirably, a simmering impatience. At the time he had attributed this to annoyance at his flirtatious overtures to the lovely Juliet, which he always maliciously intensified in Miss Greyson's presence, having guessed from the start that she looked upon his friendship with her charge with deep suspicion. In the light of recent discoveries he was inclined to believe now that her impatience had stemmed from a desire to be done with the dawdling pace of the ride and to enjoy a good gallop.

A softened expression came into his dark eyes as he

studied the performer still lost in her music. What a monumental task she had set herself and what a demeaning experience! It would be difficult enough for a proud young woman to place herself in an inferior position, but to have to submerge her entire identity, lose herself as it were, must be galling in the extreme. From his short experience with the confident and slightly arrogant Miss Spicer, he would not have thought it possible, but his better acquaintance with Miss Greyson made him regard the seated figure with a new respect.

She repeated a phrase once, twice, and then brought the selection to a close, dropping her hands into her lap.

"Thank you for the private concert. I have enjoyed every moment I was privileged to hear."

The figure at the pianoforte had started at his first words, and she turned toward the speaker, but not, he was quick to note, before her left hand darted out to pick up the spectacles lying on the instrument. She replaced them on her nose and faced him primly.

"You startled me, sir. I did not hear Penniestone announce you."

He grinned at the implied censure in her tones and started forward. "Don't blame Penniestone, Miss . . . Greyson. I would not allow him to interrupt a beautiful rendition of one of my favorite works."

Miss Greyson rose from the bench and met him midway in the room, laying her hand reluctantly in his extended one before gesturing toward a chair, her pique at being unknowingly observed submerged by the necessity to perform the duties of a hostess.

He smiled at her blandly, perfectly aware of her reaction, and waited till she was seated herself before taking the chair she had indicated.

"I regret that Miss Brewster is not at home at the

moment, sir." Her annoyance at his perception found its way into her voice and infuriated her. What *was* there about this man, she asked herself helplessly, that always set her teeth on edge and caused her to behave in an ill-bred manner she was certain to regret later? The very first time she met him, all her defenses had sprung to life, almost as though alerted to some danger, and she had responded by denying his simple request for a dance in a manner that still covered her with shame when she thought about it. Something in his smile challenged something fundamental inside her to resist him—she didn't understand it, but she still responded to it, because here she sat, unrelaxed and determined not to speak again until he asked a direct question.

"It seems a great deal longer than eight days that I have been away," he offered, still with that challenging smile.

Miss Greyson directed a look of polite inquiry at him before letting her gaze come to rest on the bowl of yellow roses on the Pembroke table between them. She heard his quiet laugh but kept her eyes on the flowers.

"I daren't ask you if you missed me, lest I lay myself open to a repetition of the treatment I suffered at Miss Brewster's hands when last we met."

This did bring her troubled gaze around to his face, and she answered with quick earnestness, "She was abominably rude to you, sir, but she is very young, you know, and had, or thought she had, good cause." Too late she realized where her automatic defense of her young friend was leading and her voice trailed off. "May I offer you some refreshment, sir?" she asked with an assumption of brightness, heading for the bell that would summon Penniestone.

Mr. Kirkland caught her wrist as she passed him. "I don't want anything, thank you. Won't you tell me what

173

I did to offend Miss Brewster?" He had turned her toward him with his other hand on her arm between elbow and shoulder, and after a second or two when she seemed on the brink of struggling to release herself, she met his serious look. For a moment green eyes stared frankly into brown and made the surprising discovery that they trusted the owner of those eyes despite the basic antagonism that existed between them.

"Do you recall," she began slowly, "the last rehearsal before the actual production?" Her eyes questioned him, and he frowned slightly in concentration.

"Of course, but I don't recall anything of an unusual nature, certainly not an upset that would cause Miss Brewster to nurse a grievance."

"No, no, it was nothing like that. You may remember that I was not present at that rehearsal, but when Juliet came home I noticed that she had a . . . well, a very self-satisfied air about her that I could not account for until later when she was going over her wardrobe and said . . . or perhaps *implied* is a better choice . . . implied that she expected to . . ."

He waited for an instant, then prompted, "Yes? Expected what?"

"To hear something of a particular nature from *you* at the dance after the performance."

"He gazed at her blankly. "Hear what, for pity's sake?"

She remained silent, looking steadily back at his impatient face.

"Of *what* particular nature?" Sudden comprehension flashed across his countenance, followed instantly by rejection. "Good Lord! You don't . . . you *can't* mean she expected a marriage proposal?" As she still watched him in silence, he dropped her arm, which she had forgotten he still held, and raked his fingers through his hair. He

174

made an impatient gesture with his other hand. "This is preposterous! How could she possibly have been in the expectation of hearing an offer of marriage following immediately on the heels of a . . . a draining experience like that play?"

Miss Greyson took pity on his perplexity. "Girls of seventeen do not necessarily see things in the same light as men of thirty," she stated sagely.

"But presumably girls of seventeen have the same mental equipment to reason with as men of thirty," he objected drily, "and two ears to hear with."

"Mr. Kirkland, *did* you tell Juliet at that last rehearsal that you had something to tell her—to say to her—after the performance of the play?"

Again the hand raked through the hair. "I don't know. I suppose I may have done. I intended to tell you all that I was going to Bath for a time; in fact, I did tell *you* at the dance."

The sympathy she felt for his consternation dried up instantly as she recalled the manner of his announcement to herself, and her expression stiffened. He had the grace to look discomfited for a second and took a hasty step forward, but something in her face stopped him in his tracks. "I informed Miss Brewster I was leaving for Bath also, in a perfectly ordinary conversation," he added, trying to switch her thoughts back to Juliet.

She nodded, her expression under control again. "I saw you. You told her during a waltz and she missed her step. When next you invited her to dance, she refused you even though it meant dancing a third time with Lord Hampton."

His eyebrows, which had shot up at the beginning of this detached recapitulation, contracted and his mouth tightened for a moment before he sighed in defeat.

"I . . . see. Perhaps you are correct. At least, I cannot think of any other explanation for her sudden coldness, but it still seems incredible." He sought her eyes and saw not accusation but understanding there. After a moment he said heavily, "You must know that I would not have hurt the child or wounded her pride for the world, but I must hold myself to blame nonetheless because I did seek her out in the beginning, and there's no denying I did flirt with her. She seemed older than her years at first and she's an accomplished flirt, of course, but there is no excuse for my conduct." There was no doubting his sincerity, but surprisingly, Miss Greyson laughed out spontaneously.

"There is no need to be so abject. No slightest damage has been done to Juliet's heart, I assure you; in fact, her heart should be all the better for having had her pride slightly bruised. It may make her kinder to the scores of suitors she is bound to have before she marries."

"I am relieved to hear it naturally," Mr. Kirkland replied, sounding rather more irritated than relieved at the brisk cheerfulness exhibited by his comforter. "You do not believe then that her heart is at all involved?"

Miss Greyson hid a smile at this surprising manifestation of a tender male sensibility and produced more of her offensive cheerfulness. "Oh, no. You were nothing but a romantic fancy; the child knows nothing of love yet."

"And you, what do you know of love, Miss . . . Greyson?" The mockery was back in his eyes, but Virginia was not to be caught so easily. Her countenance remained unclouded.

"I personally, do you mean? Nothing at all, but I have seen Lady Mallory's two daughters through various affairs of the heart, so I feel fairly confident of my ability to assess Juliet's state of mind."

"Then perhaps you can tell me how long I am to remain in purdah?"

Miss Greyson had returned to her chair during the last of the exchange. For the first time she looked a bit uncomfortable. "Well, I fear you may find Juliet a . . . a trifle *cool* until she is convinced no one could possibly think she ever expected or wished to be singled out for attention on your part."

"Don't bother trying to wrap it up in clean linen to spare my feelings. I gather I am to be decisively snubbed on every occasion that offers, even if her majesty has to contrive the occasions herself in a manner public enough to draw just the sort of attention to us that she should most wish to avoid."

"I . . . I am afraid this could indeed be the case for a time."

"Ah, the female mind is a wondrous thing!" He abandoned his sardonic manner and asked seriously, "For her sake should I play least in sight for a time, do you think, or would that be equally obvious—as well as depriving young madam of her opportunity for revenge?"

"My father always said it was best to get over difficult ground as quickly as possible," Miss Greyson replied with a whimsical twist to her lips. "So I would advise you to continue your normal schedule. Naturally I will do my utmost to prevent Juliet from going her length, but she can be willful at times, and the fact that she has confided nothing of her feelings in this matter to me makes me feel the blow to her pride was severe indeed."

"She has said nothing of this to you?" His keen eyes detected a very faint rise of color under whatever stuff she used on her face to disguise her complexion.

"Well . . . no. She is growing up, you know, and though we go along nicely together in the ordinary way, she has known me for less than a year. I cannot hope to be accorded the same confidence a mother might receive."

"Or that she might accord to a female friend near her own age?"

"That is true also. It's unlikely she would confide problems of a romantic nature to a spinster long past her own youth."

"And do you consider yourself a spinster long past your youth, Miss . . . Greyson?"

Behind the spectacles green eyes flickered, wrenching away from the hypnotic power of that dark, enigmatic stare, and for a moment her tongue clove to the roof of her mouth, unable to assist in forming the matter-of-fact reply the question demanded.

"Aggie, Staro and Emily are going to stay for lunch. Oh, I beg your pardon, I did not realize you had a visitor." Juliet entered the drawing room in her usual impetuous manner, followed by two of the Penrose youngsters.

While greetings were exchanged, Miss Greyson eyed her young companion consideringly. Juliet had shaken hands with Mr. Kirkland and echoed the others' welcome in an offhand manner that put an end to her duenna's hopes that a week of flattering attentions from about every young buck in the county who could find an excuse to call at Fairhill might have softened her attitude toward her former favorite.

"It's good to be back among friends," Mr. Kirkland replied now to Miss Penrose's softly murmured welcome.

"No doubt you will find it sadly flat in Essex after enjoying the more sophisticated company to be found in Bath," Juliet remarked.

Mr. Kirkland turned the full force of his brilliant smile in her direction. "Bath, like London, is always thin of company in the summer and in any case cannot compete with the attractions to be found in Essex at the moment."

"Ah, yes! I understand that Lady Eugenia is to remain at the Manor for another few weeks." Juliet deliberately misunderstood the implied compliment and immediately turned away from him to address a question to Mr. Penrose.

Miss Greyson sighed soundlessly. The foolish child obviously intended war to the teeth. As had happened on other occasions, it thus became her task to slide into the breach in hopes of obscuring whatever impression the girl was making on their young guests. "Juliet, my dear, did you remember to advise Penniestone that we shall have guests for lunch?" she asked, and when the girl jumped up to remedy the oversight, she invited Mr. Kirkland with a smile, "You will remain and lunch with us, too, will you not, sir?"

To her relief, since she did not look forward to refereeing a quarrel at table, that gentleman rose at her words and said easily, "I thank you, ma'am, but I am expected at the Manor for lunch today. I shall hope to give myself the pleasure of accepting just such an invitation one day soon." He made his smiling adieux and bowed himself out of the room in the wake of the butler, who had appeared in response to Juliet's pull on the bell rope.

The ride back to the Manor was spent in a similar mood of frowning concentration to the one that had enveloped him an hour before on his arrival, with the difference that now he had two problems to bedevil him instead of one. He had all but forgotten the snub Juliet had administered on the day before his departure for Bath, until he had mentioned it himself quite by chance in his tentative casting around for an approach to Miss Spicer. He hadn't found one, but had complicated his life still further with the subsequent discovery of the delicate situation existing between himself and Juliet. He experienced a sensation of unreality, disbelief even, as it struck him forcibly that his demeanor toward these two ladies in the immediate future was almost bound to be more false than all the playacting he had indulged in on the stage recently. For the time being he must pretend to be unaware of Juliet's active hostility while trying to keep her from creating gossip, and in his relations with Miss Spicer he must pretend to be unaware of her real identity, at least until he could be sure such a revelation would not hurt her. The smooth path of his life seemed to be developing some mighty rough stretches all of a sudden, and he did not enjoy the feeling that matters were in danger of slipping out of his control.

Those assembled around the luncheon table at the Manor that afternoon found the generally convivial houseguest a bit less communicative than was his habit. In fact, for the remainder of that day more than one individual discovered the necessity of repeating a question or observation addressed to Mr. Kirkland in order to gain that gentleman's attention.

CHAPTER TEN

The sound of voices raised in question startled the figure in the cane-backed chair from a deep reverie.

"Out here on the terrace!" called Miss Greyson, closing the book in her lap over her index finger. "I've been sitting here enjoying the mid-afternoon sunshine," she explained, summoning up a smile for the Brewster girls when they appeared seconds later at the long doors of the family parlor. Both glowing brunettes were attired in summery shades of blue today, and they made a charming picture framed in the doorway for a brief moment before joining their preceptress on the stone-paved terrace.

"Did you have an agreeable luncheon with Emily and Alice?"

The sisters chorused an enthusiastic assent that Miss Greyson found mildly surprising, at least on the part of Juliet, who generally did not trouble to conceal from her companion her views on the lack of entertainment to be found in a visit with the quiet Penrose girls. She was not left in the dark as to the reason for this unusual enthusiasm, for Juliet plunged at once into a description of plans for a picnic party on the grounds of a girls' seminary that had been famous for its gardens back in the past century.

At that time the property had belonged to a gentleman

whose passion for garden making on a grand scale had, over a period of thirty years, reduced a considerable fortune to a mere competence. His only child having predeceased him, he had willed his estate to a distant relative, but since the remaining money was tied up in a scheme to perpetuate the gardens, the disgruntled heir had promptly disposed of the burden by donating the property to the trustees of the seminary. The gardens were still acclaimed as a highlight of any tour of stately homes in the district. Juliet explained that Mr. Penrose had a close friend on the board of trustees and was thus able to secure permission for the proposed outing later in the week.

When the governess inquired as to the size of the party, she realized that some at least of Juliet's satisfaction was due to the inclusion of all the young people from the Manor, as well as those in the Brewster and Penrose households. Being acquainted at firsthand with the resourcefulness of her charge, she had not the slightest doubt that Juliet would contrive to spend some time wandering about the extensive gardens with Lord Hampton, away from her companion's watchful eye. But since Lord and Lady Teasdale would be present to chaperon the party, she could not very well make any demur, especially as Mrs. Penrose had seen fit to allow Emily and Alice to join the party. She noted the rather challenging glint in Juliet's eye but merely remarked mildly that she would have enjoyed a tour of the famous gardens herself and was persuaded everyone would have a marvelous time if the pleasant weather held.

"But you are to go with us too, Miss Greyson," said Olivia eagerly. "It was quite understood that you were to come so that Mellie and I might go too."

"What can you mean, Livvy?" Juliet's voice was sharp. "The plans did not include children, and there is no need

182

to drag Aggie with us on an eight-mile ride when Bella and Lord Teasdale are coming. Mrs. Penrose said that was perfectly adequate chaperonage."

"Yes, I know that was the original plan," Olivia explained earnestly, "but later, when Mr. Kirkland called and Mrs. Penrose was telling him about the excursion, he asked if Mellie and I might go too if Miss Greyson came to look after us." She stuck out her lower lip at the sight of her sister's darkening expression and insisted, "I did not beg to go, Juliet; I said nothing at all. The suggestion was Mr. Kirkland's. He thought Mellie and I would enjoy seeing the gardens too, and we *would*. I think Mr. Kirkland is the kindest man I have ever met—and the handsomest, too," she added with a touch of defiance, ready to defend her hero in the teeth of any disagreement with this sweeping pronouncement. "Don't you agree, Miss Greyson?"

Thus directly appealed to, Miss Greyson could only concur that it had indeed been kind of Mr. Kirkland to think of including the younger girls. She hoped neither Juliet nor Olivia would notice the lack of conviction in her tones. The second part of Olivia's statement she ignored completely, being totally unable to praise Mr. Kirkland's person while some rather nasty thoughts as to his motives for this maneuver disturbed her peace of mind.

Her glance swiveled to Juliet biting her lip in wordless annoyance at this development. No more than her companion did the young beauty attribute Mr. Kirkland's action to disinterested chivalry. Apparently she found it equally impossible to articulate her true reaction. Juliet and she, Miss Greyson mused ruefully, shared a recently acquired but strong disinclination to mention the popular guest at the Manor, though he occupied an uncomfortably significant portion of their thoughts for different reasons.

The young girl had been a trifle wary in her relations with her companion just lately, if that was not too strong a description. Certainly she was less confiding of her feelings and reactions to passing events than formerly, though on the surface nothing seemed changed. This lack of openness dated from her disappointment at the dance following the play performance, but the wariness had crept into her manner only during the last few days as a direct result of the confrontation between the companions after Mr. Kirkland's morning call on his return from Bath. Miss Greyson had taken the girl to task for her rudeness to a guest, and though she had tried to soften her reprimand by trying to communicate in a tactfully oblique fashion her understanding of and sympathy for the motivation behind such behavior, she had realized too late that this had been a mistake. Juliet's sense of humiliation had evidently been even greater than her companion had first thought. She could not bear the idea that anyone was aware of her chagrin, no matter how sympathetic.

She was bound and determined to correct such an impression. Though Miss Greyson had hastened to undo her tactical error by accepting Juliet's heated denial of any feeling of ill usage in her dealings with Mr. Kirkland, even going so far as to proffer an apology for having ever thought so in the first place, she had been afraid this hasty retreat would not suffice to put her back on the old, comfortable footing with Juliet. Subsequent events had borne out her fears. The young girl's ill-concealed displeasure at her duenna's inclusion in the picnic party was not due to fear that the presence of authority would curtail her own verbal sniping at Mr. Kirkland; she had ceased such tactics after the reprimand, though the formal politeness that characterized her demeanor on the few succeeding meetings between the erstwhile friends had been no less obvious and unnatural.

No, Juliet's present discontent probably stemmed from a desire to conceal from her too-perceptive chaperon any behavior on her part that might be considered to encourage Lord Hampton's current pursuit of her. Further observation had not altered Miss Greyson's instinctive impression that the earl was not a man to be trusted with a lovely and innocent girl. However, this was another matter, and she was in a mood to be grateful for small blessings; there was no denying it was a relief to be spared the worry over how far the child's pique would carry her in overt retaliation to Mr. Kirkland.

And that was the only thing she had to be grateful for at present, she thought, unable to keep a niggling anxiety at bay as the girls proceeded to acquaint her with all the details of the proposed expedition to Maniston Seminary. She kept an attentive look on her face, but her thoughts returned to the subject that had prevented her from reading the book in her lap earlier.

Her own position was becoming of increasing concern. Ever since Mr. Kirkland had announced his trip to Bath and offered to be the purveyor of messages to Lady Mallory, she had been trying with diminished success to convince herself that her secret was still undiscovered. At first it had been just a flash, a premonition that he knew all about her that had taken possession of her mind while she stared into his compelling dark eyes. The feeling subsided once she put some distance between herself and her tormentor. During the time he was away, she had been able to go about her daily tasks with an assumed composure that became more natural as the image of Mr. Kirkland faded. Unfortunately, her brittle facade of calm was shattered at the first sight of his disturbingly intent face on his return, and none of her efforts to retrieve it had been at all successful thereafter.

No one had ever accused her of being fanciful, but just lately, when in company with Mr. Kirkland, she had had the strangest sensation that he was willing her to confess her deception—such was the effect those eyes had on her. It was nonsensical, of course. She was allowing a natural lowness of spirits due to the deterioration of her relations with Juliet to make her abnormally sensitive. Mr. Kirkland was fond of Mellie and Olivia; it was one of the things she liked about him—one of the very *few* things, she reminded herself. Certainly she had noted with approval the indulgence that characterized his manner toward the youngsters. He always spared time for them, so why could she not simply accept that he had suggested she go along with the party solely for the purpose of enabling the girls to participate in the coming treat? She had no tangible cause to believe otherwise, but the fact remained that she could not look forward to this picnic without a feeling of trepidation.

When the day for the proposed outing arrived, no one would have guessed the constant effort required to maintain her customary air of impersonal pleasantness; she had her fears well in hand. The numbers had increased in the intervening days to include Bertram and his tutor, and since the weather continued sunny and seasonably warm, it was a relaxed and merry group of young people who assembled on the south lawn eager to ride the eight miles to Maniston. Miss Greyson had experienced a slight qualm at the inclusion of Olivia, who was an indifferent rider, but it turned out to be an easy ride, and thanks to a soft rain during the early hours of the morning, the dust that usually accompanied a rider at this season was absent.

The various parties had decided to meet on the grounds

of the seminary, and the Penroses had made themselves responsible for providing the picnic feast, so the Fairhill contingent had nothing to do but get itself to the spot, using whatever means appealed. After an easy paced and mostly shady trip over reasonable terrain and good roads, they arrived at their destination almost as fresh as if they had traveled in the comfort of a carriage.

They entered Maniston Seminary through the Roman arch of a charming, three-storied Jacobean gatehouse of pink brick and stone, divided exactly in two by the entrance road. The existing house was of a later date and had been set at some distance along the avenue, Mr. Ryding explained to Miss Greyson. The avenue, lined with handsome cypress trees, was part of the landscaping plan and had been designed to curve around the site of the original structure, which had predated the gatehouse. He said no more on the subject, so five minutes later those who were visiting the estate for the first time came around a deep bend in the approach road to gaze unprepared at the picturesque ruins of an earlier building. It appeared to be a chapel or hall with one long wall nearly intact and parts of the adjacent walls still standing. One lovely Gothic window remained untouched by time, except that it was bereft of its glass, its pointed arch standing out visually against a background of old trees.

"I understand this structure dates from the late thirteenth century," Mr. Ryding offered, as the onlookers murmured their appreciation of the romantic setting.

"At least the previous owner's fortune would not have been further depleted as others were by the cost of building fake Gothic ruins," remarked Miss Greyson.

Mr. Ryding chuckled. "True, ma'am, but he found numerous other ways to dissipate it. There are some fantastic structures on the property that he did add solely to enhance his garden walks, including a Chinese bridge over a minuscule stream and a Greek temple by the lake."

Before they could move on to the meeting place, Olivia had to be firmly dissuaded from dismounting immediately to explore the inviting ivy-covered ruins, consoled by a promise that she and Mellie might return to the site after the picnic. The parties came together near a small apple orchard. The Penrose Hall group had already dismounted, and Emily and Alice were busy directing the servants in setting out tables in the shade of the trees. Since the location was several hundred feet from the stables, the preparations demanded a good deal of walking back and forth, and the young men offered their services in transporting food from the carriages once the horses were turned over to the grooms.

Thanks to willing hands and feet, the feast was nearly ready by the time carriage wheels announced the arrival of the party from Thorpe Manor. Miss Greyson had turned over the special marinated mushrooms she had prepared as well as Mrs. Murchison's popular dilled cheese bread to swell the variety of tempting offerings. When Lady Teasdale arrived bearing baskets of tarts and maids of honor, the young people of each group decided as one to fall upon the food without further delay.

Mrs. Penrose, herself past the age to enjoy sitting about on the ground, had had a number of chairs included for dining in comparative comfort, but except for Miss Greyson who thought her status as chaperon demanded it and Sir Malcolm, whose kindness led him to declare himself averse to sharing his food with the ants, the picnickers ignored the chairs and ranged themselves on rugs under the spreading trees while they gorged on slices of home-cured ham, a variety of cheeses, precooked chicken parts, and tasty fruits and vegetables.

On seeing Miss Greyson seating herself on a chair held out by Sir Malcolm, Mr. Kirkland had made a motion as if to join her at the table, but at that moment Lady Eugenia had laughingly patted the spot next to her in obvious invitation, and Sir Malcolm had dropped into the chair beside Miss Greyson. Mr. Kirkland checked his movement smoothly and joined Lady Eugenia and Lady Teasdale with a smile.

Juliet welcomed Lord Hampton, who had steered a direct course to her side, and carefully avoided her chaperon's eye. The men had dismissed the servants to their own meal, promising to wait upon the ladies in their stead, and the alfresco meal proceeded amidst much hilarity as the gentlemen leapt up continuously to satisfy the slightest wish expressed by a member of the fair sex.

From her vantage point at one of the tables Miss Greyson was easily able to monitor the entire scene while keeping one ear tuned to Sir Malcolm's gentle flow of commonplaces. She noted with amusement that Bertram and Alistair Penrose, animated no doubt by a sense of mischief, were pressing additional helpings of various foodstuffs on the younger ladies in a manner so exquisitely polite as must have aroused suspicion, had not the general hubbub and the little snatches of individual conversations kept the girls too engrossed to detect the teasing attentions. Mr. Kirkland caught her eye suddenly, and a look of shared enjoyment passed between them just as Miss Alice Penrose exclaimed, "Heavens, Bertram! No more, please! I shan't be able to walk round the gardens at all if I eat another bite."

The rest of the ladies echoed these sentiments just in time to save Olivia and Amelia from bursting with impatience to be off exploring. Those who had visited Maniston before had described some of the sights to be seen on the various walks, and with such a vast choice of attractions within the grounds it was not to be expected that everyone should wish to keep together like a flock of sheep.

Miss Greyson was aware that the two children were her special responsibility today. She had taken pains to place herself where she could not watch Juliet, hoping the girl would relax and moderate her rather obvious efforts to captivate Lord Hampton. But after an hour or so of eavesdropping she could only trust the girl's behavior would not seem so transparent to others less familiar with all the nuances of her personality. If only they could go back to those untroubled days before the arrival of Mr. Kirkland had brought Juliet's simmering coquetry to the boil! She had not gone to the lengths of ignoring the rest of the company, thanks to basic good manners, but a man of Lord Hampton's experience would be in no doubt that he was being singled out for the young lady's favors.

Since there was nothing to be done about the situation at present, Miss Greyson agreed with Olivia and Mellie that the first aspect of the gardens to be examined should be the Gothic ruin. Leaving the servants to clear away the remnants of the picnic, the large party split up into groups that merged, divided, and reformed over the next two hours as everyone explored the delights and surprises offered by the well-planned romantic gardens. There were dozens of seats tucked away in corners for quiet contemplation of a single aspect of the landscaping, so there was no danger of anyone's becoming exhausted while pursuing beauty. Olivia and Bertram were determined to miss no attraction the gardens offered no matter how obscure the location, and Amelia allowed herself to be dragged along in their energetic wake. From time to time they returned with reports of some unexpected delight to tempt Miss Greyson, who found herself hustled along at a faster pace than she would have chosen under other circumstances. Still, the children's enthusiasm was contagious, and she could always stop and sit in a particularly lovely spot while they dashed off in yet another direction.

The sun was still high in the sky, and Miss Greyson was grateful for the parasol she carried when not amongst the trees. She was alone for the moment, admiring a bed of asters and trying to shield her face from the burning rays, when a faint silver sound of water enticed her between some hedges. The next moment a soft exclamation of pleasure blended with the water's gurgle as she entered a cool area shaded by one enormous oak tree. She sank onto a wooden seat built around the trunk of the tree and closed her parasol thankfully as she leaned back and gazed with pleasure at a dolphin fountain spilling a tiny stream of water into a small pool. Blue hydrangeas bloomed at the edge of the pool and added the last perfect touch to an idyllic setting. In this spot none of her problems seemed to have any importance. She could have stayed there unmoving for hours.

Mr. Kirkland found her there five minutes later.

When Mrs. Penrose had first disclosed the plan for today's outing to him, he had suggested including the two youngest girls in response to an instantaneous conviction that Miss Spicer, with her rare appreciation of beauty, would enjoy touring the renowned gardens for their own sake almost more than any of the ladies already invited. She had been having rather a thin time of it lately and deserved a treat. Even with the responsibility of Olivia and Mellie he was persuaded she would derive much pleasure from the excursion.

As he wandered in the direction where he had last caught a glimpse of Miss Greyson's dark blue dress, Mr. Kirkland was experiencing a judicious satisfaction with the success of his plan. It was turning out to be a most pleasurable excursion; certainly nature had cooperated wholeheartedly with a perfect day, and the picnic feast itself could not have been bettered. Miss Spicer had appeared more relaxed than he had seen her lately, and if the beauteous Miss Brewster was still treating him with a touch of reserve, at least it was not so obvious as to draw unwelcome comment. If the equally beautiful and infinitely more sophisticated Lady Eugenia was demonstrating an unobtrusive but unmistakable preference for his own company, at least it redressed the balance. And since she was well up to snuff and knew the rules of the game, there was no possibility of future misunderstanding in that quarter.

For a moment a brooding expression settled over his countenance as he considered his friend. Mal had said nothing to the point, but he had an uneasy hunch that his quiet, reserved host had been knocked in a heap by a pair of beautiful but calculating blue eyes. If rumor spoke truly, both Hampton and his sister needed to marry money, and he knew himself to be a far richer matrimonial prize than poor Mal. It had taken a bit of adroitness to slip away from the lady a few moments ago, but he had used the children as an excuse when Malcolm and young Penrose had joined them in the grape arbor. Even if he did not discover Miss Spicer's whereabouts, the solitude was welcome at present.

The sound of running water somewhere close by chased personal thoughts out of his head. He slowed his pace and glanced around for the source, coming into the clearing as Miss Greyson had earlier. He saw her before she was aware of his presence, and it struck him of a sudden that she was a lonely figure, though at the moment she looked happy enough in all conscience, sitting relaxed with her back against the tree and her hands resting motionless in her lap. Though those abominable spectacles concealed her eyes at any distance, he knew when she perceived him by the involuntary straightening of her back and her mouth. A nicely curved mouth, he observed coming closer, despite the stuff she used to blur its outline and drain its color. The heat of the day had taken its toll on the disguise, however, and the rich natural color of her lips was rather enticing as they widened into a resolute smile when she rose, frustrating his intention of joining her on the bench.

"Isn't this the loveliest, most peaceful spot imaginable?" she remarked softly, indicating their surroundings with a wave of one white hand. "I'd be quite content to remain here for hours, but I'm afraid it's time I caught up with Olivia and Mellie again."

"Stay a bit longer," he urged. "The girls cannot come to any harm here, surely."

Her laugh didn't ring quite true, but she answered easily, "You do not know Olivia if you can say that, sir. Bertram told her there is a tower on the grounds that is over one hundred feet high, and she is determined to climb to the top. She will try to bully Mellie into climbing with her if I am any judge."

He returned a light answer, suiting his pace to hers as she reentered the path, knowing he had only himself to blame for her reluctance to spend any time in his company. He was strongly regretting the retaliative impulse that had led him to tease her so unmercifully in the past, but though he longed to reassure her that she had nothing to fear from him, somehow the words refused to form themselves into sentences. He feared she would avoid him totally or, worse yet, run away again.

So they compared notes on their impressions of the gardens. It seemed Mr. Kirkland's grandfather had been acquainted with Henry Hoare, who had created a famous romantic-classical garden at Stourhead in Wiltshire. From what his father had told him of a boyhood visit there, he would deem Maniston to be contemporary and similar, though on a somewhat reduced scale. Miss Greyson confessed that she had seen nothing to compare with Maniston in the area around Bath, but when Mr. Kirkland tried to turn the conversation to her life in Bath, she brought it back to the present with a determination that would have been quelling had he not sensed the fear that lay beneath her formal manner. Fortunately, at that moment the trees thinned, the path widened, and they came in sight of the tower Bertram had described. The scene that met their disbelieving eyes dispelled any constraint along with any consideration of personalities.

The tower was not as tall as previously reported but stood well over fifty feet high. It was of red brick and was circular in form with a crude narrow stairway winding up the outside with no other support than the tower wall itself. Virginia noticed all this without really noticing at the time; her eyes were glued to two figures, one only a few feet from the top of the tower and the other just appearing in view from the back of the structure about two thirds of the way up.

"Oh, my God!" she breathed, and opened her lips to call out to them. Instantly a hand covered her mouth and another gripped her shoulder.

"Don't make a sound!" warned Mr. Kirkland in a hoarse whisper. "You could startle them into falling." The horrified watchers stood rigid, side by side in the blazing sunshine, but Virginia suddenly felt a chill creeping over her body. She shivered, and the man at her side enfolded her more securely within that strong, comforting arm, though his eyes never left the two figures so far above them.

"How in the merry hell did they ever get up there?" Mr. Kirkland muttered in a fierce undertone that tickled Miss Greyson's ear. "The fence that surrounds the tower must be eight feet high and it's clearly posted."

Virginia had to try twice before she could produce a sound. "It was Olivia—she's such a willful child. Oh, whatever possessed her to attempt such a foolhardy stunt!" She gasped and closed her eyes tightly as the girl at the top missed her footing and stumbled to her knees just below the opening to the roof of the tower.

"You can look, she's made it." Mr. Kirkland removed the icy hand clutching his sleeve and took it into a warm clasp. "Coming down will be more difficult and dangerous. As soon as Mellie gets to the top I am going up after them. Wait right here."

Two pairs of eyes shifted as one to the younger girl. After a charged instant Virginia clutched the hand holding hers so convulsively her nails dug into his thumb. "She must have frozen; she hasn't moved an inch since we arrived!" The panic in her voice earned a sharp reprimand from her companion.

"That won't help, girl. Get a hold of yourself. I'll bring them both down safely." He freed his hand and gauged the height of the wooden fence with narrowed eyes. Before Virginia could move a muscle, he had leaped on it in one spring and scrambled over the top.

"Simon, be careful!" The words were wrenched out of her and it's doubtful she was aware of uttering them. The sound of Olivia's voice calling to Amelia drew her glance from the running man disappearing around the side of the tower. She could hear the intrepid Olivia urging her friend to finish the climb, promising her a glorious view, taunting her with being a baby; but Mellie's replies—if she made any—were too soft to reach the ears of the anxious governess.

The younger girl was crouched in a kneeling position, one hand on the narrow railing that connected the widely spaced balusters and one hand on the wall itself. Her head was turned toward the wall, and she appeared frozen indeed. Olivia's urgings became a trifle strident as the very real danger for both girls finally began to impress itself on the elder. The stairs were barely wide enough for one. It would be perilous for someone to try to edge by another person, especially since the railing was broken in several places. Even had the railing been intact, the distance between the balusters was great enough to allow a full-grown horse to slip through, let alone a slimly built child. At that point it was a sheer drop of nearly fifty feet.

Miss Greyson called in clear authoritative accents, "Olivia, be silent and stay right where you are. Mr. Kirkland is coming up to help Mellie down first. You are to stay put until he comes back for you, do you understand?" She waited until the surprised and subdued girl signified agreement before speaking in soothing tones to the paralyzed youngster crouching against the wall.

"I know you are frightened, Mellie, but you are perfectly safe. Mr. Kirkland will be there in just a moment now, and all you have to do is obey him. You don't have to look down at all if it frightens you, just do exactly as he tells you. Will you do that, my dear?"

She could not be sure that her words penetrated the fog of terror that enveloped the child. There was no audible reaction, and she was about to try again when Mr. Kirkland came around the side of the tower to stop short a couple of steps from the sprawled figure. He made no attempt to touch the child initially. That he was talking

196

softly to her was evident to the woman below, but strain as she might to hear, no sounds reached her. She gripped her hands together tightly, pressing her knuckles against her mouth, watching for some sign of movement in the child. The stairs were so narrow and winding that carrying her down was not an attractive option except as a last resort.

Glancing up, her eyes found Olivia leaning over the edge of the wall around the roof of the tower as she peered silently at the tableau beneath her. It seemed a nerve-stretching eternity before the silent spectators saw the small hand that grasped the rail unclench slowly and drop off the rail. Virginia released a painful breath as Mellie turned her head the tiniest bit toward Mr. Kirkland, who smiled encouragingly at her. There appeared to be more conversation and directions before he extended his hand and Mellie, after a palpitating pause, put hers in it. She was drawn carefully to her feet, still facing and clutching the wall; it was another minute or two before either hand-linked figure made any further movement. The woman on the ground bit her knuckles and concentrated on willing the two to begin the descent.

In due course they did this. The man went first with his left hand on the railing, his right holding the left hand of the young girl. Mellie continued to face the wall when not watching her feet, which she placed on each step as her rescuer's foot left it. Her right hand never left the wall during the long, awkward descent. When they disappeared from view, Virginia repeated her warning to Olivia to remain where she was before she headed around the base of the tower to where the stairs began.

A broken section of the fence showed clearly how the children had gained access to the structure. Virginia climbed through herself and was waiting at the foot of the

197

tower when Mr. Kirkland led Amelia down the last steps. Her heart went out to the trembling white-faced child. When she opened her arms, Mellie rushed into their safety and burst into tears. The woman was still petting the distraught girl and murmuring soothing platitudes when Mr. Kirkland reappeared with a shamefaced but slightly defiant Olivia five minutes later.

Obviously her rescuer had already delivered himself of a homily on the wanton foolishness of the escapade, for which Miss Greyson could only be grateful. She was too drained of strength to attempt anything of the sort herself and was becoming rather alarmed at Mellie's continued weeping. The child was in danger of making herself sick.

"There, there, Mellie—here is Olivia. You are both safe. It's all over now. Stop crying, my child." She succeeded in raising Mellie's chin from her shoulder so she might see her friend, but the sobs had scarcely abated at all, and she cast a glance of worried appeal at Mr. Kirkland, who was wiping his streaming forehead with a handkerchief. It was Olivia who came to the rescue, however.

"Don't be such a baby, Mellie!" she exclaimed bracingly. "You'd have made it if you had listened to me. I told you not to look down. You missed the most beautiful view all over the gardens, and I saw a grotto over there which I intend to visit, but I won't take you if you don't stop blubbering."

This somewhat heartless diatribe achieved what Miss Greyson's gentle solicitude could not. Mellie's sobs lessened and stopped. She mopped her woebegone face with Miss Greyson's handkerchief and bent eagerly to her friend. "A real grotto made of shells? Do let us hurry, Livvy! That is, if you have no objection, ma'am?"

"And off they sail on a new adventure, blithely leaving two wrecks on the shoals," Mr. Kirkland commented dryly as he took Miss Greyson's elbow and assisted her back through the hole in the fence after the girls had hurried away. "If I'd dared take the time to search for that, I'd have spared my coat a tear." He paused to brush some dirt from the shoulder of his blue coat and flipped a finger at a small rent in the sleeve.

"Sir," Miss Greyson said earnestly, "I have not thanked you yet for coming to the girls' rescue in such a splendid manner. I am truly grateful and so will be their parents. They are in my care today, and I must hold myself grossly negligent of their well-being."

"Nonsense," he cut in ruthlessly when she would have continued in this vein, "you could never have known there would be an actual hazard in a pleasure garden. The less said about this little episode the better." Once again he was the well-dressed, imperturbable man of town, though his skin tones were still heightened after such exertion in the broiling sun. "Let us head for a shadier walk. You know," he remarked conversationally, "the still unknown but undoubtedly heroic fellow who takes on that formidable child has my wholehearted sympathy."

Miss Greyson sighed. "Yes, she is a rare handful, a most indomitable girl, except about horses. She would deny it at the stake, of course, but she is secretly afraid of horses."

"I hope the hypothetical husband keeps her chained on one until he can train her in conformity."

For the first time since the discovery of the girls on the tower staircase, Virginia relaxed. Her spontaneous laughter was low and musical. "No wonder you are still unwed, sir, with such an attitude. No doubt you are seeking a meek, downtrodden creature without an idea to call her own who will be delighted to do just as you dictate in everything."

"You wrong me, Miss Greyson," he replied, meeting

the laughing challenge with a disarming grin that faded to seriousness as he held her mocking gaze. "My wife will be full of spirit and courage. She'll—"

"There you are, Miss Greyson! That little fool of a—" The red-haired lad coming around a bend at a fast clip broke off abruptly as he noted Mr. Kirkland's presence. He came up to them and substituted lamely, "I believe Juliet is in the rose garden if you should wish to join her, ma'am. Lord Hampton is being so kind as to conduct her around."

"Thank you, Bertram. I have been hoping to come across some roses myself. Would you keep an eye on Olivia and Mellie for me? They went looking for a grotto of some sort a few minutes ago."

Bertram bowed and left them, secure in the knowledge that Miss Greyson had taken his meaning. So, too, had Mr. Kirkland apparently, for as they changed direction to head for the rose garden, he remarked calmly, "There is no cause for alarm, you know. He wouldn't be such a fool as to do anything that would thrust a spoke in his own wheel."

"No, of course not, but she is very young and a trifle heedless at times. I do not wish her to get herself talked about. It could be ruinous." She hesitated, then asked bluntly, "Is Lord Hampton a fortune hunter?"

Mr. Kirkland appeared to choose his words with care. "He comes from an old and respected family. It is rumored that he is deeply in debt, but I have no exact knowledge on that subject." After a significant pause he added deliberately, "Sir Reginald would have better information than I."

"Thank you," she said with real gratitude. "It is no bread and butter of mine, but I have been a trifle concerned of late. You relieve my mind."

200

"You take your responsibilities too much to heart, Miss Greyson. You are not, after all, Miss Brewster's legal guardian."

"No, but she is at a difficult age and she is having a rather hard time at the moment, and that is more or less your fault, you know. Oh, I do not mean to imply that any blame attaches to your conduct," she added hastily as he started to protest, "or that you have anything to reproach yourself with, but you did pay her decided attentions you must admit, and the fact that she read more into them than you intended and feels herself so humiliated now is behind her current recklessness."

"My reaction to Miss Brewster's beauty was an honest one; she has a face like a flower and a lovely, graceful body." She could hear the self-mockery creep into his tones. "This is only the third time in my life I've ever been bowled out by a woman's looks, and one of them was not even a beauty in the strictest sense of the word. Perhaps I should have known at once that an essential part of the child's appeal is that dewy innocence that accompanies extreme youth and that can never substitute for other qualities with a man of my years. For that lack of insight I must hold myself accountable." He slowed his pace to a crawl and turned to face her with a lightly pleated brow. "Has it not occurred to you, though, that your charge's current behavior stems from a deep-seated vanity and a rather disaffecting determination to attach every man who crosses her path? A few setdowns won't do her any harm."

"No, but after the way she has been cosseted and admired all her life it is understandable surely, if not laudable, that she should overreact to such a signal disappointment. In time I hope to bring her to recognize her motives and to own her mistake. She is vain, but not heartless and not totally selfish, though I admit her propensity for coquetry is worrisome to a chaperon. Even that can be attributed in large part to youthful spirits. When she really gives her heart, she will change."

He shrugged and made no reply, but the skepticism in his face said much. They resumed walking and after a short silence Miss Greyson ventured, "What happened to the other two?"

"I beg your pardon?"

"You said you had three times been bowled out by a woman's looks."

He laughed in genuine amusement, and little gold specks lighted the dark eyes. "Well, I was fairly young the first time, but I believe if my enchantress had had as much elegance of mind as of person I'd be a Benedick today. She was a glorious golden creature with a brain the size of a pea and the interests and tastes of a milkmaid."

"And the second?"

He hesitated fractionally, then turned to her with the familiar mocking smile. "Ahhh . . . that is still an unfinished tale. I'll tell you one day, but not just yet."

"Lady Eugenia," she thought shrewdly, and then gasped as she realized she had articulated the thought. Two spots of hectic color burned in her cheeks, and she made haste to undo the mischief. "I do apologize most sincerely, sir. It was unpardonable of me to become so personal. Pray forget I said that."

"No, why?" he asked in some amusement. "In any case you are mistaken; it wasn't Lady Eugenia, though I readily concede she is a beauty. Strange isn't it, this force we call attraction between a man and a woman?"

"I . . . I wouldn't know." She answered at random, still embarrassed at her departure from the canons of good taste.

"Does that mean you have never experienced it, Miss

202

Greyson?" The mockery was gone from his face, but she found the searching look that replaced it infinitely more disturbing.

"Yes . . . I mean no, never!" she replied distractedly, determined to terminate a conversation that was fast getting out of hand, and aware even as she answered that her words were a lie. Fortunately for her peace of mind they were almost in the rose garden. She must concentrate on Juliet.

CHAPTER ELEVEN

"Oh, isn't the scent heavenly, Mr. Kirkland!" declared Miss Greyson in ringing accents. She felt his quick surprised look at her, but the reason for her increase in volume became clear as they glimpsed a drift of yellow muslin retreating down a side path. He returned a polite agreement, and they began to stroll slowly amongst the assorted rose bushes. Miss Greyson was delighted with everything she saw, pouncing with glee on a speckled variety she called Belle de Crecy, even more thrilled to discover a particularly fine Rosamunde. Mr. Kirkland ably supported her inspired performance with a look of pointed amusement that would have caused her to lose countenance had she been so foolish as to try to meet it.

It was perhaps two or three minutes before they heard Juliet calling, and they turned around, projecting pleased surprise. Miss Greyson took in every detail of her charge's appearance in one lightning summary before shifting her attention to Lord Hampton. Juliet's manner was fairly composed, but she looked like a girl who had been thoroughly kissed. Her cheeks flew two flags of color and her eyes sparkled dramatically. There was an aura of suppressed excitement about her that belied her casual manner. The yellow dress appeared decidedly crushed also, although perhaps one should take into account the heat of the day and the picnic under the trees before attributing this condition to a man's embrace. She was carrying her straw bonnet over her arm tied by its satin ribbons. One or two fine specimen roses peeked out over the brim.

Lord Hampton met Miss Greyson's glance with a slight smile and a knowing look in his cold blue eyes that made her fingers itch to slap his face. She noticed the stained handkerchief wrapped around his right hand and experienced a fleeting satisfaction that he had evidently scratched himself picking roses for Juliet. She wondered what the chances of developing blood poisoning were but dismissed the hope as unrealistic.

Juliet began compulsively expatiating on the glories of the rose garden for the benefit of Mr. Kirkland, who said all the right things and, to his eternal credit, maintained a pleasant impersonal air that helped restore her composure.

Miss Greyson took a hand in the affair. "You look rather hot, my dear, and I must confess that I am dreadfully thirsty myself. Perhaps there may still be some of that lemonade we had with our lunch."

"Now that you mention it, Aggie, I am a trifle warm," Juliet admitted. "A glass of lemonade would be most refreshing." She accepted Mr. Kirkland's arm and walked off, leaving Lord Hampton and Miss Greyson to follow.

Thanks to Mr. Kirkland's social address, Juliet was almost entirely herself, chattering quite naturally in her usual enthusiastic manner by the time they had regained the orchard. The pair behind them stayed well behind at the will of Miss Greyson, who did not permit Lord Hampton to hasten her deliberate pace. Nor did she allow the earl to take charge of the conversation; once having taken the reins into her own hands, she negotiated the conversational course with a steady eye on generalities and a light touch, nicely blending humor and observation. Not for nothing had Virginia served as her father's hostess for nearly five years. Lord Hampton's initial efforts to steer the talk to Juliet's charms, whether in the hope of embarrassing her chaperon or eliciting information, were skillfully parried by one as adept and practiced in verbal fencing as he. It was not until he had escaped the nonprepossessing companion of his quarry that the self-assured earl realized that he had divulged more about himself than he had learned about Juliet.

Between them Miss Greyson and Mr. Kirkland saw to it that Juliet and the earl did not have so much as one additional minute of privacy during the rest of the afternoon, even though the gentlemen from the Manor rode back partway with the Fairhill party. More tired by her afternoon's adventures than she wished her governess to know, Olivia accepted a seat in the carriage that had brought the ladies from the Manor, which relieved Miss Greyson of one of her responsibilities and freed her to concentrate on the other.

Her thoughts were not comfortable ones, and the result of her deliberations was likewise neither comfortable nor to her liking. Her first reaction had been to continue to ignore the matter, trusting that the near discovery today and Juliet's own sense of propriety would combine to see that such familiarities ceased entirely. However, the information she had gleaned from Mr. Kirkland regarding Lord Hampton's desperate financial position, allied to the distrust she felt of his character, represented too great a danger to the inexperienced girl. She would be contemptible indeed if she allowed the fear that another confrontation with her charge would irreparably damage their shaky relationship to weigh in the balance against Juliet's whole future.

Lately the conviction had been growing that her days with the Brewster family were numbered. The position had been a haven for her during those first few heartbreaking months of loneliness, and she had grown fond of all the youngsters, but a parting was inevitable in any case. Sir Reginald had intimated that he was considering a girl's seminary for Olivia after Juliet's presentation in preference to a restricted regime in London, since the child would not be able to participate in the bustle of social events that would absorb all her sister's time. If she did not alienate Juliet beyond reason, there was every likelihood that Sir Reginald would give his employee an excellent character and perhaps even recommend her services to a family of his acquaintance.

There was little time to dwell on her own barren future during the ride back to Fairhill because it was necessary to hold up her end of the desultory conversations that broke out when the going was slow enough. Juliet became rather silent as the distance from her home and a probable accounting of her behavior diminished. Miss Greyson was aware that the girl had directed several speculative glances at her companion on the way. Without doubt she was trying to assess just how much her chaperon had seen—or guessed—of her tryst with Lord Hampton amongst the roses, but Miss Greyson maintained a serene, impersonal facade and, ably aided by Mr. Kirkland, kept the conversation moving smoothly on trivial matters.

It certainly did not come as a surprise when Juliet pleaded fatigue on their arrival and declared her intention of retiring to her room for a rest before dressing for dinner. Virginia said nothing whatever in reply but presented herself at that young lady's bedchamber door as soon as she had freshened her own appearance. Juliet, enveloped in a vastly becoming pink wrapper, opened the door herself.

With difficulty she controlled the frown that accompanied her recognition of her caller and forced a casual greeting.

"Don't you feel the need of a rest after such an active day, Aggie? I for one am tired beyond all bearing." She patted her lips to cover a delicate yawn, but her companion refused to accept this pointed dismissal.

"What I have to say won't take long, then you may rest." She moved inside the door and shut it behind her. Juliet did not ask her to sit down and remained standing herself, her face a closed book. Miss Greyson studied her coolly for a moment, then dispensed with preliminaries.

"Don't trouble to deny that you allowed Lord Hampton to kiss you in the rose garden today, because I cut my wisdoms many years ago and you would be wasting your breath. If you continue to travel the path you are treading at the moment, you may well find yourself betrothed to the earl before your comeout—if your father should fear that your complete want of conduct has left him no choice. Think well before you decide, my dear Juliet, if this is truly what you want. Yes, you would be a countess, but since the entire ton has long been aware that Lord Hampton is deep in debt and must make an advantageous marriage, where is the triumph for you in being regarded as the means for him to reestablish himself? Everyone will say, with justification, that the triumph is his, and if word of your current behavior got out, they might also say, with equal justification, that you had set your cap for him."

At the beginning of this blunt speech Juliet had gone beet red, but soon the color faded, and she was white with anger, defiance, and fear by the time Miss Greyson had thrown her final shaft. There could be no doubt that all of them had gone home.

"I don't believe you! How would *you* know about Lord Hampton's debts? You are saying this to frighten me!"

The enormous blue eyes were staring, her lips were trembling and pale.

Virginia knew a surge of relief that at least Juliet wasn't in love with Lord Hampton. Her reaction would have been very different if her feelings rather than her self-interest had been involved. She was careful to maintain a stony exterior, however, the memory of the way Juliet had rejected her sympathy on another occasion still sharply with her.

"You need not take my word for this. Ask your father for confirmation. I did not come here to pull caps with you, Juliet, merely to show you where a continuation of today's actions could lead. Now I'll leave you to your rest." She was gone on the words, shutting the door quietly behind her.

The tempestuous beauty stood rooted to the spot for an instant, staring at the closed door in disbelief, her face ashen and her fists clenched at her sides. Aggie had whisked herself out of the room without allowing her to give utterance to any of the justifications and protests churning in her mind. Suddenly she was released from her temporary paralysis, and she dashed across the charming blue and white apartment to fling herself down on the big bed, where she relieved a burning sense of frustration by indulging in a lusty but short-lived bout of weeping. In less than ten minutes she had cried herself into an exhausted sleep from which she was roused by her maid when it was time to dress for dinner.

It was a rather quiet group that gathered about the dinner table that evening. Bertram, it was true, was full of the day's events, but the female members of the family displayed much less than their habitual vivacity. Both girls agreed that Maniston's grounds were beautiful and assured their father that they had found the picnic excursion a vastly diverting experience. They answered all his queries willingly but had little to offer unprompted. Miss Greyson and Mr. Ryding took up the slack with their customary skill, though Miss Greyson was not insensible to the growing puzzlement on the part of the tutor at the unusual respect the young ladies under her care were according to any opinion she might offer tonight.

Considering the state of hostility in which she had parted from Juliet, Miss Greyson had been prepared for a difficult hour when next they met; in fact, it had been a monumental task to assume an air of serenity to conceal her own abysmal lowness of spirits, a task that was only made possible by resolutely banishing all personal concerns and concentrating on the necessity to uphold her position in Sir Reginald's eyes. She too found the girls' propitiating attitude incongruous until it dawned on her that both Olivia and Juliet were anxious that certain of their activities at Maniston today should not be brought to the attention of their papa.

There was a certain piquancy to the situation, she reflected with humor, but it relieved her mind of its most pressing concern. If Juliet had wholly discredited her revelation concerning Lord Hampton, it was extremely unlikely that she would have adopted this conciliatory manner. The cautious hope was born that the girl would retreat somewhat from her open encouragement of the earl's attentions.

It was still a difficult evening with all three females ill at ease in each other's company. Mercifully it was mutually agreeable to make it a short one. The young men had departed after dinner to fulfill a mysteriously unspecified engagement, though Olivia, who added eavesdropping to her other accomplishments, later confided with ineffable scorn that they were bound for a mill in the next village, adding that she quite failed to see the entertainment value in watching two low, vulgar persons attempting to knock each other unconscious. Sir Reginald retired to his study and the ladies, after a praiseworthy charade of engaging in amicable conversation for an hour, retired with unspoken but shared relief to their various bedchambers.

An hour later Virginia was compelled to acknowledge that the early bedtime was at best a mixed blessing. True, the Brewster girls had been awkward company this evening, but her own thoughts were proving equally so, and from them she had so far been unable to escape. Closing the book of sonnets in her lap, she glanced around the comfortable apartment dimly lighted by a lamp at her elbow and wondered how much longer she would be safely installed here. She experienced again that sense of time running out and felt helpless to slow the process.

Today had been the most eventful day in weeks. On the heels of the fright over Olivia and Mellie had come Juliet's indiscretion with the earl, and between the two incidents the most significant and alarming event of all—the unwelcome discovery that she was no longer indifferent to the potent appeal of Mr. Simon Kirkland, if indeed she had ever been in that infinitely desirable state. It was a stunning discovery and in the circumstances, a most unwelcome one. When she considered the number of eligible suitors who had paid assiduous court to her in her salad days without making the least impression on her heart, she was much inclined to rate her intelligence extremely low. She had begun to think herself immune to those flutters that attacked most of the females of her acquaintance in the days before her father died. While he lived, marriage had held no real allure for her. Afterward any hazy notions of lost possibilities were swamped in the grimmer reality of having to make her own way in the world. She had certainly not spent her time at Fairhill mourning any loss of matrimonial prospects.

Until now. Today's revelation had struck her like a thunderbolt. How could she have been so stupid as not to have seen whither she was drifting? She had clung to her original dislike of Mr. Kirkland, knowing it for no more than an irrational whim, and had drifted into a dangerous friendship with her eyes wide open. How had the significance escaped her of the frequency of late with which her glance would meet Mr. Kirkland's in an instant of shared amusement or understanding? Why had she not been aware that she *waited* for that spontaneous, unself-conscious smile that wiped all the mockery from his face and gave him such a different character from the one he presented to the world? At her age she should have recognized the initial symptoms, should have known that her pleasure in helping him organize the theatrical production stemmed from more than satisfaction of a job well done. She had felt that their minds and tastes were attuned but hadn't had the wit to see the danger in this line of thinking so she might draw back before it was too late.

The chair rocked violently as its occupant rose with the haste of someone who had been stung by a wasp. Unseeing eyes watched its motion gradually slow down and stop; their vision was directed inward. *Could* she have drawn back somewhere along the way and averted this present torment of loss and longing? Or would it be more accurate to say that some instinct for self-preservation had impelled her to do just that in the instant of meeting Mr. Kirkland's challenging gaze for the first time in Bath, and that once met again she was irretrievably lost? For uncounted seconds she savored the knowledge that she might have won his affections in Bath, but the thought was more bitter than sweet, given the present and permanent condition of her hopeless ineligibility.

She had been standing motionless in the middle of the room but now wandered over to the window to pull back one of the draperies and stare out at the moon-washed grounds. It was eerily beautiful at this hour with all color drained out of the lawns and foliage, and it was perfectly suited to a mood of aching melancholy. The clock on the dresser had chimed eleven times before the woman at the window replaced the curtain and began to make her preparations for bed. She removed her clothes and folded them methodically, donned a plain white bedgown, and rinsed her hands and face without recourse to a mirror. It was only after removing the ubiquitous cap, symbol of her current and future spinsterhood, that she approached the mirror with brush in hand. The rich chestnut hair crackled as a result of strong rhythmic brushing before the woman ceased her mechanical efforts and bundled the mass up under a nightcap, which she tied under her chin before climbing wearily into bed.

To confound her expectations of staying miserably awake all night, she fell almost at once into a deep sleep. Undisturbed rest, however, was not in the cards for her this night.

A knock at the door partially penetrated her slumber, but it was not until an anxious voice accompanied another louder knock that Virginia struggled up from the depths.

"Yes, who is it?" Her seeking hand grouped for the lamp until she realized she had no way of lighting it.

"It's Juliet, Aggie. Will you come to Livvy? She's had a nightmare or something and I cannot soothe her."

"Of course. Do you have a light?" Miss Greyson, her spectacles shoved on her nose, was scrambling into a wrapper after which she felt her way to the door and turned the key. The light from the candle Juliet held was sufficient to show them the way to the corridor where the girls' bedchambers were located:

"Did you say Olivia had a nightmare?" Miss Greyson, busily engaged in retying the girdle of her wrapper more securely about her waist, was unaware of the swift survey being made of her person by the girl at her side, but she turned her head in question when no answer was immediately forthcoming and encountered a fixed blue stare.

"Oh . . . yes," Juliet said, removing her glance to the candle in her hand that flickered dangerously until she shielded it with her other hand. "She woke up crying. I had not been asleep so I heard her right away. When I went into her, she was crying out that she was falling, or someone was falling. She wasn't very coherent and she was a good deal upset. I tried to calm her, but she is still weeping. I was afraid she'd make herself sick so I came for you."

"I'm glad you did. Do you have any idea what time it is?"

"After one."

They were crossing the threshold of Olivia's room, but Miss Greyson paused for a second. "You were awake at this hour? Do you feel unwell?"

Juliet shook her head vigorously. "No, I was . . . thinking."

They were near enough to hear Olivia's sobs by this time, so Miss Greyson was unable to pursue this disclosure. She merely desired Juliet to place the candle on the bedside table before returning to her room.

"Should I not remain in the event you require assistance?" the girl said doubtfully.

"Thank you, my dear, but I believe I know what caused this upset. You had best try to get some sleep."

"Very well." Juliet placed the candle on the table and withdrew, though not without another long look that roved over her companion's face and lingered on the hair escaping from under the nightcap. At the door she turned back once more. "Good night, Aggie," she said quietly.

Miss Greyson returned an absent reply, her attention already engaged in scooping up the girl huddled in the middle of the bed into a comforting embrace. During the whole of the climbing escapade Olivia had remained cool and seemingly unafraid, but here was a delayed reaction that was every bit as severe as Mellie's fright.

It took Miss Greyson the better part of an hour to calm the tearful girl and restore her to a semblance of normalcy with repeated assurances that no one believed she had meant to endanger her friend. Olivia gradually grew sleepy again, but it was after two A.M. when the governess returned to own bed after satisfying herself that both girls were finally sleeping peacefully. She scarcely dared hope that the eventful day had at last come to an end as she blew out the candle and crawled back under the blanket.

CHAPTER TWELVE

As sometimes happens after a period crammed with significant developments, the days following the excursion to Maniston were remarkable only for their uneventful character which, as far as Miss Greyson was concerned, was all to the good. All three ladies were feeling rather jaded the morning after their disturbed night. It was a relief to have no formal appointments to keep and rather a rarity lately to be able to spend the day in pursuit of mildly pleasurable activities on their own. Olivia and her teacher whiled away a considerable period amusing themselves at the pianoforte, and Olivia even went so far as to devote a half hour to the much neglected harp. Juliet was also in an unaccustomed mood to enjoy solitary activities. In the morning she insisted on doing all the flower arrangements herself, and after lunch she wandered off with a large sketchbook and a box of watercolors.

It was a rare day that saw no one call at Fairhill, however, and that day was no exception. Both Mr. Kirkland and Lord Hampton arrived (though not together) in time for tea to find two of Juliet's local admirers already in attendance. The son of the house and his tutor, accompanied by Mr. Alistair Penrose, wandered in a few minutes later from a day of fishing. Their arrival was greeted warmly by Miss Brewster and Miss Greyson, who welcomed the latest additions to the impromptu tea party for much the same reason. Although she gave no sign of it, each lady was well aware that at least one gentleman in attendance was desirous of monopolizing her attention, and in each case the lady in question was avidly desirous of avoiding such a tête-à-tête.

Of necessity the conversation was kept fairly general. Bertram and Alistair were discussing plans to ride to Smithfield to spend a day at St. Bartholomew's Fair. On overhearing this personal snippet, Juliet gave a little bounce of eagerness and indicated her desire to visit the famous annual fete as well.

"Don't be ridiculous," Bertram said flatly, a look of superiority sitting oddly on his youthful countenance and doing him no good whatsoever in his elder sister's eyes. "Girls of your quality don't go anywhere near such a spectacle. The place will be teeming with the great unwashed, including a good number of pickpockets and thieves. Not your style at all."

"Then why are you going," retorted his incensed sister, "if it is so dangerous and objectionable?"

"Because it will be famous fun, that's why, with sideshows and freaks and bruisers taking on all comers. Besides, Chris will be with me."

Juliet turned the full force of a wheedling smile on Mr. Ryding. "If Miss Greyson were there and you and Staro escorted us, surely we should be safe enough. I have always wanted to go to a fair."

"My dear Juliet," said her companion coming to the tutor's rescue, "nothing would induce me to step foot on a fairground even if I were escorted by a regiment of militia. The smells and the dust alone, not to mention the milling crowds, would make your head reel within ten minutes."

"I don't see why," Juliet insisted stubbornly. "If it is just a question of rubbing elbows with the vulgar, why everyone with the price of admission can go to Astley's Amphitheatre or Vauxhall Gardens, and it is perfectly permissible for girls like me to visit these places."

Mr. Ryding leaned forward and said earnestly, "It is quite different at a fair where everyone is milling around constantly, I assure you, Miss Brewster. The rougher element cannot be counted on to keep a distance. You could not be comfortable in the crowded conditions that apply at such events."

Juliet opened her lips to protest further, but her companion intervened in tones of finality. "Let us speak no more of this, Juliet. It is out of the question." With a warning glance that caused her charge to color, she bent her attention to a remark of Lord Hampton's. The other gentlemen tripped over themselves in their eagerness to turn the disappointed beauty's mind to other matters.

No further reference was made to the fair then or later. Nor did Juliet confide to her companion any of her feelings regarding the determined pursuit of her by Lord Hampton. With a sense of relief that the girl seemed intent at last on discouraging the earl, Miss Greyson forebore to infringe on her privacy with even the most oblique question about the situation.

Sitting on a stone seat in the garden a day or so later with an unopened book in her lap—lately she seemed unable to concentrate on a book—Virginia's thoughts were, as happened with distressing frequency, concerned with the parallel predicaments in which she and her charge found themselves. Each was employing all evasive tactics possible under the rules of civility to avoid a private conversation with a man she had previously encouraged, in the case of Juliet and Lord Hampton, and at least been on easy terms with in the case of herself and Mr. Kirkland.

Once she had admitted her own *tendre* for Mr. Kirkland, Virginia had decided such evasive action was the only course open to her consistent with maintaining her pride intact until she left Fairhill. She had no idea why Mr. Kirkland should seek out her society unless her recurrent premonition that he suspected her identity was based on fact, which alarming thought she tried to avoid confronting. As far as Lord Hampton was concerned, she could only trust that it would not take many more snubs before he would accept the fact that the hand he sought in advantageous marriage had turned against him. She frowned, suddenly recalling the expression on his face the other day when Juliet had declined to walk in the garden with him on some transparent excuse. The smooth charm had been conspicious by its absence on that occasion, and she had to admit to a feeling of unease that permeated the atmosphere each time the earl called.

At this point in her reflections she raised her head as she heard light footsteps on the gravel on the far side of the hedge that walled in a formal garden. Someone was pacing slowly along the path. The luxuriant hedge did not permit her to see the individual on the other side, but presumably he or she was also seeking solitude. She returned to her unproductive musings until other, firmer footsteps announced the arrival of a second person in the garden.

"At last, Miss Brewster! Penniestone informed me I might find you walking in the garden at this hour. May I offer my arm? What a delightful prospect this is!"

At the first sound of Lord Hampton's unmistakable drawl Miss Greyson had risen from her seat with the half-formed intention of foiling any designs on his part to get Juliet alone.

"Good afternoon, Lord Hampton. Yes, it is a pretty place, but I have been here long enough to feel the heat of the sun on my head. So foolish of me not to have worn a hat. Let us return to the house. I'll call Aggie and we'll offer you some refreshment."

To one who knew her as intimately as the woman on the other side of the hedge, Juliet sounded a bit nervous, but on the whole she had handled herself well. The listener prepared to head for the house herself in order to arrive before the couple, but Lord Hampton's next words halted her in her tracks.

"I don't care for any refreshment, thank you. No mere food or drink could compare with the refreshing sight of you in that blue dress that so enhances your magnificent eyes. I have been longing to get you all to myself for almost a sennight. Cruel fatality to lead me such a dance when you must have realized my eagerness to be with you again! Say you feel the same, my dearest one!"

"I . . . I think we had best return to the house immediately, my lord. I should not be here with you alone."

"I can recall another occasion when you did not object to being alone with me in a garden. Indeed, you seemed more than content to remain with me. Can it be that you were toying with my feelings? I refuse to believe it of you."

"Lord Hampton, it is ungentlemanly of you to remind me of that . . . that unfortunate incident when you must see that I regret it!" The panic in Juliet's voice had given way to rising indignation.

"How can you wound me so? I thought that you returned my affections. I *know* that you do! This missishness is unlike you."

"I did not mean to mislead you. Perhaps I . . . I mistook my feelings," Juliet declared wildly. "You took me by

221

surprise that day, but the truth is that I do *not* return your affections, sir."

"I can make you respond; I did before. Trust me, my love."

"No! Let me *go!*"

Miss Greyson estimated the distance to the nearest gap in the hedge as better than thirty feet and decided to make her presence known vocally. Before she could carry out her intention, however, another voice intervened curtly.

"You heard Miss Brewster, Lord Hampton. She has made it abundantly clear that she does not return your affections. To persist in forcing your attentions on her is to offer intolerable insult."

In their absorption neither the antagonists nor their hidden audience had heard Mr. Ryding's approach. Now Juliet gasped, whether in embarrassment or relief the woman behind the hedge could not determine, but there was no mistaking the chagrin in the earl's reply.

"Very well, I apologize, ma'am, for annoying you with attentions I had every reason to believe would be acceptable to you. I'll relieve you of the embarrassment of my presence immediately. I bid you good day, ma'am . . . sir."

The sound of his footsteps moving away caused Miss Greyson to relax, but evidently the form of the apology did not satisfy Mr. Ryding, for suddenly Juliet pleaded breathlessly: "*No!* Please, sir, let him go! Do not trouble yourself further on my account, *please.*" She added in a humble voice her companion had never heard before, "Perhaps I deserved what he said."

"*You* to deserve censure from such a scoundrel—the very idea is ludicrous! He should be horsewhipped for trying to take advantage of your innocence!"

"I cannot let you say such things when they are not

222

true, but I am excessively grateful to you for coming to my assistance just now. Please do not say any more, I *beg* of you."

"I promise I'll say nothing to distress you, only let me escort you back to the house. It is very hot in the sun and you have had an unsettling experience."

Miss Greyson sank back down onto her seat as their footsteps receded. There was no need now to advertise her presence; in fact, in view of the malaise existing between herself and Juliet, it would be as well to forget she had overheard the preceding exchange. At least there was one worry less to confront her now. Lord Hampton was too shrewd to throw his cap over the windmill. They would see much less of him in the future, thank heavens.

As she slowly retraced her path to the house a moment later, a thoughtful expression came over her features. The notion would intrude that they might merely have exchanged one problem for another. To her ears it had been beyond question that Christopher Ryding had betrayed his feelings for Juliet in that last scene. She could only hope that Juliet had been too preoccupied with her own embarrassment and distress to detect the fervent note in his voice when he had addressed her. It seemed there was no end to the complications this summer had wrought in the pleasant life at Fairhill.

Still, on the surface life continued quietly. Juliet was a bit subdued but evidently quite content to remain passively at home for the time being. Though she made no mention of Lord Hampton's attempt to maneuver her into a trap from which she could only emerge betrothed, her attitude to her companion warmed considerably from the recent chill.

The two ladies were cozily ensconced in the small room used for breakfast two days after the incident in the garden. Olivia had been invited to join Amelia in a visit to a friend of Lady Wrénthorpe's, and the stay-at-homes were utilizing the time to make a pattern for a new reticule for Juliet. That is, Miss Greyson was engaged in that prosaic task. Juliet was puzzling over a knitting pattern that refused to come right. She looked up ruefully after recounting her stitches.

"This is the third time I've attempted this part, Aggie, with three different results—all wrong! Can you find my mistake?" She held out the rose-colored mass in exasperation, and silence reigned for a few moments while Miss Greyson concentrated on the pattern. At last she found the mistake and corrected it. She was showing Juliet how to go on from there when Penniestone entered on a quiet knock.

"Mr. Elliott has called to see Miss Greyson. I have put him in the small saloon, ma'am."

"Thank you, Penniestone, we'll join him presently." Miss Greyson's voice lost none of its calm assurance, but she directed a beseeching look at her companion as the butler went out again. However, that young lady gathered her knitting together hastily and jumped up, her face all demure mischief.

"He's not here to see me, Aggie. I shall take my work to my room for a while. Shall I have Penniestone serve tea?"

"It's too bad of you to desert me like this, Juliet. Won't you please come and support me?" she wheedled. "I am persuaded Mr. Elliott meant to inquire for both of us."

Juliet giggled but declined to play gooseberry, a gratuitous remark that called forth a reproachful look from her duenna. "I simply cannot face a half hour of Mr. Elliott's prosing today, Aggie," she demurred. "I'll offer you some advice though. Watch your step. Bella says he's looking for a wife who'll put the skids under that sister of his. She has made herself thoroughly disliked in the village with her sharp tongue and domineering ways. Of course, if you play your cards right, you could be mistress of the rectory." Juliet whisked herself through the door on another giggle, leaving Miss Greyson to follow reluctantly, a small crease between her brows.

In the face of other worries lately she had rather allowed the minister's partiality for Agnes Greyson to slip from her thoughts. He had not called in the last week or two; in fact, she had only seen him once since the night of the play. On that occasion he had pressed a date upon her for tea with his sister, an engagement she had not scrupled to break on the pretext of a sick headache when the time had arrived. No doubt he was here to name another date for this meeting. Well, she supposed she would have to go this time for the sake of common civility. Her dragging feet had brought her to the door of the small saloon; she sighed gustily and pinned a false smile to her face as she entered.

"Good afternoon, sir. How nice of you to call."

Mr. Elliott popped out of his chair like a cork from a bottle and bounced over to seize her hand before she had taken two steps into the room. He carried the hand to his lips and kissed it with a fervor that Miss Greyson could only regard as excessive.

"Dear lady, at last! It has been an age since last we met. You must forgive my seeming neglect of the inhabitants of Fairhill. I assure you nothing less than being confined to my bed would have kept me from paying my respects before this."

Miss Greyson tugged gently at her hand until it was released, though not without reluctance, and she made polite inquiries as to the state of the minister's health.

225

"I fear I suffer from a long-standing predisposition to colicky disorders. Every now and then there is nothing for it except to take to my bed for an invalidish spell. I make no complaints," he added, an expression of pious resignation causing his thick lips to contract horizontally and expand vertically to a degree that produced an inward shudder of revulsion in the woman watching. "In general I have been blessed with good health, and thanks to my sister's devoted nursing, I trust I come through these painful episodes with little permanent damage to my constitution. Hermione oversees all food preparation in the kitchens, you know, and allows no one else to select the fruits and vegetables that come to the table."

Virginia seized on this reference to his sister to forestall any possible detailing of his dietary requirements. "I was sorry to have to cancel my appointment with Miss Elliott," she said hurriedly, feeling that the setting of a new date for the tea drinking was to be preferred to learning the intimate details of the man's constitution.

"Naturally Hermione is most eager to reschedule your visit. She would have accompanied me today had I not let fall a hint that I was desirous of obtaining a private interview with you. I daresay you may have guessed the reason." Those repulsively fascinating lips widened to reveal large irregular teeth.

Dismay spread through Virginia with the rapidity of ink spilled into water, and she found herself desperately regretting the absence of the voluble Miss Elliott, a situation she would have dismissed as ridiculous only an hour ago.

"You should have brought Miss Elliott with you," she replied, striving for a tone of light raillery. "After all, we hardly know each other well enough to have anything of a private nature to discuss."

The unsubtle hint passed him by and he remained undaunted. "My dear Miss Greyson, in your innate modesty which I heartily admire—please do not think otherwise— you underrate yourself. Anyone who has witnessed over a period of months, as I have been privileged to do, the beauty of your character, your generosity to others, your denial of your own pleasures to give pleasure to others, must be held to know you more thoroughly than you know yourself."

"You are mistaken, sir. I am a very ordinary person and do not deserve these extravagant compliments."

"I shall not allow you to be a proper judge of what you deserve, dear lady," he rebutted with heavy gallantry. "Your humility, to which I would almost apply the term saintly, did I not fear to offend that modesty to which I have already referred, blinds you to the worth of your own character. Nothing I have seen in your behavior over many months of observation would preclude your becoming the worthy partner and helpmeet of a man dedicated to the service of humanity, in short, a man of the cloth."

In a desperate attempt to avert the declaration hovering on his tongue she replied repressively, "It is very kind in you to say so, sir, but in any case I am quite happy in my position in this household. If I have any talent at all, it is an affinity for teaching the young. I have no thought of marriage."

"Naturally a woman of your obvious breeding would not have the indelicacy to dwell on such a subject until a gentleman had given some indication of his sentiments toward her, but though teaching is a worthy calling for some, marriage is and must always remain a woman's natural sphere."

"In general I cannot quarrel with your sentiments, sir, but there *are* other callings. Your own sister has chosen to devote her energies to making a home for you and assisting you in your vocation. Other women devote themselves to lives of piety and good works."

If he was disconcerted by her determination to steer the conversation away from the personal, he did not allow it to thwart his purpose for long. "My sister was not fortunate enough to have the opportunity of marrying during her youth. This is sometimes the case in this imperfect world but does not alter the fact that every woman must prefer to be mistress of her own establishment. It is a woman's privilege to take her place at a man's side and be a comfort to him on his life's walk. This is the highest calling a woman can aspire to. Anything less is in the nature of a waste of her talents. It would grieve me deeply to see you denied this station in life. Miss Greyson—*Agnes* —I would be greatly honored to make you my wife."

Virginia's heart sank to her shoes. She was no coward, but in view of such sincere conviction that he was conferring a signal honor on her, she shrank from administering the sort of setdown that she feared would be required to convince him that she did not aspire to the honor. She bit her lip and the silence lengthened.

"I have taken you by surprise I can see," Mr. Elliott said kindly, "but indeed, dear lady, I have given the matter much thought. This is no precipitate action on my part. I would not insult you with an impulsive declaration about such an important decision." He was inching forward in his chair, which was at right angles to hers. "I beg you to say the words that will make me the happiest of men."

Virginia allowed herself a quick glance at the smooth bulbous head with its smooth pomaded hair and the thin colorless eyebrows that didn't seem to register against the ruddy expanse of flesh. He was smiling and those beady little eyes all but disappeared in the folds of flesh as his neck had disappeared in the folds of his neckcloth. She returned her eyes to the contemplation of her shoes, took a deep breath, and plunged.

"Believe me, sir, I am deeply sensible of the honor—the very great honor—you have done me in wishing to make me your wife, but I am afraid it is out of the question. I think of you as a friend, but I do not cherish for you those warmer feelings that are necessary for marriage. I am truly sorry." *There!* She had done it. She risked a peek at him, and her eyes widened in surprise. He was *smiling*!

"I take it by 'warmer feelings' you refer to those of a romantic nature. I honor you for your candidness, but believe me, my dear Agnes, such sentiments are totally unreliable and do not in any way promote a successful union, for they often preclude a real understanding and appreciation of the true character of the person so regarded." The smile broadened and became more condescending. "It is of much greater importance to hold the prospective partner in respect and esteem. As a minister I have too often seen the unhappy results of the so called love match. A woman who marries for companionship will find this quality much more enduring than ephemeral romantic leanings."

"I am sorry, sir, but I could not contract to marry without feeling something stronger than friendship or respect for the man who would become my husband."

"But my dear Miss Greyson—Agnes—I never meant to imply that there is no place for such feelings in marriage, merely that they must not be the primary consideration *before* marriage. Afterward it is to be hoped that mutual respect and closeness in daily living will engender just such lasting sentiments. It would be my duty and pleasure as your husband to teach you to esteem me in the fashion you regard as desirable."

Virginia snatched back the hand he had engulfed in two

damp pudgy ones and rose agitatedly to her feet as he started to go down on his knees before her chair.

"I am sorry but it would not work, we should not suit," she stammered distressfully. "Oh, pray get up, sir, I beg of you. Do believe that I know my own mind—"

"Ahem, Mr. Kirkland."

"I trust I don't intrude?"

Virginia turned a flaming face toward the men who had entered so softly that the occupants of the room were oblivious of their presence until two separate voices pierced their absorption. The butler's dry cough had alerted her, but it was upon Mr. Kirkland that her embarrassed glance alighted, and on contact she felt almost scorched by the fury of that inimical regard. An instant later he was strolling into the room wearing his customary satirical smile, and one might have imagined that momentary rage. She was aware that Mr. Elliott at her side had swarmed to his feet but for once seemed incapable of speech.

"Of course you don't intrude, sir," she replied in a reasonably cool tone. "Mr. Elliott was just leaving, but he . . . he dropped a button and was searching for it." And you can't prove otherwise, she thought defiantly, meeting the mocking dark gaze squarely, only to drop her eyes a second later as she bit furiously on the inside of her cheek to control a mad desire to laugh. Mr. Kirkland had raised his quizzing glass and was leisurely inspecting the black coat of the minister.

"How very annoying. I trust you found it, sir?" he inquired with gentle solicitude, letting the glass fall the length of its ribbon.

"Err . . . yes, and now I must be going. I have already tarried longer than planned." He accepted the hand Miss Greyson held out to him and bowed over it. "We will

230

continue our discussion at some more felicitous moment, ma'am. Your very obedient servant . . . yours, sir."

The gentlemen bowed punctiliously, and Mr. Kirkland stepped back to allow Mr. Elliott to follow the wooden-faced Penniestone to the door.

The awkward silence continued even after the door closed softly. Miss Greyson seated herself with meticulous attention to the fall of her skirts and indicated a chair to her guest.

"Dear me, despite your reassurance I cannot help feeling my entrance was a trifle inopportune." There was invitation in the apologetic remark, an invitation that was refused with finality.

"Not at all, sir. It was good of you to call. I will tell Penniestone to acquaint Miss Brewster with your arrival."

"No wait! I have been trying to get five minutes of privacy with you for days." A pointed glance directed at his hand on her wrist from behind the ugly spectacles resulted in its removal, but he laughed rather harshly as she hesitated near the bell pull before bringing the hand to join the other in her lap.

"Perhaps it is just my deplorable lack of self-confidence," he drawled in accents that were not free from sarcasm, "but I have the distinct impression that you do not welcome a tête-à-tête with me any more than with the reverend." A heavy frown creased his forehead, and for the first time in her experience of him he looked to be somewhat at a loss. "There is something I have to tell you, but I'm stumped as to how to go about it."

"Perhaps you should just come right out and . . . say it," she suggested in even tones that were a triumph considering the tension apparent in the set of her head on her shoulders as though braced for a blow.

"Perhaps I should at that." Suddenly he smiled at her,

not the mocking quirk of lips, but a real smile, slightly rueful and redolent of humor and kindness. Her heart began to accelerate its beating and a tinge of anxiety crept into her eyes as he went on. "My sins have come home to roost, I fear. For some time I have been regretting that our acquaintance started off on the wrong foot. I—"

"Good afternoon, Mr. Kirkland, Penniestone told me you had called. How do you do?" A smiling Juliet followed her voice into the room.

CHAPTER THIRTEEN

Miss Greyson was in the main saloon arranging tall stalks of lilies and delphiniums in blue and white Wedgwood vases. Her clever hands were reducing the number of stems in the cutting basket by her side as they inserted one after another to fashion twin arrangements for the tables on either side of the fireplace. The better part of her intelligence, however, was engaged in a wrestling with problems that had nothing to do with flowers.

Almost twenty-four hours had passed, but she had not succeeded in banishing the two disturbing interviews to a dusty attic room in her mind. They persisted in occupying the main drawing room. Both encounters had proved highly embarrassing in nature, and the one with Mr. Elliott had sorely tried her patience also. An unwilling compassion for a rejected suitor, no matter how presumptuous his proposal, had caused her to soften her response to his offer, with the result that the minister now planned to reopen the subject when he could arrange an opportunity. At the time she had been so grateful for the interruption provided by the arrival of Mr. Kirkland, despite the attendant embarrassment, that she had not considered that she would have her refusal to do all over again. She had a horrible inkling that Mr. Elliott's conceit would make mincemeat of her desire to remain within time-honored social formulas in getting him to accept her refusal as final. A vehement shake of her head accompanied a renewed determination to think no more on the matter.

She stepped back to view the results of her artistic efforts. One vase looked just right as she placed it carefully on the rosewood table. The other needed filling in a bit more. The task was begun briskly enough, but within a minute her hands had stilled and her mind was projecting a persistent image of Mr. Kirkland as he had looked on discovering herself and Mr. Elliott in a frozen attitude worthy of a classic rejection scene. What was behind the flaming rage that he had instantly brought under control, if indeed she had not read too much into a fleeting expression? The suave mockery that succeeded his initial reaction was exactly what one would have expected from a man with his sardonic sense of humor and acute appreciation of human foibles.

During a disturbed night the same question had recurred with annoying frequency, but no adequate answer had suggested itself. The brief interview with Mr. Kirkland had been as trying, if not as embarrassing, as the longer one with Mr. Elliott. She had found it necessary to draw upon increasingly slender reserves of resolution to be able to face him with outward calm, and not solely because of the preceding scene. Foolish though the attitude undoubtedly was, she had dreaded each meeting garbed as Miss Greyson ever since making the discovery that she was in love with him. It was galling to her pride and desolating to her spirits to present less than her best appearance when in his company.

She regarded the finished flower arrangements with a somberness at great variance with their freshness and beauty, and began to gather up the fallen bits of leaves and stems. Yesterday she had greeted Juliet's appearance with a relief born of fear that she was about to have her disguise exposed, but today she was of a different mind. There would be a certain bitter satisfaction in bringing the uncertainty to an end. This going from day to day not knowing the exact moment when her deception would be unmasked was like waiting for the sword of Damocles to land on her neck. She was so sure that the sands of her time at Fairhill were running out that she had written to Agnes this morning telling her the whole story and alerting her to expect a visit in the near future. Of course, there was the possibility that Mr. Kirkland might know her secret and elect not to betray her, but it was only logical that his main concern would be for his friends. How could he reconcile his duty to them and not expose the deception?

She had just picked up the basket and was preparing to leave the room when hurried footfalls approached the door. The next instant Bertram burst in upon her, followed closely by Mr. Ryding.

"There you are, Miss Greyson! Do you know where Juliet is?" The brusque question caused her to raise slender brows a trifle. The lad was barely controlling a seething impatience that revealed itself in snapping gray eyes and a rigid set to his boyish mouth.

"Why, yes, Bertram. She rode over to spend the day with Emily and Alice Penrose. She mentioned her plans at dinner last night. Do you not remember?"

"What did I tell you?" This remark was flung at Mr. Ryding, who was looking a bit troubled now. "She isn't at the Hall," he stated for the benefit of his sister's companion. "Chris and I were at the Manor just now and Emily and Alice are there—invited for luncheon. *Staro* is *not* there, however. Alice said he rode off this morning for the whole day but was very mysterious about his destination."

As the implication of this disclosure sank in, Miss Greyson looked from the angry boy to the serious-faced tutor. "Are you suggesting that Juliet might be with Mr. Alistair Penrose?"

"It's not a suggestion; it's a certainty!"

Mr. Ryding spoke for the first time. "Bertram has the idea that Miss Brewster may have persuaded Penrose to escort her to St. Bartholomew's Fair, but surely she would not act so rashly after what was said about public fairs the other day."

"Hah! If you think that, you do not know my sister! She thrives on opposition—both my totty-headed sisters do. The minute anyone throws a rub in the path of one of their schemes, they become as obstinate as mules. Juliet was furious when everyone agreed a fairground was no place for a girl, but she saw at once there was no chance of getting round Miss Greyson or me with her cajolery. She can wrap Staro around her little finger. Lord, what a gudgeon he's become since coming down from university!"

Miss Greyson had been doing some rapid thinking, and now she addressed herself to Mr. Ryding. "I am afraid Bertram may be correct, and I cannot think Mr. Penrose an adequate protection for a young girl at such a place." The words "especially a girl as beautiful as Juliet" hung unspoken but understood between them. "I would be failing in my duty if I did not make a push to find her and bring her back. How vexatious that her father should be away just now with the chaise!"

"You have only to command me, ma'am. If Bertram would lend me his curricle, I will be pleased to drive you to Smithfield."

"Yes, of course, Chris, but I think I should go with you

instead, in case you need another pair of fists," protested Bertram.

Miss Greyson thoroughly approved of the seriousness with which Mr. Ryding received this suggestion. "Thank you, Bertram, I'd welcome your company except that I believe Miss Greyson's presence is more vital for your sister's sake, since it might well be sunset before we return. In any event we will be going to the fair together tomorrow, so you will not miss anything."

"Oh, very well, but won't three in the curricle on the way back be excessively uncomfortable?"

Miss Greyson spoke up briskly, "Yes, but that cannot be helped. We shall squeeze Juliet in between us as her fitting punishment for causing such a deal of bother. Oh, it occurs to me that they may have driven there even though Juliet rode off this morning on Betsy. She might have left the horse somewhere. Bertram, do you suppose you might find out which groom accompanied her this morning just to be sure we are not haring off on a wild-goose chase?"

"I have already done so. Robbie went with her as far as the Penrose home farm, then she sent him home and went on alone."

"No doubt they planned to meet away from the house," Miss Greyson mused. "That settles it. If you have no objection to missing lunch, sir, I should like to leave as soon as I can change these house shoes for half boots and find my hat and gloves."

Mr. Ryding, as anxious as the governess to start without further loss of time, went directly to the stables to order the horses put to the curricle. Bertram detoured by the kitchens and surprised the pair with a basket of hastily assembled bread, fruit, and cheese to ward off starvation when he saw them off less than fifteen minutes later.

237

It still lacked a few minutes to the lunch hour when Bertram looked up from the fishing rod he was repairing in the game room to greet Mr. Simon Kirkland, who entered on the heels of Penniestone's announcement.

"How do you do, Bertram? Penniestone tells me neither of the ladies is at home today. Would you and Mr. Ryding care to join me in a ride over to Lawson's farm this afternoon to look at that chestnut gelding he's been puffing off?"

Ordinarily an invitation to accompany Mr. Kirkland would have been accepted with alacrity, since that gentleman's prowess in all sport made him something of a hero figure to the sixteen year old, but the necessity for keeping today's events from becoming known in the neighborhood caused Bertram to fumble around for an excuse.

"I regret, sir," he explained, "that Chris is not here right at present; he's doing an errand. I do not know precisely when he'll be back. I shouldn't like to keep you waiting."

"I'm in no hurry," Mr. Kirkland said with a lazy grin. "I wouldn't refuse an invitation to lunch while we await Mr. Ryding's return."

Instant consternation appeared in the boy's face, but he swallowed and said courteously, "Of course, sir, you are most welcome to have lunch, but I do not think . . . that is, I hardly know when Chris will be returning."

Mr. Kirkland had been drawing out his snuffbox, but although he flicked the lid open with a practiced movement of his left hand and proceeded to take a pinch of the aromatic mixture with his right, his eyes remained fixed on the youngster with a new intentness.

"Is something wrong, Bertram?" he asked sympathetically.

"No, of course not. What could be wrong?"

238

In the ensuing silence the tiny click of the snuffbox closing caused the boy to jump.

"I don't know," the man answered slowly, "but something I believe. When did you say Mr. Ryding would return?"

"Perhaps not until sunset," Bertram said swiftly, hoping his persistent guest would take himself off on hearing this.

"I see. A rather time-consuming errand, in fact." The dark eyes narrowed thoughtfully as the color rushed up in the boy's face. "Is Miss Greyson expected shortly?"

"No, that is I do not know . . . sir." This last was tacked on to bring the bald statement up to a minimum standard of politeness.

Mr. Kirkland spoke softly, almost as though to himself. "I wonder, could the simultaneous absence of Mr. Ryding and Miss Greyson have any relation to the agitation you exhibited earlier this morning on discovering that the Misses Penrose were at the Manor?" Bertram returned his stare unblinkingly. "Or perhaps it was the discovery that young Penrose had gone off somewhere for the day that disturbed you?"

"I don't know what you are driving at, sir. Staro's whereabouts are no concern of mine. Nothing is bothering me," Bertram replied stiffly.

Mr. Kirkland continued to muse aloud. "You were surprised at finding Miss Penrose and Miss Alice there, but it was not until they said Alistair was away for the day that you recollected an urgent appointment and took your leave. Could it be that your surprise in the first instance was because you expected your sister to be with the Penrose girls, and your agitation was because the fact that young Penrose was also missing was suddenly connected with something in your mind?"

239

Reading the answer in Bertram's face, he abandoned the soft tones and stated briskly, "It's my guess that Miss Brewster and Penrose have gone off somewhere and Mr. Ryding and Miss Greyson have gone searching for them. Am I right?" Then as the boy remained stubbornly silent, he said impatiently, "Be assured it will go no farther, but they may welcome reinforcements in the search. Do you have any idea where they went?"

Bertram surrendered to force majeure. "We think they went to Smithfield."

"Of course, the fair!" Mr. Kirkland frowned at the rug for a long moment and then shrugged. "It's more than likely my help won't be needed, but I'll feel better if I head for Smithfield myself." He turned on his heel and left.

It was a beautiful sunny day, though a bit humid, and Juliet enjoyed the long ride to London. Alistair had proposed driving his curricle, but she had opted for horseback since she had to wear her habit anyway once she announced her intention of riding to the Hall. They didn't hurry, and it was nearly noon before they approached the outskirts of London and saw the tents and colorful booths that proclaimed the fairground. Alistair was thinking in terms of a luncheon at one of the inns in the area, but Juliet was much too excited to wish to sit down to a meal, especially when it meant wasting precious time. They left the horses in charge of a loiterer in a field already crammed with carriages and conveyances of every description and headed for the midway area.

It soon became apparent that no one had overstated the matter when warning Juliet of the crowds and the dust and the smells associated with a fair. It was necessity, not sentimentality, that caused her to cling to her escort's arm. Once separated from Alistair, the chances of finding him again in a reasonable period of time must be slim indeed. In truth, she was a bit frightened of the crowds, but it was a rather pleasurable sensation all the same and added to the thrill of meandering slowly amongst the many temporary structures erected to house the exhibits.

Just reading banners and placards proclaiming the multitudinous marvels to be glimpsed (for a trifling sum) within the various tents was a day's entertainment. They saw the World's Fattest Boy and Fattest Girl, of a grossness that was truly astounding, standing among their normal siblings. Juliet gasped with astonishment at the performance of the man who actually swallowed fire, and she nearly swooned away with a rush of pity for the two pretty sisters billed as the eighth wonder of the world, who had been born joined together at their backs.

At this point Mr. Penrose thought it advisable to get the sensitive young lady out into the air again and restore her spirits with some refreshment. Accordingly they devoured cakes and comfits, and Juliet drank milk fresh from the cow while Alistair refreshed himself with the ale that contributed much to the area's almost indescribable conglomeration of odors. A puppet show and a performance of a melodrama, much curtailed but vigorously acted, helped restore her equilibrium still further. She was entranced with the maneuvers of a troupe of little birds trained to march like soldiers across a table. They wore tiny grenadier's caps of paper on their heads and little stick replicas of muskets were attached under their left wings. They even enacted a scene of shooting a traitor with a tiny cannon to the wonder of all who were privileged to witness this extraordinary event.

Juliet resisted the importunities of a filthy greasy-haired crone who promised her a magnificent fortune for a shilling. The thought of being mewed up in any tent of the gypsy's for even five minutes fairly turned her stomach. At her pleading look and desperate clutch on his arm, Alistair tossed the old woman a coin to assuage any disappointment at the loss of custom, and they made their escape.

When Juliet had had her fill of freaks and wonders, they paid their penny to fish for prizes in the pool and tried their hand at other skills, eventually reaping an armload of ridiculous fairings and trifles. Attracted by the screams of the patrons of the boat swings, they stopped to watch the passengers soar to dizzy heights, but Alistair could not persuade Juliet to venture into the swings, despite pointing out the secure buckling system that kept the riders safely anchored. Recalling the condition of her stomach at the stench and heat of some of the tents, Juliet was persuaded the wisest course was to keep her feet firmly planted on solid ground.

This prudent resolve was undermined almost immediately as a disembarking passenger, an overrouged young woman with brassy curls beneath a red bonnet whose huge poke was lined in purple to match the plumes on the crown, lurched strongly into Juliet, nearly knocking her off her feet.

"I beg your pardon," Juliet began automatically, but on seeing her assailant, an instinctive reluctance for contact with a woman whom despite her inexperience she recognized for a doxy caused her to draw in her skirts fastidiously, a gesture that was not lost on the other.

"Why'incha watch where you're going? Think ya own the place?" the blond snarled, clinging closer to her escort, a burly young man sporting a checkered coat over a flashy yellow waistcoat hung with a variety of fobs and seals.

On having his attention drawn to the other victim of the accident, his threatening scowl was instantly replaced by an expression of mocking admiration as he swept off his hat and made Juliet a low bow, apologizing profusely and thereby incurring the vociferous wrath of his partner, who claimed her dress had been ruined by contact with Juliet's booted foot. The gallant detached her hand from his arm without so much as a glance in her direction and turned squarely to Juliet, begging her to restore his peace of mind by assuring him she was uninjured. Alistair showed signs of wishing to call the other to account for his familiarity, but having already compared the bulk of the tall stranger with her escort's slim build and moderate height, Juliet was determined to avoid any further unpleasantness. She declared herself perfectly unhurt in a propitiating voice while urging Alistair away by repeated tugs on his sleeve. For the first time it was brought home to her that a male escort did not necessarily guarantee her safe conduct in a place patronized not only by respectable cits in their Sunday best and well-meaning working people, but also by a rougher element that delighted in kicking up riot and rumpus.

The fairground was teeming with children of all ages, too, who while less menacing than the street toughs, seemed to be completely unaccompanied and unrestrained, darting thither and yon across everyone's path and jostling anyone so misguided as to try to slow down their impulsive progress. Not five minutes later the pair found themselves caught up on the edge of a crowd that gathered like wasps around spilled food, about two youths who were pummeling each other with bare, bloodied fists.

They changed direction immediately, but it was no easy task to go against the flow of the crowd, and Juliet, in her heavy and cumbersome habit, was hot and disheveled and more than somewhat frightened by the time they were relatively clear. Much of the enjoyment of the fair had evaporated for her after two such encounters, and it was almost with relief that she heard herself hailed by a familiar voice.

"Aggie!"

Her abrupt about-face caused a large man intent on passing the dawdling couple to carom into the girl at full tilt. Having loosened her grip on Alistair at the instant of turning, Juliet made a frantic effort to avert a fall by grabbing at him again and ended by twisting her ankle sharply. Afterward nothing registered clearly for a pain-wracked interval. She was aware of Miss Greyson's brisk voice giving orders to remove her to a more secluded spot and of the disjointed apology of the man who must have crashed into her, though she never saw his face. She remembered being lifted into someone's arms and then nothing, as a renewed stab of pain sent her into unconsciousness for a brief time. Too brief actually, for the next sensation was a comforting whiff of a clean male fragrance, instantly overcome by an agonizing throbbing in the dangling foot as she was carried for what seemed an age before being gently lowered to a grassy patch of ground. It was less suffocatingly dusty here, and she gulped the fresher air gratefully and opened her eyes to encounter a concerned stare from two hazel eyes.

"Mr. Ryding!" she gasped faintly as the heat spread over her cheeks.

"Thank heavens she is getting some color back," said Miss Greyson prosaically. "Mr. Penrose, see if you can procure a glass of water for her, if you please."

Unfortunately, it was soon established that the injury to Juliet's ankle was a good deal more serious than a momentary wrench. It started to swell immediately and was obviously giving her constant pain.

"That boot will have to come off at once, I'm afraid, Juliet. The longer we wait the harder it will be for you."

"But I must ride home again," protested the distraught girl on the verge of tears, "I cannot take it off."

"You'll do no more riding today, my dear. I fear I may have to hurt you a trifle, but it will be over in a trice, and Mr. Ryding will then conduct you home in Bertram's curricle." Miss Greyson had started to loosen the boot even as she spoke soothingly, and Mr. Ryding discouraged those curious persons disposed to linger in the area in the hopes of seeing something newsworthy. If the removal operation took longer and was productive of more discomfort than Miss Greyson's optimistic predictions, Juliet endured it with exemplary fortitude, but she was alarmingly pale when at last the boot was suspended from the limp fingers of her almost equally pale chaperon. Mr. Penrose was back by that time with a mug full of water that was accepted gratefully by the injured girl while Miss Greyson conferred briefly with Mr. Ryding.

It was at this point that the party was augmented by the surprise appearance of Mr. Simon Kirkland, who took in the situation at a glance and said with brisk good humor, "All the dreary way here I told myself my presence would at best be superfluous, but something drove me on and I see my instincts have been vindicated." He smiled in sympathy at the girl sitting on her companion's shawl, then addressed Mr. Ryding. "I believe Miss Brewster will be more comfortable in the phaeton than the curricle, and my cattle are probably faster. Since it is preferable that she return with a member of her own household, I propose to exchange vehicles with you. I'll take Miss Greyson with me."

Neither Juliet nor Mr. Ryding had any objection to offer to this plan, but Miss Greyson said coolly, "You are

245

very good, sir, and as far as Miss Brewster is concerned your plan is probably for the best, but we had already agreed that I would ride Miss Brewster's horse home."

"I couldn't reconcile it with my conscience if I permitted a woman of your years to ride twenty miles or more on horseback at this hour, Miss Greyson," replied Mr. Kirkland with a bland effrontery that struck sparks in the older woman, who was constrained to suppress an overmastering desire to hit him for his unwelcome consideration. He ignored her tight-lipped silence and added, "Penrose may lead Miss Brewster's horse home, and judging by that sky, we should lose no time in setting forth." He proceeded to pick Juliet up and head for the field.

In the face of such unassailable logic Miss Greyson subsided, not without damage to her temper. Mr. Penrose, who had the worst of the arrangement by far, was too miserably conscious of his culpability in the affair to do other than agree with the decision with as much grace as he could muster, cheered somewhat by Juliet's sincere thanks for her lovely day despite the ending. His offer to locate a pillow or quilt to support her foot during the long drive was gratefully received also. Miss Greyson smiled at him warmly when he returned with a quilt purchased at one of the booths just as Mr. Kirkland settled Juliet in the phaeton. The others waited until Mr. Ryding had maneuvered this conveyance out of the field before repairing to their own transportation.

Miss Greyson, still smarting illogically from the remark about her supposed age, was resolved to initiate no conversation during her enforced journey in the company of the man who could annoy her more than any human being she had ever met, despite having captured her unwilling heart. It was relatively simple to avoid conversation at first because the driver needed concentration to negotiate his way between the vehicles and pedestrian traffic at the fair-grounds and for some time thereafter until the turnpike was reached. Miss Greyson occupied herself in gazing with awe at the variously dressed participants in one of London's annual extravaganzas. Never in her life had she seen so many people in such constant motion within a circumscribed area. She sighed a trifle regretfully for lost opportunity—there was something contagious in the air of excitement that emanated from the patrons of the fair.

"Don't repine," advised her companion, reading her mind with ease, "there will be other fairs."

"You mistake fatigue for repining, sir," she assured him in frigid accents. "What liking could a woman of my years have for the juvenile pleasures of a fairground? It has been a rather fatiguing day, that's all."

He chuckled but made no answer, being concerned just then with keeping his horses from bolting at the effrontery of a trio of dogs in chasing madly after the curricle for a distance, barking furiously all the while.

After this the silence that settled over the pair lasted for several miles until Mr. Kirkland inquired, "Are you still sulking over that reference to your years? I would never have accused you of being age conscious, Miss Greyson."

Virginia, who had been not sulking but miserably re-gretting her fate, leaped out of the Slough of Despond into which she was fast sinking, aided by a push from the mockery that had characterized his attitude to her throughout much of their acquaintance. She snapped, "I should rather say you were the age-conscious individual, sir. I assure you I have no qualms about my ability to ride a mere twenty miles on a good horse."

"Accept my heartfelt apologies, ma'am, for presuming to infer otherwise. Please believe that it was concern for

247

your welfare, not doubt of your ability to accomplish the feat, that motivated my infelicitous remark."

About to declare forthrightly that she did not believe him when his tone demonstrably belied his words, Virginia bit her lip and swallowed the retort. A quarrel might while away the tedium of a long drive, but she was aware deep inside her that she did not wish to quarrel with him. Refusing to follow this line of thinking into the forbidden area of what she did wish, she remarked primly; "How well-sprung Bertram's curricle is! And his horses move well. We should not be too far behind the others."

"I wish I could share your optimism, Miss Greyson," her escort replied with a touch of grimness. "Look behind you at that sky."

She did as he instructed and cried out in surprise, "Good Heavens! I did not realize there was a storm so imminent. How far would you say we have come, sir?"

"Roughly halfway. We are racing the storm but it is nearly upon us. Feel the breeze springing up?"

"Oh, poor Juliet! Do you think they will make it home before it strikes? Have they enough of a start on us?"

The expression in his eyes was not to be believed when he smiled at her, and his next words struck her dumb. "Did I ever mention that you are a sweetheart? Not a word of complaint about your own chances of getting a wetting, which are one hundred percent. And here it comes!" he added as the first huge drops slammed like bullets into the surface of the road. "I'm hoping to reach a lane Malcolm brought me to the pike on one day before we are soaked to the skin. There is a dilapidated barn a few hundred yards along it that should afford us some shelter. Watch for a turning on the right very shortly now."

Virginia tried to oblige, but already her spectacles were

spotted with water. Surreptitiously she removed them and wiped them swiftly on her skirt, averting her head. Before she could replace them on her nose, however, Mr. Kirkland said impatiently, "Leave the wretched things off. How you have managed to avoid walking into a door before this is something that passes my understanding, Miss . . . *Ginger Spice.*"

Even in the midst of an increasing storm he was aware of her utter stillness at his side. He waited a full minute, unable to look at her after that first quick glance for fear of missing their turn.

"What are you going to do?" No denials, no pleading, just the quiet question. Mentally he doffed his hat in tribute to her gallantry under fire.

"Do? Marry you, of course." His voice was as calm as hers had been, but it brought her head around with a jerk.

"Evidently you find this a subject for jesting, sir, but let me tell you I do not share your extraordinary sense of humor. I—"

"There it is, there is the lane! Hold tight!"

"*Mr. Kirkland!*

"Yes, yes, you many ring a peal over me as soon as we are under shelter." They had turned into the storm now, and in the short time it took to arrive at the door of the disused barn, they were both drenched. Mr. Kirkland handed over the reins without a word and jumped down to swing the huge door open. Virginia drove in and just sat there for a moment getting her breath. She watched unmoving as Mr. Kirkland unhitched the horses and led them to stalls on the far side of the barn. From his movements the part of her brain that was still functioning decided he was fetching hay for them. In a minute he would return, and she would have to think of something to say that would show him she could appreciate his grisly little joke. He would probably apologize for teasing her. Or perhaps he would ignore the subject altogether.

He did neither. She was still sitting there when he came back to the curricle. He held up his arms to assist her down, and when she was on the ground he used both hands very efficiently to remove her wet hat, the muslin cap under it, and before she realized what was happening, the pins that confined her hair. He ran his fingers through the dampish tresses, freeing them from all restraint, while she stared at him half in shock, tingling from the touch of those fingers on her scalp.

"There!" he said with supreme satisfaction. "I have been wanting to do that for weeks. Also this." She slipped deeper into a bemused state as two strong arms gathered her close and two firm lips fastened possessively on her mouth. For a moment longer she stood rigid, scarcely believing, and then abandoned thinking in favor of melting into those strong arms. Her lips quivered and returned the pressure of his for an enchanted interval as she snuggled closer into that purposeful embrace.

He raised his head a bare inch to smile at her lovingly. "What an admirable woman you are, Miss Ginger Spice, always so quick to take my meaning. I have never considered myself inarticulate, but I haven't been able to tell you ... or ask you. That disguise was so intimidating, my love. Then yesterday, when I saw the parson on his knees, I knew I had to put it to the touch."

She smiled dreamily into those bold dark eyes. "Don't call me Ginger," she said.

He shouted with laughter and hugged her closer. "Do you realize those are your first words since entering this delightful place? Scarcely romantic, and not auguring well for our domestic felicity, I would say."

The dimness of the barn did not quite conceal her blush

at his teasing. The laughter stopped. "Virginia," he murmured, exploring the sound, "darling Virginia."

The kiss they exchanged lasted even longer this time, but all too soon he put her a little away from him. "We are in a dreadfully sodden condition, my love—not that I am complaining, mind you. If it were not for your habit of taking the air during summer storms, I might not yet know your identity." He was divesting her of the wet shawl as he spoke, and he draped it over the back of the curricle seat before shrugging out of his coat and placing it beside the shawl. "They won't dry of course, but we shall be more comfortable while we wait for the storm to blow over. We won't be cold anyway. This place is airless even with the door open."

Virginia fastened on the one interesting fact. "Is that when you recognized me—that time you brought me back in the rain?"

He nodded. "I was nearly positive but I didn't know why you were masquerading as another woman."

"Then at the dance, after the play," persisted Virginia, pursuing her line of thought, "when you were so horrible to me, threatening to visit Lady Mallory, *you knew*! Simon, that was *cruel*!"

"I know," he admitted penitently, "and I offer my most humble apologies, my darling, for succumbing to my baser instincts, but I did not know the whole story at the time. Besides, I have been well punished for my actions. You retreated from me and gave me no encouragement at all. You left me no choice but to compromise you."

"Compromise me! Simon, what are you talking about?"

He waved a comprehensive hand, indicating their surroundings and the rain outside. "If the storm ends before sunset we may still return before dark; if not, we'll have

251

to wait till the moon is up. In either event people will be bound to talk."

"Not about Miss Agnes Greyson," Virginia insisted. "She is a pattern card of rectitude."

Mr. Kirkland hesitated a moment. "Come up here where we can be comfortable at least," he said, and aided her to climb back into the curricle. The contented chomping of the horses eating hay and the dripping where the barn roof leaked in several places were the only sounds within the quiet building for a time when he had taken his place at her side. All jocularity was gone from his manner, and the dark eyes that held her gaze steadily were quite serious.

"I've given this a deal of thought since realizing that I loved you." He clasped her hand warmly between both of his and compelled her attention. "It's the devil of a coil, my dearest girl, and I feel only the truth will answer. I know what you are going to say"—as she opened her lips—"but hear me out. You think if you were simply to resign your post and return to Bath, no one need be the wiser, but recollect that Malcolm is a good friend of mine. Unless I cut the connection entirely, how can I conceal a wife from him? And do not become enamored of the idea that he will not recognize you in your own identity, because he will. It is much easier to go from the plain Miss Greyson to the lovely Miss Spicer, which would be *his* task, than the reverse, which was the situation that confronted me, and he knows your voice, which I did not. Do you accept my reasoning thus far?"

"Yes." She sighed. "I am sick to death of the whole deception, but I never thought to hurt anyone, and I have grown so fond of all the children, and Sir Reginald trusts me, and . . ."

Her voice trailed off and became wholly suspended by

tears. Mr. Kirkland bent his best efforts to the enjoyable task of comforting his weary betrothed, and it was some little time before they returned to the main problem. It was not going to disappear of itself, though, so return they did eventually. Mr. Kirkland spoke decisively, "People are going to be shocked, of course, at first; but my guess is that Sir Reginald will not cut up stiff once he understands the reason for what you did. And I shall be there to detail your devoted care for his daughters should any argument or censure be ensuing."

Virginia read the resolution in her fiancé's strong, clear-cut features, and her fears and alarms dissolved magically. Eight months ago she had been completely alone and bereft, and now through some as yet uncomprehended miracle, here was everything she would need for the rest of her life in the person of one determined man.

She smiled at her betrothed through a mist of tears. "I love you, Simon; I'll always love you."

Such a pledge had to be answered, of course, and it wasn't until an awareness of something missing in the atmosphere invaded their rapture that they drew apart. "Listen, the rain has stopped, and judging by the sky, we should be able to get to Fairhill before dark."

As Mr. Kirkland jumped down to begin the process of hitching up the horses, Virginia squealed, "I'd forgotten all about Juliet. The poor child was being so brave about the ankle, but a wetting would be the last straw."

Mr. Kirkland's voice came from the corner where the horses were stalled. "If the storm maintained its direction, which was toward the northeast, they may have escaped since they would be heading due east." He made short work of hitching the pair and backing out of the barn.

"You know, Simon," mused Virginia a bit later when he had skillfully negotiated their way back onto the road,

"I have a feeling Juliet is the one person who will not be completely stunned by a change in my appearance and age. On several occasions she has studied me rather thoroughly, and I have wondered if she suspected I was trying to change my appearance."

"She will not wonder about anything if she sees your present appearance," Mr. Kirkland remarked with a significance that was lost on Virginia for a moment. Big green eyes questioned him mutely.

"All that is wanting to complete the picture are wisps of hay sticking out here and there," he continued wickedly.

"Oh, lud!" she gasped, grabbing for the chestnut mane and beginning to twist it up with frantic haste. "Where are the pins? In your pocket? Thank heavens! And my cap—where is my cap?"

"I shall take great delight in personally setting flame to that unspeakable object at the first opportunity," her betrothed warned as she unearthed it from inside her hat, which had gotten squashed in a corner of the seat. "It is a crime to cover hair such as yours."

She smiled and thanked him prettily for the compliment, but when Miss Greyson's appearance had been restored to the best of her ability—for the last time, according to her beloved—she confided soberly; "I worry about Juliet from time to time. She is so very beautiful and such a prodigious flirt! Mr. Ryding is in love with her, you know, though he contrives to conceal it from her, *so far.*"

"There is nothing you can do about that situation, my love. Her fancy may alight on a half dozen men before she makes her choice. I do know that Sir Reginald is much impressed with Ryding and intends to further his career when Bertram goes to school. I doubt whether he would countenance a nobody for his daughter's hand, however, though if Juliet were set on having him, I would hedge my bets. But enough of your beautiful and tiresome charge! Do you think, my sweet love, that we might now turn our attention to our own future?"

And, encountering the determined glint in the dark eyes quizzing her gently, Virginia meekly signified her willingness to do just that as the curricle headed at a slapping pace into the fast gathering twilight.

THE END

Love—the way you want it!

Candlelight Romances